Desne Mar

Land of Magic

Book One

M.T. HAMMERSLA

This book is dedicated to my mother who gave me my love of reading, my father who helped me realize my love of writing, and my spouse who supports me in both.

PROLOGUE

Andres felt the blade pass through his back and enter his heart. The damn coward. He should have known. He should never have let down his guard. In no other circumstance would any man get the best of him, least of all his soft and spoiled cousin. Andres felt the fool to die in this manner. This was not how he had always imagined he would leave this world. It should have been from old age or a battle in which someone younger than he, faster than he, would finally get the best of him. His biggest regret was not being able to see his beautiful wife Anya again. To hold her in his arms once more and feel the black silk of her hair as he combed his fingers through it. He wanted to once again lose himself in the depths of her dark blue eyes; the most beautiful eyes he had ever seen.

In regards to his oldest daughter Ellindria, there was so much she needed to learn and prepare for, now he would never get the chance to teach her. He had, like so many others before him, been sure that he had years in which to fulfill his responsibility to her, years that he had been looking forward to. Now none of this was to be.

He slumped to the ground; face pressed sideways into the dirt, and tried to catch his breath to no avail. The sun shone down warmly upon him and it seemed almost rude. At the very least he would have liked a passing cloud to cover him in shadow as if in sorrow at his demise. Tomlin remained standing over him, which came as a surprise to Andres since he knew Tomlin to be a coward and would have expected him to run off as soon as the deed was done. As it was, it was only the shadow of his cousin that covered him briefly when he moved and blocked the sun, yet another slight in Andres' eyes.

While his life's blood left his body Andres' mind went back to the events leading up to this day. Apparently he had no control over the direction his thoughts took him and so he just followed them wherever they led. He was dying after all. *What else was there to do*, he asked himself.

Life had been good for Andres. After all, growing up in a castle because your father was king afforded opportunities and excitement that most people could not begin to fathom. In addition, being an elf with natural magical talent and long life made living that life that much more interesting, or it would have been, if it hadn't been cut short.

Andres was in line for the throne upon the death of his father or if his father became incapacitated and ceded the throne earlier. He had not wanted the responsibility that came with the crown, but knew that he had no choice in the matter. He had also known that the day would come all too soon since his father's health was failing. Soon the mantle would have been passed to him and life as he knew it would come to an end. He had been prepared for this until the day he met Anya. Elves were notoriously arrogant, and like other kingdoms, they too had different classes of people. Anya, unfortunately, was not considered to be queen material having come from a lesser house. Andres did not care. Anya was tall and beautiful. It was her warm and caring nature that made her more beautiful still. It was a boon, in his opinion, that his wife was striking. Her long black hair and dark blue eyes was the initial draw to those that were fortunate to have met her. It was her kindness and warm demeanor that kept them there. Anyone who met Anya liked her whether they wanted to or not and she truly liked everyone in return. She had told Andres when they first met that everyone has something about them worth caring about without exception. Andres wondered if she would still feel that way when she learned of his demise and knew who must have orchestrated his death.

Andres was an attractive man in his own right and could have chosen his bride from the entire kingdom of Valsara. There had in fact been several desirable young women of the upper classes that were more than suitable to be queen by virtue of both social status and beauty. However, despite the protests, he had asked for Anya's hand in marriage, causing quite an uproar from the nobility of Valsara. It had always been understood that a queen would be chosen from among the noble's daughters and this change in protocol did not go unanswered, hence the blade now sticking out of his back. To be certain, it had taken many years for Tomlin to seek retribution, but the elves had a very different sense of time due to their longevity.

Since Andres had not yet ascended to the throne in an official capacity, his cousin Teserath, Tomlin's older twin sister, could assert her claim to it and contest his wife's right as regent until Ellindria came of age. It didn't help that Anya was not born of the royal line. Anya could claim the throne as her own due to her marriage into the royal family until such time that Ellindria or one of their other children took their rightful place. In Andres' opinion, his daughter Ellindria was most worthy of all those that could claim a right to it. He knew, however, that his wife would most likely cede the throne to his cousin Teserath based on the new circumstances. Regardless, Ellindria could claim the throne at any time once she came of age and Teserath would be obliged to step aside. Andres knew Teserath to be a good and decent woman and felt confident that if this was indeed the case, then she would do her duty to her family and kingdom.

His son, being his eldest, could challenge both Teserath's and Ellindria's claim to the throne. Despite the fact that he was next in line, Andres did not feel that his son was king material any more than Tomlin. In fact, his son and cousin were more alike than he cared for, something he had tried unsuccessfully to change. It was this very reason that thankfully he had had the foresight to have already taken steps to ensure that his son never sat on the throne. Whereas he had thought he had all the time in the world to turn his oldest daughter into the best queen that had ever ruled Valsara, he had been anxious to make sure that his son could never be king. As he lay in the dirt with his blood pooling around him, his thoughts a jumble in his head, he was thankful for that at least.

Also, knowing that Tomlin would not be the one to take the throne upon his death, but Tomlin's sister Teserath instead, gave him some measure of comfort. It briefly passed through his mind that perhaps Teserath had been party to what was taking place. As fast as he thought it, it was discarded in the next instant. He knew better. He actually felt guilty even considering the possibility and sent a silent request for her forgiveness.

As his death drew closer he felt and saw his children at different times in their lives. Like still moments in time he saw them and was awed and humbled to have been so fortunate. When he drew his last breath a smile crossed his face, his features relaxed and he felt his wife's arms around him once more. Her mouth was upturned slightly as though amused at something he had done or said; a look he had seen more times than he could count. Her eyes were an invitation to which he couldn't wait to answer. He lost himself for the last time in those blue eyes full of mischief, understanding and love and allowed their depths to take him to whatever end.

Tomlin stared down at the cousin he had just literally stabbed in the back. The peaceful expression on Andres' face, along with an actual smile, initially confused him and then enraged him. The son of a bitch! It felt as though Andres had won somehow even though Andres was the one lying in the dirt, dead at last. Tomlin's anger got the best of him and so he kicked his cousin's body over and over again until his anger was finally sated.

***

Upon learning of the death of her husband, Anya went into the suite of rooms they shared in the castle and proceeded to their private bed chamber. A fire was lit in the large stone fireplace that was situated opposite the foot of their bed. She felt chilled and the warmth was sorely needed. Next to the fireplace sat two chairs facing one another. She and Andres would sit in the chairs and share a hot drink on a cold morning or perhaps a nightcap after dinner with the family. The empty chair now sitting across from her spoke volumes and soon she began to softly cry.

Despite the fire, she was still chilled and pulled a quilt around her shoulders. She wrapped herself completely, only her hands holding the hot tea her hand maiden had so thoughtfully provided could be seen. She placed the tea down on the table next to her chair as soon as her hands began to shake when her soft cries became sobs that wracked her body. She cried as only someone who has lost a loved one could understand. She cried for what seemed like hours. By the time she calmed herself, her hot tea had gone cold. She sighed in resignation and drank from the cup anyway.

Anya took a little more time to collect herself and then called for her hand maiden to attend to her. She requested that her children be brought to her within the hour. In the meantime, she prepared a list of all that would need to be done. Andres' father the king was dying and when that day arrived she wanted to be prepared to leave. Thankfully she and Andres had spoken of the possibility and she knew what to do. The only reason they had even discussed something so remote was due to the rumors being whispered and the common knowledge that Tomlin had always wanted the throne. It mattered little that there were three children and an older sister with more claim to the throne than he.

Although Anya had no proof, she knew that Tomlin had something to do with her husband's death, be it directly or indirectly. Since Tomlin and Teserath were part of the extended royal family, they too lived in the castle. The brother and sister lived in a different wing which although was not as well appointed as the wing of the royal family, it was luxurious nonetheless. They also were provided for by the castle servants and one would think that they had all they could desire. Teserath was happy with her lot, her brother, however, would never settle for anything less than the throne itself and the power it represented regardless of how far removed he was from that very throne. Anya was well aware of Tomlin's desires and her concern for her children's welfare outweighed any desire she may have had to rule as queen. Because of the circumstances in which she found herself, Anya made plans to leave the castle and raise her children away from Valsara. Only then would she feel that her family was safe. She would raise them well away from the courts of Valsara, and although Gustaf and Ellindria would need to adjust to a simple life after living in the luxury of the castle, her youngest would have no such memories and would probably be the happier for it. She would certainly adjust more quickly because of it.

When the king died, Anya temporarily renounced her family's claim to the throne with the understanding that one of her children may wish to reclaim the throne at a later time. Then Anya did as her husband had wished and they settled down to life in the southernmost part of the neighboring land known as the Kingdom of Amjukar.

Chapter 1

Spring had recently arrived bringing with it another cold and damp night to the Kingdom of Amjukar. Draconas Callis pulled his cloak tighter around his shoulders as he hurried to the meeting place. Never had he been as conflicted as he was at that moment. The person he was to meet had in their possession, a scroll that could change lives for the better or place the realm in chaos, depending on who received the information. He would need to think on this with a clear head before deciding which direction to take. If the scroll was what he believed it to be, he would need to decide whether to share it with the council or destroy it before it fell into the wrong hands.

His leather soled boots made little noise on the stone paved streets still damp from the latest rain and he soon found himself at the moon gods' temple. The twin moons gave rise to the twin gods Soros and Somara. The sanctuaries were beginning to fill with those that would give thanks to the gods of the night charged with keeping the world safe in its darkest hours. The buildings were identical in all but size. They were simple in structure with one area open to the sky. When the moon was in position, the light shone on the statues centered there.   Soros was the brother moon and approximately twice the size of his sister Somara.   In keeping with this distinction, the buildings were proportionate to their size difference.   Draconas Callis was to meet at Somara's sanctuary, due to its smaller stature, it had fewer worshippers and so it offered a little more privacy.   He stood in the shadows of the statue of the goddess Somara and waited.   The moon goddess looked up towards the heavens; her nude form was voluptuously rendered as was the norm for most statues of the gods.   Her head was tilted slightly back.   Her face looked toward her brother when the moons were at the peak of their ascension.   Her long golden hair had a braid on each side of her face, and the back was left in long flowing waves.   A simple gold band with a sapphire stone encircled her brow.

Callis was a brave man and had seen many things in his long life, yet even he was nervous about this meeting and its possible ramifications. After what seemed like ages, and was in fact probably no longer than a quarter of an hour, his source spoke from behind:

"I may have been followed.   Earlier I left the item in the area we discussed when last we met. Wait until tomorrow to retrieve it in the event that I did not lose the person or persons that may be following me.   I do not know anything regarding the item in question, and for once I feel safer for my ignorance. Please be careful wise one. I have a bad feeling about this."

"Yes, of course," Callis replied. "Please be safe that we may meet again under different circumstances," he whispered to no one, for his source had already left the sanctuary.

Callis stayed a while longer to pay homage to the moon goddess before leaving and shifting into his Draconas form. The transformation occurred in the blink of an eye. His large dragon shape caused a downdraft of air as he unfurled his wings and took to the sky. Leaves and debris fanned out in all directions causing skittering noises across the stone pavement. He never tired of flying and was happy to do so again as he headed towards his cottage in the woods outside of the city. He would retrieve the scroll tomorrow and would decide what to do after familiarizing himself with its contents. He felt like a child, which was no small feat for him, practically giddy with the mystery of it all.

***

Although it was known as the Kingdom of Amjukar, it was not ruled by a king. Amjukar was ruled by a council of seven members and had been that way for as long as anyone could remember. Draconas Markim, a human Draconas, was the leader of The Seven. The Seven consisted of a council of humans, elves and dwarves, some Draconas' and others wizards, that were charged with the protection of the Kingdom of Amjukar and all that it entails. Draconas Markim had not heard from Draconas Callis and was becoming worried. It was not unlike Callis to leave for days at a time without anyone knowing where he had gone but he had never missed a council meeting in the many years Markim had known him. He looked to the other council members and asked if they had seen Callis. No one had seen him in several days.

"Draconas Brock, would you please hold this meeting in my absence. I would very much like to try and locate Draconas Callis; I've a bad feeling that will not leave me."

"Of course," Brock stated with a respectful nod of his head in his leader's direction.

Draconas Markim left the meeting by way of one of the large, heavily reinforced balconies used at the castle for the easy coming and going of the Draconas' in their dragon form. During his walk to the patio, Markim changed into his Draconas form. Royal blue and 50 feet in length, he looked both wondrous and intimidating at the same time. He stretched his wings and flew towards the home of his friend.

It didn't take long to reach Draconas Callis' home and he quickly changed back to his human form as he approached the front door. He started to knock but found that the door was already slightly ajar. Markim proceeded with caution into the home of his friend not knowing what to expect. He did not make it far into the main room before he saw Callis lying face down on the floor in front of the fireplace, the embers having gone cold and turned to ash quite some time ago. Markim knew immediately that there had been foul play due, in no small part, to the state of the room and what he could see of his friend. Also, because Draconas' lived several thousands of years making Callis' 3500 and more rather insignificant.

He turned his friend over and was dismayed to find evidence of torture. Draconas Callis' face was barely recognizable. He had been beaten to death. Someone had apparently used Callis' own fireplace poker as a club to cause severe damage about his face and upper body. His eyes were swollen shut and several deep cuts had bled rather profusely, drying in pools where he lay. His lips were swollen and cut to the extent that even if his friend had wanted to cooperate, chances were he would not have been able to speak. There was evidence that his ribs had been broken as well. Markim was shocked at first because nothing like this had happened in more time than anyone could remember. This was immediately followed by a raging anger over the treatment his friend had received. Under other circumstances, no one could have done this kind of harm to Callis. Draconas Callis and Draconas Markim were both humans, and although they had magic due to their Draconas forms, their magic was much more enhanced in that form and would have been impossible to wield inside Callis' humble home. Both Markim and Callis were about 50 ft. in length in Draconas form, making it impossible to change inside the quaint cottage. Markim knew that Callis must have been caught totally unaware to be unable to make his way outside to change and defend himself against his attacker or attackers. It was unclear how many there had been.

Markim looked down at his friend and wondered: Who? What? Why? It wasn't long before he stopped his pointless musing and turned his attention to the area he knew gave way to a secret room where Callis kept his most valuable possessions. Callis had not confided in him that he was in possession of something that he could possibly be killed for. He knew that if Callis had held out under questioning regarding whatever the person was after, that it would be in his secret place. He headed to the fireplace and triggered the hidden lever that opened the door to the secret room behind the wall. The room had been magically enchanted in such a way that no one would ever suspect it was there. It was a nice piece of magic provided by a previous wizard of The Seven many years before.

There were lamps hung on the wall inside the room and Markim lit a few to chase away the shadows. Draconas Callis had money, gold and jewels and could have lived at the castle with the rest of the council. He had, however, preferred his solitude in the small cottage in the woods. Everything he had of value was in this room and Markim knew that if Callis was tortured it was for something in there. He walked to a small desk and found a note addressed to him in Callis' writing. Behind the note was an old scroll that Markim put aside as he picked up the note and began to read:

My dearest friend Markim, Leader of The Seven of the Kingdom of Amjukar

If you are reading this, I am dead and obviously did not do a good enough job of covering my tracks. I am truly sorry that I did not share what I found with you and the other council members earlier. I was undecided if it was a good thing or not yet I am sure that was not my choice to make; again I am sorry. There is a scroll that I believe is worth more than all the gold and jewels in Amjukar. You must keep it safe. If you decide to act on it, I advise that you do so with all haste and only with those you trust absolutely. The contents of the scroll are written in old Draconas. I did not translate the scroll because the fewer that can read it, the better, and I knew that you would be able to read it even if your old Draconas is a little rusty my friend.

As for my belongings you are, of course, aware that I have no family so everything I have is yours. Do with it as you please. I know I have more books than any sane person could possibly read. Please keep what you will and place the rest in the castle library that others may enjoy them as I have.

I did not mean to leave this tremendous burden in your hands. Once you have read the scroll I have obviously died to protect, you will understand. I am comforted in knowing that the scroll now resides in your capable hands.

Take care my friend,

Draconas Callis of House Lory

One of The Seven, the Kingdom of Amjukar

Draconas Markim set down his friend's letter and picked up the scroll in question. He turned it over in his hands, deciding whether or not he should read something that had brought about the death of his good friend, or if he should light the scroll on fire, sight unseen. He finally came to the conclusion that only in the reading of the scroll could he possibly begin to make sense of such a senseless death. He pulled out the chair at the desk, sat down, opened the scroll and began to read. The further he read the more excited and nervous he became in equal measure. When he finished the scroll, he rolled it up securely and placed it in the inner pocket of his cloak. Once he looked around one more time for anything that he may have missed, he secured the secret room, locked up the cottage and flew back to the castle as quickly as his wings would take him. There was so much to do and he felt the beginnings of a headache from the random thoughts that flicked in and out regarding all that needed to be done. He continued to ponder on the possible ramifications of what he had just learned.

First things first, he needed to put Draconas Callis to rest and call a meeting of the council. In addition he also needed to prepare for the new councilmember of the Seven that would be arriving any day. It was not known how it worked.

18

Whenever a councilmember died or otherwise left the council for reasons of their own, someone, somewhere, would feel an overwhelming urge to make their way to the kingdom with all haste and present themselves at the gates of the castle of Amjukar. It always happened quickly. Apparently, whatever power was behind The Seven wanted seven councilmembers at all times. Perhaps it was simply a matter of not allowing an even split on any given issue. With an odd number there would always be a majority. Some believed there was magic in the number itself. Still it was only speculation; no one really knew. Occasionally those that received the calling came from other kingdoms; usually they came from among their own. The only thing known for sure was that they would come. The calling would become so intense that it would be impossible to resist.

Draconas Markim knew that never before in his life had he felt the weight of his leadership of one of The Seven as he did at this time. The scroll, his friend's death and the anticipation of a new member was more than he cared to think upon. He also knew that he had no choice in the matter. However, he had been chosen for a reason and Draconas Markim, leader of The Seven, quickly got to work.

***

The councilmembers, absent Draconas Callis, sat around the table. They had already been told of the death of Callis but not the reason. Draconas Markim acknowledged each in turn and then placed a dampening spell around the table and its members to keep anyone outside the council from eaves dropping on the meeting that was about to take place. The High Wizard Malek arched his eyebrows at this change in protocol. Most meetings were open to any who wished to attend, so the secrecy of this meeting earned guarded looks from all in attendance.

"My good friends and fellow councilmembers," Draconas Markim began, "it is with both ill and glad tidings that I have called this meeting. As you are aware, Draconas Callis has passed to the next realm of existence. A proper sending is being planned that the entire kingdom may wish to attend to pay their respects and a day of mourning will be observed." He paused here to collect himself before he resumed. "What you are unaware of is that he was tortured to death by a person or persons unknown." This comment elicited gasps from around the table. After allowing a few moments for the other members to grasp what he had just said, Markim continued. "I do, however, know why he was tortured. He was killed for the contents of a scroll that is now in my possession. I believe that if the contents of the scroll were known by those that tortured our dear friend that they would not have given up so easily. It is of the utmost importance that what I am about to tell you stays in this room. Remember, Callis was tortured to death for this information, yet he did not give it up. Please keep that foremost in your thoughts." He looked for confirmation and continued, "Without translating word for word, I will suffice it to say that the scroll in question tells of a land known as Desne Mar, which means Land of Magic or Magic Land in elvish."

Markim noticed the surprised look on the otherwise very serious and handsome face of Draconas Lias. Lias, a 2500 year old elf with long silvery white hair and violet eyes inclined his head towards Draconas Markim, "I have heard tales of Desne Mar. It is an elvish story told to children much like the fairytales told to human children at bedtime."

"Yes," Markim acknowledged, "I know of this story. I also believe, based on the scroll now in my possession, that the story is true or is at least based in part on the truth." The other councilmembers looked at each other and back to their leader. Akhena, a half human and half dwarf Draconas of 400 or more years looked at Markim and Lias and asked, "What is this land or story? I have never heard of it, and based on the blank stares of some of the others, I am not alone."

"Based on the scroll I have read," Markim explained, "Desne Mar is a real place. It is called the Magic Land for the simple fact that if the land is claimed in the manner indicated in the scroll, it will enhance the magical abilities of all who call it home. To what extent magical abilities are enhanced is not clear. It is said that even before the land is claimed, that anyone with magic abilities in its proximity will feel the effects of the additional power. The implications are mind boggling. If the wrong person were to come into this information and claim the land, the rest of the realm would be in grave danger. That kind of power in the wrong hands could be devastating. This is the reason Draconas Callis did not come to us right away. However, if the Kingdom of Amjukar were able to locate this land and claim it for our kingdom, then the prosperity and safety of our people would be greatly enhanced. I can only assume that those with any magical ability whatsoever would help to settle Desne Mar, making it an extension of Amjukar and further strengthening our kingdom."

"How do you know that this is real and not some hoax or children's story?" Draconas Lias persisted.

"I do not," Markim replied, "I do know that Callis was killed for this information. I also know that more than one childhood story is based on true events that eventually fade into legend over time. The fact that the scroll is both very old and written in old Draconas lends to its credibility as well. Basically, I feel that we have no choice other than to follow the leads provided and send a scouting party out with the authority to claim the land if it is found. Does anyone disagree or have anything else to add on this matter?"

No one spoke up and Markim continued.

"Additionally, as you know, we should all be expecting the newest councilmember soon, depending on where he or she is coming from. Please make yourselves available to welcome our new member when he or she arrives."

"I would recommend we send the scouting party once the newest member has arrived and the vote has been taken. I wish to send Commander Devin and whomever he chooses, as well as two councilmembers to oversee everything and check for magical influxes. If there is nothing else, we will meet again when our newest member arrives. Thank you." Draconas Markim nodded to each in turn and left the council chamber, once again taking his Draconas form and leaving by way of the balcony.

One by one, the others left the meeting as well. Draconas Lias shifted into his Draconas form. With his 40 feet of bright white scales, violet eyes and silver horns, Lias was sleek and fast. He flew from the balcony and was gone from sight in the span of a heartbeat. His speed was legendary.

Draconas Brock was an extremely strong and stocky dwarf. When he took his Draconas form, it was more of the same. He was about 35 feet in length with burgundy scales and amber eyes. When it came to brute strength, Draconas Brock was the one to call upon. He also took his Draconas form and leapt from the balcony. Most dwarves spent their lives in mountain dwellings and considered flying for the birds, literally. As a Draconas, Brock was comfortable both above and below ground, though truth be told, he missed his mountain home. He flew to the bottom of the central tower where a room had been prepared for him specially to simulate his underground home in the Krull mountains.

The High Wizard Malek was human and cherished being one of The Seven. He very much enjoyed his position in the community and what some people may mistake for ego was no more than pride in a job well done. Malek could come across as stuffy and stoic, although in reality he took his job and the protection of the kingdom very seriously leaving little time for moments of levity. As a wizard he could have made quite a show of disappearing but he simply left on his own two feet.

Draconas Akhena felt most at home among The Seven. Being half human and half dwarf caused problems for her from both races. She had lived a very solitary life until the calling of The Seven had changed all of that. Her colleagues seemed not to care about her half breed status and being a Draconas as well as one of The Seven changed how she was viewed by others now as well. She was tall for a dwarf and short for a human. She had the voluptuous figure common among dwarven women, as well as the blue eyes and sandy hair which was a trait from her human mother, though that was an assumption since she had never known her birth mother. She came across as strong and was considered attractive though she didn't see herself as such. She preferred to draw as little attention to herself as possible and so traveled by whichever means created the desired effect.

The Wizard Tannis, a tall elf with long black hair and extremely dark, almost back eyes, whispered a spell under his breath and was gone from sight.

***

The next two days consisted of ordered chaos. In the end, the Sending Ceremony for Draconas Callis was carried out with most of the kingdom in attendance. Callis was beloved by all and all those who could attend did so.

Draconas Callis was laid out on a feathered bed atop a platform of wood, twigs and leaves and placed inside a Sending Vessel. The vessel, a small boat adorned with flowers, lavender and objects made by the populace was launched from the castle side of the lake and once it was almost halfway across the Captain of the Archers raised his bow and let a single flaming arrow fly. The arrow hit its mark and the fire started slowly at first. Soon the entire Sending Vessel was aflame. All in attendance bowed their heads for a few moments of silence and then the celebration of Draconas Callis' life began.

The city came alive with people paying homage to one of their leaders. Most of the populace was human, and due to the shortness of their lives in comparison to those on the council, the councilmembers had been their leaders for their entire lives and felt like one of their family, perhaps extended family, though family nonetheless. The Seven were unlike most rulers in that they made themselves available to the populace regardless of status thus making the passing of any of them a truly sad event in the lives of the Amjukarans.

The other leaders of The Seven made their way through the city to bring comfort and show that although a member had left them that there would be continuity and a smooth transition. The people of Amjukar also knew that soon they would be introduced to a new member causing a mixture of excitement as well as mourning in the great city. The city continued to celebrate the life of Draconas Callis into the early hours of the morning until a new day dawned and the sun god Sol made his appearance in the sky.

Chapter 2

"Oh, Elle, I am soooooo jealous...." her sister moaned. "To think, that we finally have another Draconas in the family, after so many years. How can you even begin to think that it could be a bad thing?"

"I didn't say it was a bad thing; it's just a little hard getting used to," Elle replied. "Using my magic as an elf is different than using it as a Draconas and it takes time to realize how they work together." Elle tilted her head, her auburn locks flashing both red and gold highlights when touched by the sun. She turned to look at her baby sister Sela, an exaggerated look of exasperation playing across Elle's face. Elle was just shy of being 200 years old. Usually, if an elf evolved into a Draconas, they did it at a later age of approximately 300 to 500 years, although 200 to 700 was not unheard of. Since Sela was only 80 years old, she decided to hold out hope that perhaps one more Draconas in their family was not unreasonable.

"I want to see your Draconas form," Sela pleaded, her emerald green eyes the same shade and shape as her sister's and bright with anticipation. How could Elle say no?

Elle continued to look at her sister with exasperation though she understood her excitement. Ever since she felt the onset of the change she had experienced a multitude of emotions, although the feeling of elation was probably top of the list. She looked her sister in the eye, gave her a grin and a wink, and then looked down as the change overcame her. She could finally make the change instantaneously. For her sister's benefit, she did it gradually to allow all of the nuances to show. Once the change was complete, in the place of Elle the elf was Elle the Draconas in all her glory. Elle the Draconas was approximately 35 feet in length from snout to tail with red scales protecting her body, the scales becoming deep purple around the face and extremities. Her emerald eyes became almost jewel-like in their appearance with cat-like pupils that allowed her vision to cover an incredible distance, especially when airborne. In her Draconas form she walked on four legs. Her legs were covered with the scales that covered her main body, protecting her organs, but they were more flexible to allow for ease of movement and therefore not quite as strong. Her claws ended in razor sharp talons that were used to catch and kill prey. Her wings were tough leather-like material and lighter than they appeared. When not in use, the wings tucked in alongside her body quite nicely. When airborne, the width of her wings was approximately twice the length of her body, not including the length of her tail. Her teeth were sharp for ripping into the hide of her kills and her ability to breathe fire had several practical uses, as well as those used in defense. The two horns that curved slightly back atop her head were more ornamental in their purpose and could be used for fighting. Triangular scales protruded from the back of her head and continued down her neck. They were instrumental in helping to maintain tight turns and, like her face, they were dark purple in color. When her transformation was complete, she looked up at her little sister. Sela stared at the Draconas before her and realized that her sister, Draconas Ellindria of House Kar, was beautiful in both forms. She walked up to her shyly, as if she was someone new, and reached out a hand to caress the scales. She was amazed at their smooth yet hard texture that was cool to the touch.

Elle bellied down to the ground and looked at Sela questioningly. When Sela realized what she was asking, she practically squealed with delight. She scrambled on top of Elle's back with her feet secured at the wing joints and her arms around her neck, careful of the scales protruding there. Elle was intentionally slow in her movements lest she un-seat her sister and before long they were airborne. There was a chill in the air, yet the sun was bright, making for a beautiful day. Being in southern Amjukar, the season had already made its debut. Despite the chill, Sela was nothing less than exhilarated. Sela had magic of her own, but to be able to fly! Elle began very slowly for fear of causing her sister harm. Caution was soon thrown to the wind at Sela's laughter and urgent requests of "Faster Elle! Higher Elle!" Sela sat atop Elle's back, holding on with complete faith that her sister would keep her safe. Elle wasn't so sure she would have such faith in another and would probably require some form of saddle to hold on to. That thought brought a chuckle to her. Imagine Sela placing a saddle upon her back to go for an evening ride. Suddenly she no longer felt like a Draconas and felt more like a horse. Once again, her thoughts amused her, and when she snorted, a wisp of smoke escaped her nostrils and covered her sister entirely. This had them both laughing so hard that Elle was afraid she would definitely unseat her sister and they made their way down until they were skimming the tops of the trees. They made a few more passes of the immediate area before landing near their home. Elle changed back in the blink of an eye, causing Sela to squeal with delight once again. It had been a wonderful outing for the sisters, their joy still fresh upon their faces. Elle tousled her kid sister's hair as though she was only a child and they made their way to the kitchen to help their mother prepare the evening meal.

***

Unbeknownst to Elle or Sela, Elle's brother watched their play from a distance with a scowl on his face. Gustaf was furious. As the oldest sibling and the only son, he could not understand why Elle, of all people, had evolved into a Draconas. He would never forget the day that the mark of the Draconas, the equivalent of a dragon tattoo, appeared on the left side of Elle's face near her eye. He could not believe it. At first, he would not believe it. When a Draconas first evolves the tattoo is prominent then recedes once the person changes for the first time. One could keep the tattoo to show their status or choose not to. Or one could simply show it for ceremonial purposes, which was more common. If it had been him, as it *should* have been, he would wear it proudly at all times. In fact, it should have been him. She must have twisted some magic or done something to have taken this from him. He saw no other possible way, for was he not more deserving? He had already been cheated out of his birthright and a woman, for pity's sake, was residing on his throne. Women were the bane of his existence. His mother stated that it had been her father's wish that she leave the kingdom of Valsara if he died before ascending to the throne. He didn't believe it for a minute. Why would anyone willingly give up the rule of Valsara, the most revered kingdom in the realm? Her explanations fell on deaf ears for he refused to listen. The traitorous bitches. He would show them all. Granted, it would have been easier if he had evolved and taken the Draconas form. That in and of itself was treated with a good measure of reverence, for Draconas' were few in number. Still he fumed and thought on all that had been done to him. Gustaf needed something with which to vent his anger or he was sure he would explode like the volcanos he had heard tales of. He searched in his mind's eye and found a rabbit not far away. The cute and furry fellow sat upon his hind legs and cleaned his face and ears, oblivious to the angry elf not far away. Gustaf focused on the rabbit and with just a thought, squeezed the small animal's neck. The rabbit's heart gave out due to fear before the rabbit ran out of air. Gustaf smiled.

In the southwestern most point of the Kingdom of Amjukar, where Elle lived with her family, she found herself in her Draconas form banking towards the northeast. She was well on her way when she finally realized that she had no idea where she was going or why. She turned back towards her home, and as soon as her mind started to drift, so did her direction and once again she was headed in the same northeasterly direction. Again she changed her heading towards home. No longer allowing her mind to wander, she focused on her need to reach her family home. It was ridiculously hard to stay in the direction that she wanted, as though an invisible force was pulling her away. Despite the problem, she finally arrived. Elle's home had been built when her sister Sela was a toddler. The trees, vines and stones that made up the home had been magically coerced by her family and a few trusted friends into the grandiose structure standing today. It was tucked into a grove of trees with a swift flowing brook nearby. Each family member and friend had used their magical gift to call upon the forest's trees and vines to weave and transform into the rooms that now existed. Elle's own bedroom had originally been made by her mother and shaped by Elle. The room itself was large with the intertwined tree trunks and vines forming an impenetrable barrier from the most fearsome weather on all sides. Room was left for large windows that could be magically closed and sealed although broad leaves and vines were used for aesthetics. In addition, any indigenous flowering plants of all seasons were strategically placed both inside and outside the dwelling adding both beauty and the wondrous scent they provided. A large balcony overlooked the nearby brook where Elle spent much of her time reading and enjoying the sounds of the forest. Elvish homes are usually alive. The elves can magically enhance any vegetation to grow to any shape or size that they wish. This ability is beneficial to the elves as well as the plants and trees and those animals that depend on them. Shelter can be procured for temporary means, or to last a thousand years or more, without the devastation of forests common among the other races. This in turn allows the animal life to remain abundant for food and clothing. Unfortunately this also means that elvish land is coveted by those races that have depleted their own land of all its resources.

Elle walked into the kitchen and found her mother hovering over a pot of vegetable soup with a spoon to her lips. One often found Anya in the kitchen or the garden, the two places that gave her the most pleasure. Although Elle's mother was over five hundred years old she didn't appear to be much older than Elle herself. Unlike Elle's auburn locks, her mother Anya had black hair that fell straight down her back and blue eyes that stood out in contrast. She was a beautiful, some would say breathtaking, woman. Elle hugged her from behind and kissed her cheek. "Where's everyone else?" she asked.

"I haven't seen your brother in days. Your sister is probably practicing her water magic at the creek."

Elle could hear the concern in her mother's voice that was always evident when speaking of her brother. Then, addressing her daughter, she smiled and asked, "And how is my Draconas daughter today?"

"I had a very strange thing happen to me today. I was flying in my Draconas form when I realized I was going in the wrong direction. I turned around, and a while later, I was going in the wrong direction again. It felt like something was pulling me." Elle took a ladle and dipped it in the soup. As she brought the aromatic broth to her lips she noticed that her mother was looking at her very oddly. What she saw in her expression gave her pause.

"Why are you looking at me like that?"

"In which direction were you going that you had to turn around?"

Elle thought only a second before she replied, "It was northeast. Why?"

"I have just learned that one of The Seven has recently died. They have already performed the Sending Ceremony," her mother answered.

"I am truly sorry to hear that," Elle said and she truly was saddened by the kingdom's loss, "but what does that have to do with this new ability as a Draconas that I have yet to understand?"

Her mother sighed, "We are so isolated here. Do you recall the story of The Seven that rule Amjukar?"

"Vaguely," Elle replied, "It has something to do with a calling."

Anya nodded her head and said, "For as long as this kingdom has been in existence, there has been the The Seven. When one of The Seven dies or steps down, someone is 'called' to take their place. The calling is something no one understands. It just happens. I understand that it cannot be ignored; the call is too strong. I think, perhaps, that this is what is happening to you." Anya looked upon her daughter with a mixture of emotions: sorrow, pride, concern and perhaps a little envy for the calling was an honor like no other elevating the person's status to the equivalent of a king or queen. When Elle's mother gave it thought, she felt that perhaps it was only fitting. Elle would most likely have ruled Valsara in time had her father not been killed. In fact, when Elle turns 200, she could stake her claim for the throne at that time.

"Mother," Elle laughed, "that is just not possible. It probably has something to do with my Draconas magic. As I said, I am sure it is a new ability that I have yet to understand."

"Perhaps," her mother conceded, although she did not sound convinced in the least.

Elle left the kitchen, her appetite now gone, and went to her room. She sat upon the daybed on her balcony waiting for the usual calming effect of the brook that cut its way through the forest near her home. This time, however, her mind was in turmoil and the brook did nothing to soothe her.

She remained unsettled and decided to find Sela and offer her help with her magic lessons to keep her mind occupied. She left her home and went deep into the woods where the water pooled and her sister would most likely be found.

Chapter 3

King Baldor overlooked his kingdom, the Kingdom of Erewyth, a bored look on his handsome features. He was tall and broad with black hair and dark green eyes. A scar that began at one eyebrow and ended near the corner of his mouth did nothing to detract from his looks. If anything, the scar made him look fierce as well as handsome, a fact he knew and took advantage of in both his human and Draconas forms. He could have healed himself magically and removed the scar, but the appearance of it, in both his human and Draconas forms, was enough to give anyone pause without Baldor lifting a hand or saying a word. Baldor knew that sometimes it was the little things that made a big difference. He had gone so far as to create his own crest depicting a hovering dragon, wings back and high, claws extended, head poised to strike with a blood red scar extending down from the brow. The making of his own crest would not have been necessary had he not stolen the kingdom he now ruled. But he had, and it was.

In his Draconas form, he had black scales covering most of his form with red on the crown of his head, around his eyes, his muzzle, feet and tip of his tail. His eyes were dark green, his claws black and at over 60 feet in length, he was larger than any other Draconas known at that time. He was currently in his human form while he stood waiting for Donnal, his arms crossed over his chest, an impatient look beginning to take place of the bored one. Donnal was his first in command and was a Draconas as well. Whatever Baldor wished, Donnal made it happen. Donnal had been with Baldor since he was a boy. Baldor remembered the day that he had found the feisty kid trying to protect his mother from an abusive father. Despite Donnal's best effort, his father accidentally killed his mother in a drunken fit when a blow caused her to lose her balance and her head struck a stone. Donnal tried to kill his father in retaliation, though he was simply too young and too small. Baldor had seen the entire incident take place and asked the young Donnal if he wished his father dead. One look from the boy was all that was needed and Baldor struck the father down where he stood with a sword through the man's heart. He wiped his blade clean on the father's clothes before sheathing it. He held out his hand to the young boy who hesitated for only a moment. Baldor had then taken Donnal under his wing and was rewarded when Donnal became a Draconas like himself. Overall, the young boy grew up to be his greatest asset. He turned his gaze to the horizon and his impatience was finally rewarded when the Draconas form of Donnal landed on the balcony of Baldor's private quarters. Like King Baldor, Donnal was also a handsome man as well as an impressive Draconas. In Draconas form, Donnal was a good 55 feet in length, almost as large as Baldor. His scales were the color of sand, gradually becoming darker towards the tips which were a chocolate brown. When he changed back to his human form, he stood almost as tall as Baldor. His hair was the same sandy brown color as his scales. His eyes were a light brown with gold flecks. A square jaw completed the package. He was a handsome man by any standards. Unlike his king, however, he had no interest in such things. He was also a very serious man who had no family ties, a fact that made him all the more desirable as Baldor's right hand man. Sometimes, however, King Baldor thought that perhaps it would be better if Donnal had a family. It was always better to have something or someone to hold as collateral if the need ever arose. Nevertheless, Baldor trusted Donnal more than anyone he had ever known; perhaps even more than his daughter.

Donnal gave a slight nod of his head. "You sent for me my king?"

"I have received confirmation that our sources were unsuccessful in acquiring the information that I wanted. I believe I know what the scroll was in reference to but I have only a slight inclination and no actual details. The morons that were sent killed Draconas Callis before obtaining the information. I will personally see to it that they are aware of my displeasure."

Donnal stared straight ahead. His king's definition of displeasure would cause anyone in the know to blanche and beg for mercy if directed at them. It was one of King Baldor's most used understatements. Donnal knew that the men that were sent would soon wish that they were dead. He also knew that their wish would be granted – in time.

He stopped his thoughts cold to erase the image they brought and asked, "Do you wish for me to see to this personally then?" Donnal looked at him.

"Yes, I do. Travel to Amjukar and find out what you can. Callis must have left the scroll to one of the other members and I want it. Make sure you contact me in private with any updates. I am counting on you, Donnal. I have a feeling that this is of great importance, and I will be less than pleased if it is already too late."

"Of course, my king, I shall ready myself and leave at first light." Donnal turned on his heel, changed into his Draconas form and flew into the night.

King Baldor pulled a cord that summoned the deaf mute tasked with taking care of his every need. He was not born a deaf mute; he was made that way to serve his king. Baldor preferred that the servant who would meet his most personal needs be without the ability to read, write, speak or have need of a woman. Removing the man's tongue, penis and burning his eardrums was to ensure that he could not betray the king. Using simple gestures that the servant recognized, he sent for his evening meal and the night's entertainment. He was most definitely in a truly foul mood. He was not used to people not coming through for him. Quite honestly, they were usually too scared to let him down. His temper was well known and anyone that was remotely acquainted with the king knew that to fail was to die. Frankly, he was surprised the idiots had returned. He needed someone to work out his aggressions on and made it known to his servant that he would be availing himself of such after indulging in the feast that was laid out before him. This object would be a particular girl that had been used for this very same reason before.

She arrived by a side door that remained unseen when flushed with the wall when it was closed. It was unseemly to have servants roaming the halls. They travelled by the tunnels built into the walls, giving guests the illusion that their food and toiletries arrived and were removed as if by magical means. She entered his room, and he grinned to himself when he saw the look of fear on her face. Her fear fed his hunger as well as his power, and so he took his time and enjoyed the feast before him while she watched. One of his favorite pastimes was bringing a young girl to his room and making her wait while he sampled the many meats, breads, fruits and cheese that made up his dinner. He would throw out in one night what the girl would give most anything to have as her meal for the next month or more. Lording his wealth over others truly amused him. The girl was on the skinny side due to a lack of adequate nutrition making it all the more enjoyable to Baldor when he discarded a piece of bread for being slightly stale or an apple that had a small bruise. The girl couldn't help lament the food being tossed away like so much garbage when it was better than she had eaten in her entire life. He also knew that in the morning, when he would wash for the day ahead, she would grab as much as she could from the trash and tuck it away in the folds of her skirts. She thought he was oblivious, but of course he knew all. It amused him to know that she had to remove it from the trash. Still, on some perverse level, he believed that he was doing her a service and expected a service in return. Once he had finished his meal, he turned to her and said, "You know what it is I want." She had been here before and readied herself without a word, for she knew that Baldor wanted complete obedience and he wanted it silent. She stood before him shivering, not from the cold, from what she knew was to come. He would use her in ways that she would have never dreamed of, if not for him, and prepared herself for the pain and humiliation that was to come. Baldor looked her over and his mood was improved. The night was looking up.

***

As a Draconas, Donnal's best mode of transportation was himself. Flying in his Draconas form would be the fastest way to pass over the Krull Mountains that acted as a natural barrier between the kingdoms of Erewyth and Amjukar and were home to the dwarfs of the Kingdom of Moe Din. On the other hand, he didn't want to call attention to himself, and as a Draconas he would definitely be noticed since they were few and far between. He decided that flying over the mountain was a risk worth taking and then he would obtain a couple of horses from the breeders near the border. He would then continue his journey with the horses, using one then the other, allowing one to rest and therefore make better time. He packed only what was necessary to include sufficient coin for expenses and any bribes that may be required. When he was ready to depart, he changed into his Draconas form. His clothing, satchel and additional belongings became a part of his Draconas form; a magic that he never understood but appreciated for its usefulness. He took to the sky and flew east into the rising sun while behind him Soros followed his sister moon Somara from the sky and the sun god Sol began to make his appearance in the direction Donnal was headed.

Chapter 4

Elle woke up in a strange bed. Fear and confusion muddled her thoughts as she sat up and pulled the blanket to her shoulders. The fog began to clear and she remembered leaving her home to see her sister Sela. She remembered getting lost in her thoughts...going over what her mother had told her and what it could mean. She also remembered thinking the whole thing ludicrous. She could recall changing to her Draconas form and then....nothing. She remembered nothing after that. She looked around at the room she was in, although the word "room" was hardly appropriate for what she saw. It appeared to be more of a suite of rooms. In many ways it reminded her of her old rooms in the castle of Valsara. She had successfully pushed all thoughts of her time there to the back of her mind. At least she had until now. The rooms were rather large with a very large balcony that overlooked...what? Once she confirmed that she was fully dressed in clothes of her own, she rose from the bed and walked over to the balcony. What she saw astonished her. Spread out below her was the heart of the city in the Kingdom of Amjukar, and her viewpoint was from inside the castle. She had been to the city many years before and she recognized it. Ellindria of House Kar was in a castle once again. It was surreal. It brought back even more memories she thought long suppressed. A noise coming from the door startled her and she turned towards the sound.

"Oh good ye be up!" exclaimed the plump and friendly woman at the door. "I brought ye something to break your fast and ask if ye be needin' anythin' else." She beamed and added, "Me name is Margaret, you can call me Maggie."

"How did I come to arrive here at the castle?" Elle looked at her with confusion.

"I'm sorry me lady I don't be knowin' that, but I'll have Draconas Markim come see you straight away." Before Elle could ask anything more, off she went.

Elle began to relax. She knew where she was and she knew that she was safe. In addition, she realized she was so hungry that she felt weak and faint. She attacked the food laid out before her without regard to the use of utensils and ate as though she was raised without any manners whatsoever. When she thought on it for just a moment, she grimaced and was glad there was no one around to see her behavior. Once she was done with that, she cleaned herself up as best she could with the wash basin in the room and sat down to wait for Draconas Markim. The longer she waited, the more nervous she became. After all, Draconas Markim was one of The Seven. Not only was he one of The Seven, he was the leader for the love of the goddess. Who was she to have an audience with the leader of The Seven, in a bedroom no less? At one time, they would have been equals, now those days were gone. The more she thought on it, the more mortified she became. She felt like a fraud although in truth she was not. She wished that she could be dressed in accordance with one of his station and she could meet with him in a more formal setting, although she was unsure of why he would want to meet with her in the first place.

Elle had practically worked herself into a frenzy and jumped straight up when a knock came at her door.

"Come in," she called out with a squeak in her voice, causing her to blush from head to foot.

Draconas Markim walked into the room with Maggie close at his heels. The first thing that Elle noticed was that he was slightly taller than average with dark brown hair and light brown eyes. He had both a wise and kind countenance and she liked him right away. He wore an easy smile, but she could tell that he had concern lurking in his eyes as well. What that concern was she was not privy to, although she didn't think it had to do with her. Most people wouldn't notice, but Elle was especially attuned to the feelings of those around her. It was one of her magical gifts as an elf.

Draconas Markim walked across the room and indicated the chair across from her at the table where she was seated.

"May I?" he raised his brow in question.

"Of course," she stammered, "please have a seat."

Markim sat down and studied her for a moment. She steadied herself under his scrutiny and he smiled at the effort.

"Draconas Ellindria of House Kar, welcome to the capital of the Kingdom of Amjukar. I hope you find the accommodations to your liking." At her nod, he continued, "As the most recent member of one of The Seven, I am sure that you have questions and I am more than happy to answer them."

At the startled look that came across Elle's face, Markim realized that he had an unknowing member of one of The Seven.

"It's Elle, if you please, and I do not understand what is happening." she managed to say.

"I now realize that this is somewhat of a shock to you. I do not know if you are aware of this. One of our members, Draconas Callis, has died which caused an opening in The Seven." She nodded confirmation that she was aware of Callis' death and he went on. "Once there is an opening in The Seven, a call is received by someone to fill that position and that call was answered by you. Do you remember coming to the capitol and presenting yourself to the guard at the gate?"

Elle began to automatically shake her head "No," but stopped as the flicker of a memory came to her. She had changed into her Draconas form to get to her sister faster. She then had an overwhelming urge to fly north and east once again. She tried to fight it, though it was no use.

Once she gave in to the urge, the next thing she remembered was changing to her elven form as she walked to the castle gate. The guards had been expecting her and opened the gates at her arrival. The trip had taken a few days of straight flying with little or no rest and no food, which was why she had arrived both exhausted and famished. She was led without question to a suite of rooms where she fell upon the bed and instantly went to sleep. Elle looked at Markim once everything settled into place in her memory. Draconas Markim saw the change in her features and knew that her memory had returned.

"The castle was alerted to my arrival, although I was unaware of my destination. How?" she asked.

"Our councilmember, the High Wizard Malek, was keeping a lookout for our newest member and had a vision of your flight to us. Your appearance in both Draconas and elf form was given to the gate to be on the lookout."

"I'm still not sure I am one of The Seven. Assuming that I am, why me? I am young by elf standards. I have a good amount of magical ability, although nothing compared to those of the Seven and others that are not. Again, why me?"

"It is not our place to question the reason the Kingdom of Amjukar chooses one person over another. I will tell you, however, that each time someone has been chosen they have brought something to the council that was sorely missed or needed. I assure you that at this time in history, you are exactly what the council needs." His sincerity rang forth; he believed what he was telling her with all of his being. For this reason alone, Elle began to feel that perhaps there was no mistake; that she was meant to be one of The Seven. She sat back in her chair expelling the breath that she hadn't realized she had been holding. Draconas Markim looked across the table at the beautiful elf. He saw the long auburn hair with gold and red highlights, thick and wavy and tucked behind one pointed ear. Her eyes were large, almond shaped and emerald green, framed by thick lashes that made her eyes stand out all the more. Draconas Markim had lived a very long life and had known many beautiful women. However, he was looking at one of the most beautiful women he had ever met. He also had a strong feeling that the beauty of this woman was in abundance not only on the surface but inside as well. In addition, he read her as one with a moral center and a good strong character. He had always been good at reading people. It wasn't a magical gift, just an instinct that happened to be extremely accurate. Elle could read his emotions and started to blush. Markim became embarrassed when he saw that he was making their newest member uncomfortable and so he turned away.

"I know you have questions and a lot to get used to. Please spend the day as you see fit. We will have a dinner tonight in your honor and tomorrow we will need to put some things behind us and move forward on others. I hate to be cryptic and I wish we had more time to allow you to come to terms with all of this." He turned to Maggie, who was waiting by patiently, and gave instructions to ensure that Elle had everything she needed before he headed out.

"What if I do not want to be one of The Seven?" Elle asked, causing him to pause at the door.

He stopped in his tracks and looked over his shoulder at the young elf, "The Kingdom of Amjukar chose you for a reason. Do you really want to say no?"

Elle sat down heavily on the chair and watched Markim turn and walk out the door.

Maggie indicated the time she should be ready and assured her that she would have the proper attire to wear in time for dinner. Elle needed to gather her thoughts and decided that a flight around the castle to better acquaint herself with her surroundings would be an ideal distraction. She changed into her Draconas form and flew from the balcony.

The castle sat upon a small island in the middle of a large lake which served to act as a natural mote. The castle was square in shape with a tower at each corner allowing for a complete view of the surroundings and was manned by the castle guards. A slightly higher tower rose up from the middle of the four walls and was home to The Seven, their meeting room, library and various other rooms as were needed. An elevated walkway connected each of the four towers on the walls directly to the center tower for The Seven thus allowing fast and easy access in times of crisis and for the sake of convenience. An inordinate number of extremely large balconies were evident in all of the towers, along with one for each wall, to allow the Draconas' the ability to gain entrance to the castle while bypassing the lengthy time it would take to reach the gate and ascend the towers' winding steps. Two bridges allowed the majority of the people, not aided by the ability to fly, access to the castle. The largest bridge was made of stone and could easily allow two carriages to pass each other with room to spare. At approximately three quarters of the way to the gate of the castle, was a larger area with another guard tower. Once a person was cleared to pass through, they would then cross over the drawbridge to make their way through a lengthy tunnel, the top of which was adorned with several murder holes. At the end of the tunnel was the final and largest gate, beyond which there was a large courtyard surrounded by shops and street vendors bustling with activity. The second bridge was directly opposite the main bridge leading to the back of the castle. It was a much smaller bridge, large enough only for one carriage at a time and a pedestrian or two, which caused a need for an outcropping at the gate to allow for one carriage to pass another before crossing the drawbridge portion ending at the back gate. That gate was smaller and was also guarded at all times. The back bridge was a faster route into the castle and was used for the most part by those delivering goods and those that had daily business there whether in an official capacity or not. The outer walls of the castle were wide, allowing ease of passage and use of arms by the guards that walked along the top of them while keeping a lookout for any potential threat or breach. The castle was built with the intention of keeping out the average person. If the castle was attacked by a Draconas, dragon or any other that had the ability to fly over the walls, measures were taken to man the walls with specially built weapons made for piercing the thick hide of such invaders. Water gardens were located around the castle grounds, as well as gardens for flowers to decorate the many rooms and vegetables for the castle kitchen. This arrangement would be extremely beneficial in the event of a siege. The castle and its surrounding area were nothing short of a small city inside the much larger city of Amjukar. Also, known only to The Seven, there existed tunnels built under the castle and the lake where the water was not as deep. The tunnels ran parallel with the bridges and continued well into the countryside in a copse of dense woods. The entrances were magically sealed and concealed. The tunnels were built and maintained for emergency use only. The less they were used, the less chance of an enemy becoming aware of their existence.

After another pass and a quick tour of the city proper, Elle flew back to her suite of rooms to find a hot bath and change of clothes awaiting her arrival. She stripped down and stepped into the large tub, a sigh of contentment escaping her lips. She soaked in the tub until the water grew tepid, then quickly washed and dried herself. A long dress of elvish custom was left for her to wear to dinner. The silk dress was a lighter shade of green than her eyes with small jewels and beads in floral patterns about the neck and sleeves. It was beautiful and she felt beautiful wearing it. She brushed out her hair until it was dry and placed it in a simple braid that draped across her left shoulder. Shortly after, Draconas Markim came and escorted her to dinner.

***

The dining area was smaller than was custom. It was centrally located to the suites occupied by The Seven. The roaring fire in the hearth gave the dinner an intimate feel. Candles and lanterns were strategically placed in the event that additional lighting was needed. The heavy drapes were drawn closed on the large balcony keeping the chill of the night out and the warmth in.

Draconas Markim placed Elle by his side at the table. The other councilmembers were already in attendance and after everyone's cup was filled, he spoke:

"My good friends and fellow councilmembers, I would like to introduce you to our newest member. Please welcome Draconas Ellindria of House Kar. I ask that each of you make time to answer any questions she may have and join me in making her feel at home. He turned to Elle and began the introductions.

"Since you and I have already met, suffice it to say that I am Draconas Markim Lloyd and leader of this council. To my right is Draconas Brock of the Kingdom of MoeDin of the Krull

Mountains and 3ʳᵈ son to King Druek. At his side is the lovely Draconas Akhena of no house."

Whenever someone had questionable origins, or they were unknown, it was commonplace to refer to oneself in such a manner. Draconas Akhena smiled at Elle while at the same time Draconas Brock grunted his acknowledgement of her presence as Markim continued: "Next is Draconas Lias of House Del Corone and then you have High Wizard Malek Whitestone and Wizard Tannis of House D'Lory. Usually the council is fairly even between Draconas' and wizards; although it appears that once again the Draconas' have the majority. Now that the introductions have been made, let us break bread and toast our new member for tomorrow we have much to discuss and prepare." Draconas Markim raised his glass and together they toasted the newest member to The Seven.

Elle looked around at everyone there. She felt overwhelmed. She was in the presence of the most powerful people in the kingdom, and they had just accepted her as one of them. She was in a similar position to what she would have inherited, only here she was one of seven and somehow she found that to be comforting. Her musings were interrupted by Draconas Brock.

"How long have you been a Draconas?" he asked.

"Not long; I just changed for the first time a few months ago. As a matter of fact, when I got the calling for The Seven, I assumed it was just another part of being a Draconas that I had to learn to control. I barely remember getting here. This is all new and scary if truth be told."

Akhena looked at Elle with sympathy. Being a half dwarf, half human Draconas had its own special problems that Akhena was still learning to work through. She had been the only female on the council for some time and was hoping that she and Elle would become good friends. Akhena's childhood caused her to be cautious in opening up to people, but she instinctively felt that the newest member of the seven could be an important part of her life and was looking forward to spending time with her. If she could be so fortunate, perhaps Elle would be more than a friend and be like the sister she had always wanted.

High Wizard Malek pulled Markim aside and whispered, "She is so young and inexperienced as both a Draconas and as an elf. Her abilities as a Draconas are completely new and untested. Are you confident that she will be able to participate and keep secret the scouting mission we are about to undertake to look for Desne Mar?"

Draconas Markim watched the newest member as she spoke with Akhena and replied, "Not only do I feel that she is up to the task; I am considering sending her along with one other member. We need to make sure that The Seven are represented in this and it would also allow her time during the journey to practice her magic. As a Draconas, she will also be beneficial in the protection of the scouting party. I ask that you allow me some leeway and trust in me on this

55

matter. I have a strong feeling about this and would appreciate your support. I suggest that we discuss all options at the council meeting tomorrow and put it to a vote. Now enjoy the evening, my friend, for tomorrow will be here soon enough. "

The drinks were flowing freely and Elle began to learn more about the people that were to become a large part of her life. Councilmembers only left upon death or if they voluntarily relinquished their position for personal reasons or if unable to perform their duties. The Seven had been this way for as long as recorded history and longer still. All members of The Seven were magical, be they Draconas' or wizards. Not all Draconas' became members of the Seven, just as not all wizards became members. Draconas' were few in all races of the realm, and it was constantly debated as to what made one person a Draconas and not another. Their magic differed, nevertheless, whatever magical abilities they had were great. Wizards were slightly more numerous and their magical skills varied greatly in both ability and the magical composition each wizard possessed. Some wizards could do only the simplest of magic, while others could command the elements and more. Elle was an elf and therefore had natural magical ability. Becoming a Draconas enhanced all of her magical abilities and added more that she had yet to discover. In time, Elle would realize just how much she would change and had changed already.

Elle made a point of speaking with each of the members, and during a conversation with

Akhena, she was happy to find out that the suite of rooms she was currently residing in were to be hers permanently. She was also told that she could have any changes made that she wished, including the removal or moving of any walls. Apparently having wizards in house made for easier home improvement, and since the castle was marble and stone, not trees and vines, she would not be making those changes on her own.

Eventually the dinner party broke up and Elle and Akhena walked together back to their rooms since their suites adjoined one another. They made small talk on the way and wished each other a good evening when they reached their destination.

Elle stepped inside her room and sat heavily on the bed. Her mind was reeling with everything she had seen and heard, making her feel as though she had had more to drink than she actually had. According to the whispered conversations and quick references, there was a very important council meeting tomorrow. Somehow she knew that her life was about to change once again; for better or worse remained to be seen. She looked into the mirror at her reflection and watched the myriad of emotions cross her face which was, to her chagrin, an open book. 'I need to work on hiding my feelings,' she said aloud to no one and readied herself for bed.

Chapter 5

Gustaf was beyond angry. Elle's new status as one of The Seven was not yet common knowledge, but he knew; he had his sources. He had always guarded his thoughts when in the presence of Elle because of her ability to sense emotion. He was at least fortunate that she was in the capital, far from her home, or his emotions right now would have been too easy to read until he got them under some kind of control. His mother had been giving him looks that made him feel exposed and he liked it not at all. Their father had been killed not long after the birth of Sela and was not a factor in their lives. Baby sister Sela was nothing more than a silly little girl in his estimation. Gustaf had left his family home to live on his own, which was unheard of among the elves. Due to their long lives, the family usually lived together until each child married, at which time they would build their own home and continue the same tradition. Since Gustaf was not living in his rightful home in Valsara, he believed it was his privilege to live where he saw fit. Gustaf could tell that their mother knew that there was more than one reason that her son left the family home, and he knew that her love for his sisters was greater than her love for him if she loved him at all. It didn't matter, though, for he loved no one, no one other than himself. If he were truthful to himself he would have to question that love as well.

As the day passed, Gustaf continued to chew on the circumstances that were contributing to his anger and discontent adding more fuel to fire his hatred. Not only was Elle a Draconas, he repeated to himself over and over again, she was now one of The Seven. The loss of a kingdom had been only temporary for his sister. She now helped rule another and would once again live in a castle. The prestige, wealth and power that the position would provide would go to the one that had wronged him. He raged for hours on end. Few animals within his striking distance were left alive. He reached out to each and every heartbeat and killed them with a thought. Not all animals fell prey to his tantrum. Larger animals simply felt scared and left the area or stayed away altogether. Gustaf continued to fume and the scavengers ate well that day.

***

That morning the council reconvened and came to order with the addition of their newest member. Draconas Akhena sat next to Elle and gave her a reassuring smile. Elle appreciated the gesture; she was nervous and was afraid that it was obvious to all. Draconas Markim began:

"All of you, with the exception of our newest member," at this he looked at Elle and continued, "are aware of the reason for this meeting. I would like to start by bringing Elle up to speed and then making the final decision on how to proceed."

"Elle, as the others are already aware, Draconas Callis was killed. He was killed for information that is now in the possession of this council. The scroll speaks of a land known as Desne Mar." "Land of Magic," Elle whispered and Draconas Markim continued, "Exactly, the Land of Magic or Magic Land. Some people believe that this is simply a legend and nothing more. I myself had never given it a second thought until now. However, based on the information we now have, I disagree. I believe this land exists and would like to send a scouting party to find and claim it for our kingdom." He paused and directed the rest of what he had to say to the council. "If this land does exist, then it is imperative that we claim it first. If word of this gets to King Baldor, we could be in a race for our lives, assuming of course that the land can do what is written."

"What is it that the land can provide?" asked Elle although she had heard legends of this land as well and had an idea.

"According to the scroll, the land has the ability to enhance or increase the magical ability of those that claim it as their home. If King Baldor came into this knowledge, he would not stop in his quest to be the first to find this land · if it exists · and use it not only to increase his own power, but to take over all the kingdoms of the realm. Of this I have no doubt. We are all aware of the power he has without the added benefits of this land. We know that Baldor has spies among us, as we have spies among his court, and if word were to reach

60

him regarding Desne Mar, I cannot bear to think of the possible consequences."

"You speak as if this is a known and sure thing, yet you also speak as though the place is unknown." Elle stated, "I am unclear on exactly what we should undertake and where."

"You are correct in that we do not know exactly where Desne Mar is located, if indeed it does exist, however, based on the information at hand, we have a good idea of the area. In order to find the land, someone of magical ability must be part of the scouting party because only magic can find magic and only magic can claim the land. We must be careful in our selection of who we send as well. That person must be true of heart and innocent of nature to ensure that the land does not corrupt them or that they do not corrupt the land. There is a passage in the scroll that leads me to believe that the land will change based on the nature of the magic that claims it, leading me to believe that if that magic is evil, then the land will become evil as well. That being said I feel that among this council both Draconas Elle and Draconas Brock would be best suited for this mission with the addition of our most trusted soldiers. I base my recommendation on the fact that Elle is not entirely new to power, having had some form of it as an elf her entire life, and therefore she is less likely to be intoxicated by it. I also sense a basic goodness in her that I believe will be of great importance. Most importantly, as we are all aware, the land called Elle to the council at this time. As in the past, the call has always been to someone whose talents were greatly needed at that time. I don't believe this is a coincidence. Additionally, I have complete and total trust in Brock to do what is in the best interest of the entire realm to include humans, dwarves and elves. We must of course put this to a vote. Does anyone have something to add before the vote?"

The Wizard Tannis spoke up: "Based on what you are telling us, perhaps Draconas Callis was correct when he thought that the scroll should possibly be destroyed to ensure that it does not fall into the wrong hands."

"To some extent I agree with you," replied Draconas Markim, "and truth be told I had that idea for a brief moment myself. However, what if this is not the only reference to Desne Mar and the next one is found by Baldor or his people? I think that this has come to us at this time to move forward before anyone else has the opportunity. The magic in this land is ancient and has a mind of its own. We of all people should know this to be true, having heeded to its call once before. We would do well to listen to it once again."

High Wizard Malek started to object then simply shook his head and was quiet.

"I would like to accompany Elle on this quest," announced Draconas Akhena as she spoke up. "She is new to all of this and I believe that I am better equipped than anyone else to help her through the changes she is facing. I mean no offense, Brock." She indicated him and then turned to Markim and said, "Assuming of course that Elle finds this arrangement satisfactory."

Everyone turned to Elle, expectantly awaiting her decision. She was not afraid of the trip. She felt overwhelmed. Everything was happening at once and she hadn't had time to even process the fact that she was one of The Seven.

"I have been a Draconas for only a few months and one of The Seven for a day. Now you wish to entrust me with something that could be the most important event in recent history. I do not feel worthy and am afraid that I will not meet this council's expectations." Elle fell silent not knowing what else to say.

"It is for the very reasons that you just stated that I feel you are perfect for this task." Markim spoke with quiet conviction: "Had you believed yourself equal to the task, I would call you arrogant and rethink my reasons. Now, you will have additional security and a councilmember to help you along the way. I think that your training as an elven Draconas would benefit from the trip you are about to undertake. Which councilmember attends you can be decided by you or this council, if you prefer. Elle, I know this is all new to you and your thoughts are in turmoil. If this land does exist, then we need to begin this journey now. What say you?"

Elle knew that she really had no choice. "If it is the will of the council, I will go." She replied.

"Excellent!" Draconas Markim cleared his throat and continued: "Before we finalize the

63

details of the trip we also need to discuss the ceremony expected by the people, regarding introduction of their newest councilmember. Under normal circumstances, there would be much pomp and circumstance with several days' preparation to be followed by seven days of celebration. Obviously this would cause a delay we cannot afford at this time. If it is acceptable to the other members of the council, I would suggest that we make an official announcement to introduce our newest member, and inform the public that the official celebration would be extended to 10 days and take place at the end of the harvest, providing us a few months to bring this to conclusion. Perhaps we can change things so that this will be the norm from this day forth. We can indicate that this is to ensure that the farmers will not have to miss precious planting and reaping times heretofore and they will also be in a position to supply the celebration with fresh produce, meats and cheeses. "

The Wizard Tannis was normally quiet, but in this he spoke up, "I have good friends that farm the land or raise cattle, and although the celebration ceremonies are rare, they do cause a hardship to them at certain times of the year. I feel that this change, although for a different reason, will be well received by those that are affected most. The general populace will most likely be upset at the delay for a reason to celebrate, yet it is a sound idea."

"Thank you, Tannis. Shall we vote? All in favor?" Draconas Markim looked around the table and watched as each member, save for Malek, nodded their assent. Majority rules applied to all council meetings, and so Elle was voted to yet another change in her life.

***

Sir Devin, the Commander of the Knights of Amjukar, stood over 6 feet and had a lean muscular build. He wore his brown hair short and his face sported a thick mustache, but no beard. His gray eyes looked over the newest recruits to the Knights of Amjukar and he frowned. The kingdom had become complacent in recent years. As he reviewed the recruits, he saw only boys. Gone were the days when boys became men at an early age from necessity, and he wondered if perhaps that was a bad thing. He knew that on the other side of the mountain range King Baldor's armies were pushed relentlessly to perform beyond most human's capabilities. It was also whispered that Baldor had his wizards enhance the abilities of his most revered fighters through regular doses of magic. Whether this was true or not Sir Devin was not sure, however, he knew that it was in the Kingdom of Amjukar's best interest to prepare as if it were. He looked over at his closest friend, confidant and 2nd in command Sir Borg, and based on the scowl evident on his dwarven features, he knew he was thinking the same thing. Borg was all dwarf; short in stature with dark hair and eyes set in a heavy brow. His bulbous nose could compete with some of the best tracking dogs in the kingdom. Devin and Borg, ·· human and dwarf ·· made quite the show to any who saw them for the first time. One would think that due to Sir Devin's demeanor, which

65

caused most people to instantly like and trust him, and the gruffness of the dwarf that made him standoffish, would mean they would have little in common. It was their very differences, however, that made them the best of friends. What one lacked the other had in abundance, which came in handy in any situation whether it be a bar fight or eluding a traveling thief.

"What do they expect us to do with this lot?" Borg grumped to his friend as he always did after his review of the new recruits.

Devin grinned at his friend, then turned a serious face with which to address the new recruits. "Welcome to the Knights of Amjukar training," he began and was interrupted by a runner from the castle. He excused himself, pulled Borg along with him, and the third in command took over the recruits with a question in his eyes. Devin had no clue as to the reason for the interruption and shrugged his shoulders in reply.

"What is this about?" Devin queried.

The runner apologized for interrupting and told Sir Devin that he was simply asked to bring him to Draconas Markim straightaway. He looked at Sir Borg and indicated that his name was not mentioned, but Devin cared not and insisted that he attend as well unless Draconas Markim himself requested that he leave. The runner shook his head slowly from side to side, eyes cast down, as if to say 'it's on your head' and motioned for them to follow.

Once inside the castle, the runner took his leave and Devin and Borg proceeded to Draconas Markim's quarters. The castle was large and Borg found himself walking double-time, as usual, when he was with his long legged friend. Normally Devin slowed down as a matter of habit. It was more than unusual to be requested for an audience with a member of The Seven, however, and Devin was both curious and concerned, causing him to quicken his step.

When he approached Markim's quarters, he was told to enter and he found him waiting for his arrival.

"Ah, I see you have brought Sir Borg with you. Excellent. When I speak of this, you will both hear firsthand since you will both be a party to what I have to say. Please sit and pour yourself a drink that we may get down to the purpose of this visit."

"Thank you, Draconas Markim. How may we be of service?" Sir Devin asked.

"Please, Devin, in private call me Markim; we have spoken of this before, many times I might add." He saw the stubborn set to Sir Devin's jaw and sighed, "The consummate professional as always and the reason I have asked you here." Markim looked at them both, then used the dampening shield to keep the risk of being heard to an absolute minimum. Although Devin and Borg were not magical, they could feel a shift in the room and knew that something had changed.

"Don't worry," Markim began, seeing their silent exchange, "I simply cast a shield to keep our conversation from being overheard. I have asked you here to take part in an expedition that may lead to nothing or may lead to the betterment of this kingdom and the people that live in it. What I am about to tell you cannot be told to another person. As of this moment, only the members of the council are aware of what I am going to disclose to you. However, as with any secret, the more people that know, the more likely it is no longer a secret. I cannot stress this enough. Do not speak of it even in your sleep." He paused and looked pointedly at each of them to bring his point home and continued: "There is purported to be a land known as Desne Mar or the Land of Magic, and we are in possession of a scroll that gives an idea of where this land is located and what it would mean to those that would lay claim to it. I know you are aware of the death of Draconas Callis. What was not common knowledge was the fact that he was killed for the contents of said scroll which is being sought by someone else. Unfortunately, we have no idea who the person or persons are, nor whom they represent, although it would be easy enough to make an educated guess. We are reasonably assured that the exact contents of the scroll are not known, which gives us a slight edge. Fortunately my good friend and comrade Draconas Callis was both strong and intelligent and the scroll did not fall into the wrong hands. The council has also attained a new member in his place. Her name is Draconas Ellindria of House Kar although she goes simply by Elle. She is new as a Draconas and new to the council. I believe her to be our best choice for claiming the land. You will accompany Draconas Elle and another member of the council Draconas Akhena, to look for this land. The fact that someone killed Draconas Callis trying to obtain this scroll leads me to believe that perhaps someone may have an idea of the scroll's contents and is simply waiting until they see what steps we take. You may enlist as many or as few men as you feel appropriate. No one other than yourselves, Elle and Akhena will know the exact reason for the expedition. I recommend that you refer to it as a new training method that is being tested to avoid any unwanted queries. Do either of you have any questions?"

"Where is this land supposed to be located, and how will we know when we have found it?" Devin spoke up.

"According to our information, the land is in the barren desert wasteland south of our kingdom and the Kingdom of MoeDin of the Krull Mountain range. It is believed to be close to the old elvish lands before they were destroyed. Both Elle and Akhena are magically gifted and should be able to locate the land when they get close enough. I think that Elle's magic being both elvish and Draconas will be of more assistance."

"Why do we want to be claiming a barren wasteland?" Borg's gruff voice boomed unnaturally loud in the dampening field.

"According to the scroll once the land is claimed by someone of magic it will be transformed.

We can only surmise the extent of the transformation. I feel that if this is as big as I believe, then I would hope the change would follow suit."

"When are we to leave?"

"Will two days be sufficient to gather your men and supplies?"

"We can be ready on the morrow if you will it."

"Then it is done. I will make sure that Draconas' Ellindria and Akhena are ready and at the front gate by dawn. Thank you."

Sir Devin and Sir Borg bowed to Draconas Markim and made their way out. They had much to ready by dawn.

***

Donnal sat at the Horse Head Inn and lifted a pint while observing his surroundings. For the most part, the patrons of the establishment were humans with an elf and a dwarf thrown in here and there. He was listening with his Draconas senses for anything out of the ordinary, but there was nothing to be learned from this place. Unfortunately, his brooding good looks gained him unwanted attention from the barmaid, and Donnal had to resort to being rude to fend off her advances. He finished his meal and was once again on his way. The horses were a good breed and with proper care they would be able to endure the journey ahead without incident. Donnal abhorred mistreatment of the majestic beasts of burden and he knew this caused much amusement to his liege who felt that all was placed here to serve his needs. Perhaps King Baldor was right, though Donnal still felt an affinity for the animals which they could sense. This was a good thing because the horses could also sense the Draconas form within the man, and this would normally give them good reason to be extremely skittish.

Donnal knew that his best bet to find out anything of import was to make his way to the capital of Amjukar, contact their local informants and bribe castle guards or other servants more interested in gold than loyalty. Frequenting the local hangouts of the castle guards off duty would likely provide him with additional details concerning the death of Draconas Callis..... at the very least.

He felt that time was slipping by and he pushed the horses to the max short of causing them harm. When he felt that the horses were in danger of coming up lame he slowed them to a walk and found a good area to set up camp. He caught a few hours' sleep before setting back out after seeing to the horses' needs and assuring himself they were ready to travel. He couldn't explain it, but he knew that he needed to increase his already arduous pace and began to rethink not using his Draconas form. Instead, he pressed on.

Although Donnal was a Draconas and flying was, without a doubt, his favorite way to travel, he had missed traveling on horseback. Airborne one could see far and wide, yet the subtle nuances of the places one traveled through went unnoticed.

He enjoyed the smell of the rain and the freshly turned earth caused by the horses' hooves. The air was much different on the ground and was so resplendent with smells that it was almost a tangible thing, whereas the air higher up was thinner and without substance unless you flew through a cloud. Donnal actually flew through clouds intentionally when in his Draconas form. If they were especially thick clouds, the water drops could be significant enough to feel as if he were standing under a waterfall. Once through, he would use his fire to dry and warm himself and the result was a feeling of being both clean and refreshed. Despite the feeling of time running away from him, Donnal allowed himself to slow for a short time to enjoy the sensations for just a while. He patted the side of the horse's neck and leaned into her to enjoy her scent as well. For just a short while Donnal allowed himself to just feel and his mind was free from all thought.

***

Elle rose early though she had slept little the night before. She was to begin a journey today that she felt ill-equipped to deal with. As an elven Draconas, she was more than capable of taking care of herself and her magic was in a constant state of growth. What concerned her most was the responsibility. Just days ago she was responsible to herself and her family alone. Now she was told that she was responsible for the welfare of an entire kingdom and to some extent, the realm. It was ludicrous. Elle had come to terms with a smaller place in the world many years ago.

Apparently, her life had taken on a life of its own and she was just along for the ride. She looked at herself in the mirror as she dressed for her journey. Maggie had laid out her clothes and for that she was thankful. She dressed in a comfortable and serviceable outfit that would allow her to both ride a horse with ease and change into her Draconas form. The outfit would simply appear and disappear as needed, this being a more practical part of the Draconas magic and was one of the only magical properties that all Draconas' had in common. She placed her auburn hair in a long thick braid, although a few strays escaped to frame her face. Her emerald eyes looked frightened to her and she set about trying to look more deserving of her new station.

She felt the presence of Draconas Markim before he appeared at her door, and so she was ready when he was admitted. She tried very hard not to listen to other people's emotions. Sometimes emotions were plain to see and any fool would know them for what they were. Elle could tell that Markim found her attractive and was trying not to show it. She was no child, but he was a good deal older, whether he looked it or not, and it bothered him that she affected him so. Perhaps it was good that she was leaving the castle for a while.

"Are you ready, Elle?" he asked her.

"I'm not sure that I'll ever be ready, although I am packed and dressed if that will suffice," she teased and found that she was not as afraid as she was just moments before.

Markim returned her smile and said, "Akhena is waiting by the gate. She appears to be very excited about this. I am glad the council agreed to allow her to accompany you."

"As the only other female of The Seven, and a Draconas as well I am sure we will have much to speak of and teach one another."

They left her suite that was still so new to her. They both could have changed into their draconas forms and made their way out much faster, but there was something about using their own two feet and taking the time to descend to the bottom floor of the castle and out the front gate that was lost otherwise.

Chapter 6

The journey she was about to undertake became all the more real with the sight that greeted her outside. Other than Akhena and herself, there were more than 50 knights waiting to act as escort. Some had seen a few years and others didn't appear old enough to shave. She would later find out that this had been intentional. Sir Devin decided to use this opportunity to have some of his more seasoned knight's help with the training of the knight cadets on an actual mission instead of the reenactments they usually used in the training yard. All of the knights, both young and old, had been handpicked by Sir Devin and Sir Borg for their level headedness as well as their skills in combat or the potential they had shown. He did not want a full contingent, yet he also felt it necessary to have enough in attendance to make an impression on anyone or anything that they may encounter or that may wish to interfere with their plans.

Sir Devin rode up holding the reins of a dapple gray mare for Elle and a lovely chestnut mare with white socks and nose for Akhena. Introductions were made and the girls mounted up.

Draconas Markim gave last minute instructions to Sir Devin, then pulled Elle and Akhena aside, "I want to make sure that you committed everything to memory from the scroll. Devin is aware of the approximate area of Desne Mar, as are the two of you. Please remember that he cannot find the land without magical assistance. I expect both of you to work on the development of your magic on the way. Assume that you are in a race for this land because we are not aware who else may know of this or may find out. I am sorry you have been given little choice in this matter. Please be careful." He squeezed Elle's hand and looked at her with a guarded expression. He seemed to have some sort of inner struggle and when his decision was made, he squared his shoulders and addressed Elle once more after pulling her aside.

"I know that you are Ellindria of House Kar, true Queen of Valsara, and it was your father's desire that you would lead your people when the time came."

Elle looked at him in surprise; no one ever spoke of her family's background to include her own. It never occurred to her that someone would know who she was.

Draconas Markim continued, "I knew your father well. He was one of the best swordsmen and overall fighters I have ever known. It could only have been treachery or overwhelming forces that could have taken him down in his prime. I was very sorry to hear of his death." He bowed his head in respect then continued, "The other elves on our council are well aware of whom you are as well. We did not say anything to the other members of The Seven feeling that it was irrelevant. I will leave it to you to reveal what you wish about yourself in your own time. I believe you are destined for great things, Draconas Ellindria of House Kar, one of The Seven of the Kingdom of Amjukar, rightful Queen of Valsara, and look forward to seeing what will become."

With that he then turned to Akhena and gave her a look that she knew meant to convey: 'watch out for her.' Taking his Draconas form, Markim returned to his rooms in the tower of the castle. Elle was speechless as she watched him depart.

"Shall we go?" Sir Devin asked as he gave his horse leave to head out. Sir Devin took lead; Sir Borg brought up the rear and soon they were on their way.

***

Draconas Markim made his way back to his suite of rooms where he found the High Wizard Malek waiting for him in the common area.

"They have gone?" Malek asked.

"Yes, I just saw them off. I am surprised you did not attend." replied Markim.

"I do not know how I feel about any of this," Malek stated. "Draconas Callis kept this to himself and didn't come to the council right away for a reason. I see something coming, and it is not clear, which leads me to believe that King Baldor and his dark wizards may be cloaking whatever it is from me. His powers have grown to an extent that concerns me more than I care to admit."

"I understand how you feel, but my point on this is clear. Someone knew that Callis had something in his possession. Whether they knew what it was or not we have no way of knowing. However, at some point this will get out. Already too many people know and that's the people we trust. Who else? I told Draconas Elle to make all haste because I feel that someone else will be looking for Desne Mar if they are not already doing so. If this land exists we cannot allow it to fall into Baldor's hands."

"I am sure you are right," replied Malek, "however, I am a wizard. It is not in my nature to trust and I need to consider all options before acting unless it is something I have already prepared for. Let us hope that a young elf maiden and a young dwarf/human female are the right choice for a quest of this potential magnitude." The High Wizard Malek turned on his heel and left the room.

Malek found himself outside the quarters of the Wizard Tannis. Although Tannis was an elf and Malek was a human, the fact that they were both wizards and the only councilmembers not a Draconas, did not exactly make them friends but made them closer than would be the norm. With his wizard sight Malek knew Tannis was already waiting for him, so he entered Tannis' quarters.

"I see that everyone was up with the sun this morning." Tannis directed Malek to have a seat. He knew he was tired, considering Malek preferred to sleep in and walk the castle at all hours of the night.

"Who can sleep with everything that is going on?" Malek replied.

"Did you see the party off this morning?" Tannis asked.

"You know better. Have you thought about what we discussed last night?"

"I have," Tannis stated simply.

"And?"

"I agree. Leaving this in the hands of two young women, one of whom has no experience with anything like this, is asking for trouble. I would recommend we go ourselves, but we cannot go against the will of the council. We could, however, send our own scouting party to help ensure the success of finding this land that I still am not convinced exists. The question is who can we send? Who can we trust enough to do this? Some magical ability is a must or they will be unable to locate the area. They should be loyal to you or me. It would also be best to be able to send someone that could blend in to the "training mission," preferably someone that was already slated to go." Tannis smiled widely.

"You have already placed someone, haven't you? Who is this person?" Malek stared hard at Tannis.

"My brother Cylus was chosen by Sir Devin himself. He knew only that he would be involved in a new method of training that is being tested. The knights were not told the details, just given a general direction. I pulled Cylus aside when I found out he was going and told him just enough for him to realize how important this all is. He will keep an eye out and report directly to me until they reach the wasteland. As an elf he has magical ability, and as my brother his loyalty is to me before all others. Do you approve now?" Tannis allowed for a slight grin.

Malek visibly relaxed. "How old is your brother?"

"Approximately 150 or more years I believe."

"Why he is not even of age yet – not much better than the girls we have now," Malek snorted.

"Perfect for our needs I assure you. You know I'm right. Now if you don't mind I have things to attend to and I'm sure you would like to return to your bed."

To which Malek replied, "I don't know when I will be able to sleep again."

***

The expedition was underway. Draconas' Elle and Akhena were in the middle of the trail of horses at the insistence of Sir Devin. Devin and one of his elven knights led the party while Borg took up the rear. Elves have an uncanny sense of their surroundings, which is why Sir Devin placed one in the front of the party. Also, although Sir Borg was average size for a dwarf, he had a tendency to see more than the average person, making him ideal in keeping an eye on everyone from the rear. Many a knight in training had learned their lesson when trying to get something over on the dwarf. His reputation was such that only the new recruits were fool enough to try anything. They started out on the paved roads of the kingdom and the horses made good time. Even the trail they were headed to in the forest was well worn and easily traversed. The trip would take an unknown amount of time and they would need to hunt on occasion to supplement their provisions. Devin had told all in attendance that they would need to travel light, and take only the supplies absolutely necessary for the horses and themselves.

They continued at a good clip until they arrived at the edge of Fallon Forest. Fallon Forest was named for a wizard that once called it home many years before. The forest took a southerly route providing good cover for the first part of their journey. There was a slow moving river that meandered through the middle of the well-travelled path. Two horses could easily walk side by side on either side of the river travelling north or south. The trees provided much needed shelter and the river provided fresh water for drinking and bathing. Having started at sunup, they paused midday to eat and to rest themselves as well as the horses. Being near the most northerly section of Amjukar, they were in the beginning of spring and days were more than likely to be cold and wet. The place that they chose to rest was a little off the path, yet still close enough to the fresh water and provided a thick canopy of leaves overhead in the event an afternoon shower were to catch them unexpectedly. They were fortunate in that at this particular time, the rain had let off and the sun shone through the forest canopy in areas not quite as dense. Many of the knights took advantage of the lull in the rain and found pockets of sun in which to warm themselves. No fires were lit because this reprieve would be brief. Deciding that they would also take advantage of the unusual sun, Akhena took a seat next to Elle on a large rock near the river and offered to share her rations.

"Thanks, but I have already eaten."

"How are you faring?" Akhena inquired.

"That depends on what you are referring to: the fact that I am a new Draconas, a new councilmember of The Seven, or that I'm on a quest not of my own choosing?" She picked up a stone and watched as it skipped along the top of the water before finally sinking.

"All of the above?" Akhena playfully asked. She also chose a stone and threw it, although instead of skipping across the top as Elle's had, it sank immediately, drawing a laugh from them both.

They sat in companionable silence for a short time with Akhena trying unsuccessfully to skip a stone.

Elle appreciated her new friend trying to bring levity to the situation and after yet another sinking stone she said, "The time on the road will allow me opportunity to adjust, I suppose. I would like to take my mind off of everything and focus on my training. Tell me, Akhena, how long have you been a Draconas and one of The Seven?"

"To the shock of everyone, including myself, I became a Draconas when I was not more than 45 years of age. Approximately 50 years after that, I received my calling when the Wizard Catarina stepped down after only 600 years on the council. It is my understanding that her kingdom is on the other side of the sea, and she was called home to take her place as Queen among her people at the death of her brother who had borne no heirs. She was the only woman on The Seven for a very long time. I have been on the council for several years which have been the best years of my life despite the fact that I also was the only woman for that time."

Elle thought on this for a moment. Apparently it was not uncommon for someone destined to rule to be called to The Seven. She wondered.... *If she had already assumed the throne of Valsara, would she still have been called? Had that ever happened? In what manner would the kingdoms involved handle such a quandary?* Food for thought on the long ride ahead.

After tucking the thought away to retrieve and review another day, she once again turned her attention on her new friend, "You are so young, Akhena, to have become so much."

"Not so young as you would think. Before I was a Draconas I was simply a half breed, half human ·· half dwarf. I never knew my parents and grew up with a human woman that acted as a sort of substitute until I left to make my way in this world although I was still rather young. I am quite sure that my leaving caused her no grief. In fact, I am sure that she was relieved to be done with me. She has never tried to make contact with me, even when I was indoctrinated into The Seven. Honestly, I have had no contact with her since the day I left and would not know how to find her. That part of my life is over and I am thankful for it. She felt as though she were beginning to brood, something she was quite good at, and pushed it down before continuing.

"As a human, my life expectancy was about 200 years. As a dwarf, my life expectancy was 400 years or more, so becoming a Draconas at 45 years of age might be considered a little early if you were to average the lifespans of the two races. Now we are Draconas' and can live for several thousands of years. It still boggles my mind!"

Elle studied Akhena and wondered if Akhena believed herself to be an attractive woman. Elle considered her so, perhaps not in the classic sense, but there was something about Akhena that made you take a second look. She appeared shorter than she really was due to her voluptuous figure and stocky stature, though she wore it well. Her hair was a sandy color, thick and always in a braid that stopped at the bottom of her back. Her face was square with a strong jaw that suited her, considering her build. It was her eyes, though, that drew you in. Her eyes were a crystalline blue with a dark blue ring around the iris. There was a guarded look in her eyes at all times and Elle hoped that one day they would be such good friends that at the very least the guarded look would no longer be there in her presence. Elle started to ask another question when Sir Devin said it was time to move on. It did not take long to pack up and they were once again on their way.

No one noticed when Cylas stepped away from the rest of the knights and made his way into the woods. He checked that no one followed and he spoke through the tree by placing his hand on the bark and giving a simple message – "All is well."

Chapter 7

Gustaf had left several hours earlier deciding to make his way to the capitol. He would make contact with people he knew to see what the word on the street was. Then he would show up at the castle and announce himself as Elle's brother. How could she possibly turn him out; they were related after all. If he couldn't be a Draconas or King of Valsara, then the least he could do was try to take advantage of the fact that his sister was not only a Draconas, she was also one of The Seven. There had to be something in it for him. He had stopped at his family home just long enough to help himself to supplies for his trip, clean out the emergency fund his mother kept hidden in an old teapot and to obtain a horse. He was unaware, nor would he have cared, that at that time his youngest sister Sela had seen him taking the supplies and knew that he had not taken the time to visit with their mother. Although Sela was young, she knew that her brother was "off" and had the good sense not to approach him or make him aware of her presence. She stayed hidden in the shadows until he was gone.

The horse was skittish around Gustaf, which both annoyed him and made him smirk with satisfaction. He used to practice his magic on the farm animals and perhaps this horse had been one of the recipients of his training. He didn't care so long as the animal didn't try to unseat him. He stayed to the main roads that led to the capitol seeing no reason to hide his passage. When he came to a small tavern with a few beds, it was closing in on dusk and he decided to call it a day. He tethered his horse and went inside. It was dark inside the tavern and would take most men a minute or two to adjust to the poor lighting. Gustaf was an elf, and his sight was almost as good at night as it was during the day. He made his way to the bar and requested the old man behind the counter to have someone care for his horse and provide him with a room for the night. He took a pull of the ale placed in front of him and made himself aware of his surroundings without appearing to do so. From his vantage point at the bar, he could see the entire room and part of the kitchen. It was the girl in the kitchen that piqued his interest. Gustaf knew that he was handsome and could be charming when it suited his needs. He believed he was a decent judge of character and could tell that the lovely girl waiting on a food order for the regular seated at the end of the bar would take some persuasion to warm his bed. Her blonde hair, hazel eyes and voluptuous figure would be worth the effort. He downed his drink and handed her the mug for a refill when she approached him.

"Thank you..?" Gustaf left the question open.

"Please enjoy, good sir," she replied shyly. "Me name is Kate."

Gustaf continued, "I would be honored to have you join me, my dear Kate. Perhaps you have a break that is due or your shift is coming to a close?"

She bowed her head and blushed at being flirted with by the handsome stranger, when it was usually a married local, and replied, "If you're quite sure, I'd be happy to sup with you when me shift is over...if you can wait but an hour."

Gustaf stopped himself from showing his aggravation; he hated waiting for anything or anyone, especially some foolish girl, but said, "I would be most happy to wait until your shift is over, although I have to oversee some travel preparations and will return."

Her face fell because she didn't believe he would be back but Kate remained ever hopeful. Gustaf requested a boy be sent to his room to run some errands and he headed there himself.

As it turned out, the hour was well spent and he found himself prepared for the morning's departure at first light. He headed back to the common room and the girl lit up at the sight of him returning for her. He purchased her dinner and coerced her into a few glasses of wine. Gustaf ignored the looks he was getting from the tavern owner. If he didn't mind his own business Gustaf would teach him how. When the girl was obviously intoxicated, Gustaf lead her to his room. Once they were inside his room and the door was shut and locked behind them, the poor girl sobered at what she knew was about to take place.

"Kind sir, I've 'ad me a wonderful night, but feel it's past time that I retire to me room. I fear I've 'ad a bit too much to drink. I'm not used to drinkin.'"

Gustaf had known that this time would come and he was ready.

"Are you a tease girl? You knew what I wanted when you followed me up here. No one forced you to come to my room."

"No, sir; I swear, sir, I just started working 'ere when me father died. I'm not knowing the ways of men and women, sir. I've never been with a man, sir."

"Why do you think I asked you to my room, girl?" Gustaf had a predatory look in his eyes that she hadn't noticed before. It caused her such fear as to mute her voice. He picked her up and threw her bodily onto the bed. She began to cry and Gustaf laughed. He ripped her gown and she cried harder for it was the only decent gown she owned and now it was beyond repair.

Before Gustaf could lift her skirts there came a banging at the door.

"Go away." He yelled through gritted teeth.

"Open this damn door elf and allow the girl to leave, or every man in this tavern will have a go at you." The tavern owner was clearly agitated and Gustaf was under the impression that he meant every word. Gustaf could hold his own in a fight and had his magic to help level the odds, yet he knew that he was pressing his luck if all of the regulars that he had seen earlier were ready to defend her honor.

Gustaf was angry once again. He called on his magic and began to take the air from the girl that lay there so helplessly. The panic that came immediately when she had thought herself saved was at least something he could enjoy for a few moments. Her eyes were wide as the banging commenced at his door. Only when he could hear that they were striking the door with a large object did he finally give in.

"I'm coming, I'm coming. No need to bust your door down. If you do so, I refuse to pay for unnecessary repairs."

He allowed the girl to breathe once again and flung the door open to admit the angered owner and patrons.

One look at the frightened girl with a torn dress gasping for breath and they were ready to kill Gustaf on the spot.

It was all the tavern owner could do to keep blood from being spilled. His concern was for the welfare of the girl, and he was afraid a confrontation would most likely bring her to harm.

The tavern owner looked at Gustaf, his hatred on the surface and something that Gustaf could respect and said, "I strongly suggest that you pay the girl for the dress that you have ruined. I also strongly suggest that you are out of this room and far away by first light."

Gustaf smiled wickedly and replied, "I would be happy to oblige. If you would be so kind as to have some rations for the road and my horse saddled and ready I will be on my way before first light as you request." He flipped a coin at the girl as though she were a common whore. At first she refused to take it but one look at her dress had her swallowing her pride. She picked up the coin, placed it in her pocket and ran to owner, placed her arms around his ample waist and cried into his apron.

The owner bit his tongue at the gall of the damn elf and gave a brief nod of his head in acknowledgement.

***

Donnal finally arrived at the capitol without incident only to find that a training party had been assembled and left just a few days before on an expedition. No one seemed to know the exact nature of the expedition other than for training purposes, which quite frankly made no sense whatsoever. His sources at the castle spoke of meetings using dampening spells, which was unheard of in the Kingdom of Amjukar, and a new Draconas of The Seven that had gone on the expedition along with Draconas Akhena. It all added up to a secret that Donnal was determined to uncover, for he believed that it was too coincidental not to have anything to do with why he had been sent there. As much as he wanted to stay in the capitol, he felt compelled to catch up with the party and observe what was said and done. He would need to replenish his supplies and would head out at first light. He wasn't worried about catching up to them, it took the larger party longer to make and break camp as well as use time for any breaks they might take. He could easily make up the lost time. He found a place to stay the night, quench his thirst and appease his appetite. Donnal kept an ear open to all whisperings going on around him and overheard someone asking questions about the expedition. From what he could tell, the man was more than a little irritated that the newest councilmember had left and therefore was no longer at the castle. Donnal glanced in the direction that the conversation was coming from and saw a tall elf that was probably considered handsome. Donnal could tell that the elf was dangerous as well as mean in spirit, although the elf tried to hide it. Donnal was immediately curious about this elf that showed so much interest in the latest addition to The Seven and decided to make his acquaintance. He may not know of the training expedition or what it entailed, but perhaps he could shed some light on one of the members of the party. There was no such thing as too much information. He made his way over to where the elf sat and pulled up a stool beside him.

He requested a drink for himself and the elf and queried, "I am looking for some information. Would you care to join me in a drink or two while I ask a few questions?"

Gustaf looked Donnal over and knew that this was not someone to take lightly. "I will be happy to allow you to buy me a drink, but I make no promises in having answers for you."

"Fair enough," Donnal replied and downed the remainder of his mug. It was refilled by the bartender who also brought another for Gustaf as requested. Donnal looked at the elf and said, "My name is Donnal, and you are?"

"Gustaf of the House of Kar." He raised his mug in a toast that was more than a little sarcastic.

"I am seeking information on some people, as well as an expedition, that left the city a few days ago. Any information would be appreciated," Donnal said as he glanced at the money pouch he had attached at his waist.

"What kind of information are you looking for?" Gustaf asked as he eyed the pouch.

"Anything and everything. I need information on the newest member of The Seven, and more importantly, I am seeking information on the nature of the expedition that recently left."

Gustaf scoffed, "I can tell you all you want to know about the newest member because she is my sister. The expedition is a simple training mission and of no importance."

Donnal inclined his head towards his money pouch once again and asked, "Would you be willing to give me some information on your sister...?"

"Ellindria," Gustaf finished for him. "Everyone just calls her 'Elle,' which is disrespectful to our family, if you ask me, but no one does, and no one else seems to care.   Never mind all that, what do you want to know?"

"Everything."

"She thinks she is better than me because she became a Draconas. Now that she is one of The Seven, she will be an insufferable bitch. I don't know what magic she used to make this come about but I intend to find out or at the very least get what is owed me now that she is in this position. After our stupid bitch of a mother allowed our cousin to take the throne of Valsara, I believed that perhaps my fate lay elsewhere, or why would I be cheated of my crown? But no, my sister is the one blessed by good fortune." Gustaf warmed up to his topic and continued, "I came here to gain entrance to the castle and take advantage of her station only to find that the bitch had already left and they will not give me leave to enter the castle without her approval. Can you believe that?"

Gustaf failed to tell Donnal that the crown was to go to Ellindria for he refused to believe it himself. His delusions of grandeur would never hold up if he faced the actual facts. It was much easier for someone such as him to believe that he had been duped, for to believe otherwise was to admit he was deemed unworthy. Who would be the object of his hate and anger then?

Donnal smirked to himself. Gustaf was delusional if he thought his sister could magically conjure herself to be a Draconas, not to mention one of The Seven. It was impossible. The magic was old and was part of this world. No one could manipulate it in that manner, not even King Baldor had that kind of power. However, Donnal nodded his head in agreement with Gustaf because he planned to use him for as long as he proved to be beneficial. He also did not feel it prudent to let Gustaf know that he, like his sister Elle, was also a Draconas, for Gustaf would most likely be jealous of him as well and would be of no more assistance.

Donnal played into Gustaf's delusion, "Your sister, Elle, sounds like she took this from you somehow. Perhaps if you come with me, we can observe and learn and maybe find a way to get it back." Donnal didn't tell him that the training mission was more than it appeared to be. Gustaf was prone to anger and when angered he apparently ran his mouth and Donnal didn't want this information to become public knowledge.

"What are your reasons for following the expedition?"

"My reasons are my own. Will you accompany me? I will pay all expenses."

Gustaf thought about his current prospects and decided that he could do worse than to follow this man, at least for a while.

He looked up at Donnal who was taller by a few inches, held out his mug for a refill and asked, "When do we leave?"

**

King Baldor flew to the training grounds where his soldiers were being tested in all manner of combat. His Dark Wizard Balquin was overseeing the soldiers to choose those that would be made into something more. The fighters didn't know exactly what was entailed. They knew it would make them stronger and harder to kill and that's all they cared to know. Perhaps if they knew the full extent of the transformation that would take place, they would not be as eager to be one of the chosen.

Baldor hovered while he tucked in his wings, came to land beside the Wizard Balquin and watched the combat commence. Although he changed into his human form the soldiers in attendance were no less intimidated. King Baldor was no one to be trifled with and it was common knowledge that he would kill a man for any or no reason at all. It was the inability to anticipate his thoughts or actions that kept all in his presence on guard and alert at all times. A moment's lapse in diligence could end in one's death.

Baldor settled in to watch and was pleased to see that several of the fighters were incredibly large of their own accord. Some not blessed with bodies made for fighting made up for it in strategy. It was painfully obvious which ones would simply become front line fodder or food for the dragons that he kept imprisoned for his own needs. When the time came, he knew that the dragons would have no choice but to do as they were told or their eggs would be destroyed. Dragons only produced offspring once every thousand years, and this event had just recently occurred. If the eggs were not allowed to hatch, the dragon race would be greatly diminished and in danger of dying out.

Baldor looked down at the dark wizard and asked, "Have you made a selection of those you wish for me to consider for the transformation?"

"I have, my king. Do you wish to meet them?"

"Bring them here."

The Wizard Balquin called an end to combat and spoke with his magically enhanced voice. "When I call you, please step forward. Green 1, Green 2, Green 3..." He continued the count until he had addressed four colored groups numbered 1-20 and a last color group numbered 1-21, allowing for an even number when the king chose their commanding officer from among them. All other soldiers were told to return to their current assigned areas.

King Baldor laughed out loud, "I applaud you Balquin, eliminating their personal identities. Very efficient. I wish to look them over one at a time."

"I want everyone in order by your designation. This is how I expect you to line up or approach myself or your king at all times. One by one you are to step up to King Baldor for review. Do not speak unless spoken to. You know what it is expected of you."

The soldiers lined up and approached Baldor as requested. He looked them over as he would any property he owned. He looked them in the eye and none could keep from averting theirs, none that was until Red 3. Red 3 stood his ground. He was not the largest in the group, but there was an intelligence in his eyes that was evident to the king. He appreciated intelligence because he felt that it was in such small supply.

"What is your name?" Baldor asked.

"Red 3" was the reply.

"I did not ask for your designation; I asked for your name."

"My name was Andal," he replied.

"Your name is Andal once more," the king spoke, "Lieutenant Commander Andal, to be more specific. I am making you the leader of this group and wish to have an actual name to refer to."

"As it pleases my king, thank you."

Baldor turned to Balquin and said, "I want this man, Andal, briefed on what I expect from my commanders. I expect you to begin on the transformations immediately. I want our new leader to be modified according to his new station. I trust I don't need to explain myself."

"No my king, it shall be done." Balquin turned to leave.

King Baldor stopped him in his tracks, "I believe that something is coming up that we must be ready for at once. The time for "getting it just right" is over. Administer the change as it is now. No more waiting. Am I clear?"

"Yes, my king," the wizard conceded.

The group, which King Baldor would refer to as his Baldoran Horde, was led to their new quarters to begin their transformation. Lieutenant Commander Andal was placed in separate quarters of his own, as he would be given special attention.

The group of men stopped to watch their king change into his Draconas form and fly back towards the castle. King Baldor was not only the largest Draconas in the realm; he was also the most powerful magically. He feared nothing and no one. He would find out what The Seven were hiding and snatch it right out from underneath them. Once back in his quarters, he reached for the amulet around his neck and called out to Donnal to learn of his progress.

***

Donnal and Gustaf were well underway tracking the trail of the party that a blind man could follow. Although the party started out a few days before, Donnal felt confident that they would catch up with them soon despite the addition of the whining companion he now had in tow. If Gustaf wasn't complaining about his sister, he was complaining about the weather or whatever else had his attention at the time. Donnal was beginning to wonder if any insight Gustaf gave him of his sister would be worth the aggravation of having him along. Most elves were as one with nature and very family oriented, so Gustaf's attitude was a constant surprise. They had stopped to rest and eat, and once again, Gustaf found something disagreeable.

"This squirrel is stringy and overcooked. Is there nothing else?"

Donnal glanced in his direction, "If you do not like what is prepared, feel free to hunt and cook for yourself."

"I can kill an animal with but a thought," he bragged. "Perhaps I will kill and prepare a nice fat rabbit and you can eat my share of the squirrel."

"As I just said, feel free to prepare your own supper," Donnal stated dryly.

"You said that you would take care of my needs on this trip…" Gustaf whined.

Donnal looked at Gustaf and came to the conclusion that this man was a waste of air. However, he knew that if he dumped him now, he would be constantly looking over his shoulder because Gustaf would continue in the same direction. Better to have the enemy in your camp where you can keep an eye on him than at your back where you are constantly on alert. He shook his head in disbelief and threw a piece of jerky to the elf.

"I want to get a move on as soon as you finish eating. We have almost caught up with the party from Amjukar and I'd like to try to do so by nightfall."

"I'm tired and need a break."

"I agreed to cover your expenses, not to act as your nursemaid. We are heading out shortly." Donnal began to pack up, not looking to see if Gustaf would follow suit or not. He had had enough.

***

Elle was lost in her own thoughts when Sir Devin approached and startled her.

"My apologies, Draconas Ellindria," Devin bowed.

"No need, and for the umpteenth time please call me Elle," she smiled at him.

He was always caught off guard by her beauty, as most men were, and it never failed to embarrass him. He cleared his throat and said, "We'll be stopping soon to set up camp for the evening as soon as we come to a good spot I know of just up ahead."

"Thank you."

Sir Devin returned to his men and gave orders for the evening's preparations.

It wasn't much later that they arrived at their destination. There was something soothing to Elle about the hustle and bustle of the camp's activity when it came to readying themselves for the night. Tents were pitched; wood was gathered, and food was prepared. There was an ordered chaos about it and she was impressed at how quickly they had fallen into a routine with everyone falling easily into their role. A large bonfire was started and the game that had been caught in route was added to the rations on hand. They did this every night to conserve their rations in the event that the mission took longer than was anticipated. The knights assumed it was for practical experience. Many of the knights were from privileged families and had never had to hunt for any reason other than sport. Several smaller cooking fires were lit and smaller groups from within the whole took care of their own dinner and entertainment.

Elle walked throughout the camp and made an effort to stop at each cooking fire and talk with those around it. She took the time to try and commit their names to memory and asked if there was anything within her power to make their life a little easier on the trip. The one request that was repeated over and over was getting Borg to back off their training. Each and every time she gave a knowing smile and promised that there would come a day when they were thankful they had such a dutiful commander.

The men all adored her. Not only was she easy on the eye, she was good at heart. It was obvious to them all that she took them seriously and did not look down on them as she had every right to do.

The men also liked and respected Akhena. Akhena was more like them and in many ways had the mannerisms of a man. Akhena had become "one of the guys" in their eyes and she was genuinely glad for it. It was a big deal to the half dwarf, half human. Not only did she have a home among The Seven, she apparently had a home among the Knights of Amjukar as well.

Elle and Akhena spent their days riding side by side and talking of whatever came to mind. They worked both together and separately on their magic and were becoming fast friends.

Akhena's magic was entirely due to her becoming a Draconas, and she had learned to use it well. She had the ability to move objects with her mind and had been practicing on larger and larger objects over time. The larger the object, the quicker she would tire, so working on her stamina while wielding the larger objects was her primary focus. She could also wield an axe with a ferocity greatly enhanced by her magic, although as half dwarf her strength was also inherited.

Elle's magic was both elven and Draconas in nature. Her elven magic allowed her to ascertain the feelings of those around her and now sometimes to the extent of hearing their thoughts. She could cause trees, vines, flowers, vegetables, etc. to grow or move in any way she desired. With the addition of her Draconas magic, she could grow things in seconds or minutes that with only her elven magic in the past would have taken days, weeks or even months. She also found that she could manipulate the elements, causing rain where there is sun and wind where no breeze stirred. As with all magic users, the larger the task, the more stamina was needed, requiring Elle to work on her strength and stamina as well. Each day she practiced or tried something new and was often rewarded with a new ability or a vast improvement on one she already had. It was exhilarating and she didn't realize that the rate at which her magic was growing was unheard of. That day, she called a horse to her with only a thought. As much as she might like to determine the extent of this particular ability, she had not tried it on a person, knowing in her heart that it was wrong in so many ways.

One of Elle and Akhena's favorite pastimes was watching Sir Borg. The girls had learned to set themselves in a position to be able to watch him in action. The gruff dwarf was constantly drilling the knights en route. He would often come up behind some poor unsuspecting soul and engage him in combat. Not once did a rookie or a veteran get the better of the dwarf, and more often than not, they were made to look the fool. Sir Borg was persistent because he knew that sooner or later they would face a very real threat and he wanted them to be prepared. The knights knew only that they were on a training expedition and felt that Borg was simply a hard taskmaster with no sense of humor. Elle and Akhena knew different. Borg had a very dry sense of humor and the subject of that humor was often the knights themselves. He spent the evenings regaling them with tales of the poor men that made them look less than knightly to the amusement of Devin, Elle and Akhena. Being half dwarf, Akhena found herself spending more time with Borg and began to think of him as a father figure or favorite uncle. Borg was not one to show emotion, but it was clear that he was becoming very protective of Akhena, falling into the role of the father she so desperately wanted. They were often seen speaking with each other when Elle was busy elsewhere. Elle and Sir Devin were happy for them both.

That evening was like the others with one exception. Donnal and Gustaf had caught up with the party and were listening quietly nearby. Gustaf wanted nothing more than to waltz into camp and confront his sister. It took a lot of talking and more coins than Donnal wished to part with to convince him not to do so. They listened to the talk around the camp gleaning nothing of importance.

"We're not going to learn anything here toni· ..." Donnal stopped speaking when he saw one of the men split off from the group and he decided to follow him." He gestured to Gustaf to wait for him with their gear.

He slipped quietly through the forest and followed the elf Cylas, who was making sure to get a good distance from the camp to make his daily report. As an elf, Cylas had excellent eyesight and hearing. As a Draconas Donnal's eyesight and hearing was better still, even if he was in his human form. He followed Cylas from a distance and listened when he made his report. He spoke to a tree and his family's magic allowed the transfer of messages from tree to tree. "So far everything has been as would be expected. Draconas Elle has been practicing her magic, and it is whispered that it is growing at a tremendous rate. I will try to learn more about her magic and keep you informed."

Donnal knew instinctively that Elle was important and could be the key to what was going on. He would stay close to the party to learn what he could and follow Cylas at night to learn what he knew as well. He was glad that Gustaf had stayed at their camp. He could only imagine the tantrum that the bitter elf would have if he knew of his sister's increasing abilities. He headed back to get some sleep for he felt in his bones that things were about to become interesting.

In the castle, back in the Kingdom of Amjukar, Draconas Markim did what he was best at and paced inside his rooms. It had been several days since the expedition party had left and he couldn't help but wonder at their progress. There were also whispers coming from the Kingdom of Erewyth of an army of magically enhanced soldiers, the purpose of which was unknown. They had enjoyed peace for so long that Markim was concerned about the rumors and the preparedness of Amjukar's army. He had sent for the next in command of the forces, due to the absence of Sir Devin and Sir Borg, to ensure that all was being readied as if for war. He informed the lieutenant that he wanted all of the knights and soldiers training as if combat were imminent. He honestly wasn't sure if that may be the case and didn't want to be caught with his defenses leaving much to be desired. He was also a little concerned at the newly formed "friendship" between the wizards Malek and Tannis. They had served on the council for several years, and only now had they begun to spend time with each other. It made Markim nervous to feel that something was going on that he knew nothing of. As the leader of The Seven, it was his responsibility to know everything going on in the kingdom, and he wasn't sure he knew everything that was going on in his own council. The question was whether to ignore this new alliance or confront Malek and Tannis to find out if there was something he should be made aware of. He had known them both for a very long time, and though their personalities were not conducive to becoming good friends, he felt that they both had the kingdom's best interest at heart. Perhaps he should satisfy himself with that knowledge and trust that if there was something he should be party to, then he would be. On that thought he decided to let it go for the time being.

***

The High Wizard Malek and the Wizard Tannis had indeed been spending more time together as noticed by Markim. For the most part, Tannis simply relayed any information he received from Cylas, and they spoke about the new abilities Cylas was aware of where Elle was concerned, although he was not aware of all of her abilities. Malek felt that Elle was receiving too much, too soon and could become reckless if things continued the way they were. At this rate, her magic would become something of legend and without equal in the history books. Tannis, being an elf as well as a wizard, felt that Elle was better equipped to handle that which she was coming into, although he had some reservations as well. Having Cylas reporting to them gave them a sense of some control, but was it enough? They decided not to take further action unless it seemed warranted. Of course, with the rumors coming from Erewyth, further action may be required soon.

Chapter 8

The party had been travelling for several days, and as expected, there had been no problems to contend with north in the Fallon Forest. The further they travelled south, the greater chance they would have of running into trouble. Forest thieves, goblins and others that travelled outside of the law to earn their way in the world sometimes made the forest their home, and the majority would traverse the well-worn path looking for an easy mark. This had been one of the things that had been taken into consideration when Sir Devin was tasked with determining the size of the group that would go on the mission.

Sir Devin sent one of his senior men ahead to scout the area they would be travelling through within the next hour or so, as was his custom. It wasn't much later that the scout came back with news of a band of goblins ahead with a few prisoners. It was unclear whether the prisoners were human, elf or dwarf, but it was clear that they were being held against their will and would most likely be the goblins' next dinner. Sir Devin knew that making their destination was of the utmost and primary importance, but could not in good conscience leave the prisoners to their fate. After obtaining confirmation on the distance and layout of the land in which the goblins had settled, Devin called the knights together to form a plan of attack.

Elle and Akhena would take their Draconas forms for this fight and attack from the air.

Donnal, listening from nearby, was privy to the conversations and decided that if he played it right, this would be the best way to keep an eye on the group by integrating himself among them. He spoke to Gustaf regarding his plan and prayed that the belligerent elf would heed his instructions.

Sir Borg was positively buzzing with excitement at the prospect of a good fight. His hands clenched and unclenched his war axes, while his feet shuffled side to side. Other than the training sessions he'd had over the years, there had rarely been reason to fight and kill for one's very existence. Goblins? Could life get any better? He pulled his axes from his belt and twirled them in anticipation with a grin on his face that was rarely seen.

Sir Devin laughed and shook his head at his friend and lieutenant. Only Borg, or any dwarf for that matter, would whistle in happy anticipation of the upcoming combat. Devin pulled his sword and was comforted by the feel. He checked for all of his throwing knives and sheathed the sword when he was satisfied all was in its proper place and ready for action.

The knights were also preparing for the upcoming battle. The veterans knew that goblins could be deadly opponents, having fought them in small skirmishes before. The rookie knights felt confident that they could walk in, defeat the band of goblins, save the prisoners and walk away unscathed, soon to have songs written about their feats by the local bards. To them this was simply a nice break in routine. They would soon learn a difficult lesson. Fighting, any fighting, was a bloody ordeal for all involved and the romantic notion of it portrayed by those same bards would be quickly dispelled.

Sirs Devin and Borg quietly made their way close to the clearing where the goblins had set up camp and had a rather large fire going. They could make out the prisoners being held with their backs tied to trees at the edge of the clearing, although they were in shadow and Devin could not tell what race they were. The difference in the races could change the way they approached the rescue. If the prisoners had been dwarves, they would feel confident in the dwarves' ability to protect themselves when the majority of the other goblins were engaged in combat. All elves had some form of magic to help them, but humans could be a wild card. They went with the assumption that the prisoners were humans and planned their attack accordingly. Those that were expert with a bow remained at the edge of the woods where they had some measure of cover, and were close to the clearing in the trees where they could pick off the goblins one at a time. Elle and Akhena would change into their Draconas forms and attack the goblins as a dragon would, using teeth, claws and fire. The other knights would slowly make their way toward the goblins' camp and surround them as best they could, considering the goblins' superior numbers. After the archers shot their first volley to thin out the enemy, those waiting in reserve would attack.

The band of goblins numbered well over one hundred strong and although they were considered to be somewhat lacking in intelligence, they were tall, broad, fierce and strong. Standing at just about seven feet, some slightly shorter while others were taller, they had large claws extending from their blockish fingers and sharp serrated teeth perfect for cracking bones. The grayish brown goblins were intimidating to even the most accomplished fighters. What they lacked in intelligence they usually made up for in sheer numbers and brute strength.

Sir Devin easily removed the goblins' lookout who had been more interested in sleep than his duty. Devin was surprised they had one at all, or perhaps the goblin simply wandered from the main group and found a tempting place to rest. He gave the signal and the archers raised their bows. A second signal called for the release of the arrows. When the arrows rained down on their targets, the sound of the goblins' screech of anger and surprise blocked out all other sound and sent all manner of animal life, still in the vicinity, running in every direction.

Sir Borg could contain his eagerness no longer. Calling out his clan's war cry, he ran directly into the middle of the clearing and the goblins gathered there. One would think that due to Borg's short stature that his participation in the fight would be short lived, so to speak, especially in comparison to the much taller and larger goblins.

The opposite, however, was proven true. He was incredibly fast and agile making his way between the goblins and taking them down with his axe and his war hammer. His first blow was usually aimed at the back of their knees and was followed by an axe to the chest, back or head. His movements were controlled and precise, allowing him to fell his opponent with minimal energy. He was a lethal fighting machine and was enjoying himself immensely. His shorter size proved to have an additional benefit when fighting the goblins. There was such a difference in their height that the goblins would accidentally hurt their own when two or more attacked the dwarf at the same time. In the end it became apparent that the goblins were spending more time trying to stay clear of the dwarf instead of engaging him in battle. All the while, the dwarf repeated his battle cry and cheered himself on with the death of each goblin unlucky enough not to remove himself from Borg's path in a timely manner.

Despite Borg's flurry of activity, there were still a large number of goblins with which to contend. Elle soared from atop the canopy breathing fire at those goblins still caught in the open. She was attacking in her Draconas form for the first time. As a matter of fact, Elle was fighting for the first time, whether it be as a dragon or an elf. Although she was a beautiful Draconas with her red and purple scales, she was also a ferocious dragon sporting sharp teeth and claws. This was also the first time Elle had used her fire for something other than cooking or warmth, and she was amazed at how natural it felt to her. After noticing the Draconas' in their midst, the goblins were no longer as keen on fighting to keep their dinner and most began to make a break for the woods. She opened her maw once again and blew her fire on the goblins that were fleeing for cover. Right after Elle made her appearance, Akhena followed suit and they crossed each other's path raining down as much destruction as they could while avoiding being mauled or maimed by the goblins they were pursuing. The goblins' preferred tools of combat were large rocks, crude spears and daggers for the most part. Goblins weren't particularly skilled in the use of any particular weapon and were, in fact, more likely to claw, bite or bludgeon. Because of this the goblins were ill prepared and outmanned by the Draconas' both in brute strength and skill. Had a few more Draconas' been among their group, the goblins would have taken off immediately and not tried to engage in the fight at all.

Elle and Akhena were trying to avoid setting fire to the forest by targeting the goblins in the clearing. The two Draconas' worked in such a way as to keep the goblins running in circles in the clearing while trying to find an opening to exploit. They began with the outside of the clearing and laid down a swath of fire between the goblins and the trees. With each pass, they tightened the circle. Sir Devin had to physically remove Sir Borg before he became trapped with the goblins. Borg grumbled at having his fun interrupted, but finally made his way to the outside while the girls continued to corral the goblins still standing. Out of desperation, several of the goblins ran through the wall of fire hoping to reach the other side despite the heat of the dragon flames. Those goblins were brought down by the archers or the knights waiting for just such an action. If one of the goblins entered the forest and was on fire, it would be next to impossible to keep that fire from spreading. Those that were still in the middle of the circle of fire were finally consumed by the flames that closed in on them. Once the majority of the goblins had been eliminated, the knights began to finish those that were left. Screams were heard from both sides as metal, rocks and arrows found flesh and bone. The veterans were prepared for the strength of the goblins. The rookies' overconfidence ended in a few deaths and more than a few injuries.

Akhena landed and made her way to the prisoners. At first the prisoners were afraid and taken aback by the Draconas. Most people had never seen one in person. Akhena quickly took her natural form and the prisoners visibly relaxed. Using her axe, she cut through the ropes tying them to the trunk of the tree and yelled over the noise for them to follow her. What turned out to be a human family with a husband, wife and three children followed Akhena without question while trying to avoid the fighting on all sides. Akhena moved quickly with the family in tow.

Akhena turned to check on her charges when she saw two goblins from the corner of her eye. She turned towards the goblins that, in a panic, had changed course heading directly in her direction. Had they known that the smallish woman in their path was one of the draconas' they had just fled from, they would have altered their course. Akhena readied herself for the onslaught when a man she did not know ran from the woods and came up from behind them. With the ease of one with much practice, he pulled his sword and removed the first goblin's head with one stroke of his blade. The other goblin turned towards this new threat and was rewarded with the loss of an arm, followed closely by his head as well. A single stroke removing the head of a goblin was no small feat and although Akhena was leery of this stranger that had just come to her aid, she was also impressed.

The man, whom they would later learn to be Donnal, turned away to join the main fighting and continued the attack on the few remaining goblins. Where Borg was quick and decisive, Donnal was fluid and graceful; his kills had the appearance of a deadly dance.

Elle saw the entire incident take place and her eyes widened in disbelief as yet another man entered into the fray. Her brother was here, in this clearing, fighting the goblins alongside the stranger and the knights. What purpose he had to be here at this time and place was a question better left for when the fighting was over. She shook off her trepidation and got back to the matter at hand.

Elle banked towards a small party of goblins. They were trying to make their way to the cover of the forest and were close enough that fire was no longer an option. Using her wings to stall in the air, she hovered over the largest in the group. She extended her legs out and grabbed the goblin. Her talons were sharp and sank deeply into the flesh of the belly. Elle rose up, the goblin scrambling for purchase that just wasn't there, until she gained sufficient altitude. She dropped the dying goblin to the ground and with a quick turn of her long neck, she bit the head off another before he could raise his weapon. Having led the humans out of harm's way, Akhena rejoined the fight and they made quick work of the few that remained. Any goblins still alive had fled deep into the forest by then and were no longer a threat.

When the fighting was over, it was almost as though by design. Everything stopped at once and the party of Amjukar found themselves standing in the middle of a blood bath covered by fire and ash. Both goblins and knights lay dead amid the clearing and in the trees. Some of the wounded were among the dead and crawled to separate themselves. Those left unharmed, or at least reasonably so, went to their aid while others went about ensuring that the fires were completely out.

The dead were piled up in the middle of the clearing and a fire was set to dispose of their remains. The knights that had lost their lives were placed away from the main camp for a proper burial or fire in the morning, depending on the race of each knight. Elves preferred a cleansing fire which is also favored by most that evolve into their draconas form. Both humans and dwarves preferred burial. Those that were injured were taken to a large tent being temporarily used by the healer.

Still in their Draconas forms, Elle and Akhena, without having to communicate their desire to one another, set off deeper into the forest far away from all of the activity to find a deer or boar. Neither Draconas had ever fought in their dragon form before but they instinctively knew that the camp rations would not be sufficient to satiate their hunger. It was not long before they came across a few deer in another clearing further west and picked out a mid-size buck. Instinctually, they knew not to take a doe. There was a good chance that, being spring, any doe they chose would most likely be pregnant. When they had finished their small feast they returned to the camp.

Elle had never before taken a life. At the time of the fight, instinct took over as well as her Draconas nature, and not once did she hesitate. Now, however, the fight was over and Elle felt as though she would vomit. Considering the buck she had just helped consume, it was an unappealing thought. Sir Devin came to her side and gave her a look that told her it was normal to feel as she did and waited for her acknowledgment that she would be alright before returning to the task at hand. Elle glanced at the bonfire making quick work of the corpses there; then turned her back to it, for it surely would not help how she felt. As she began to walk away, she remembered her brother. It was time to find out what he was doing here. She didn't need to see him to know where he was. She only had to travel in the direction that her brother's angry thoughts were coming from. Once she turned towards Gustaf, her eyes fell on him and what she could only assume was his traveling companion. She took a moment to speak with Akhena regarding the care of the family saved from the goblins before turning her attention to her brother.

Elle assessed the man with her brother, trying to get a read on him. She knew her brother's nature and assumed that anyone traveling in his company must be someone to be wary of. She had to admit, though, that the man standing with her brother was rather striking in appearance. Additionally, one could not discount the fact that the man was an accomplished warrior with the swordsmanship of a master. Elle could also agree that her brother was considered handsome in a cold and dark way, some women finding him irresistible for the bad boy image he portrayed. Elle knew, however, that it was his true nature, not some persona he wished to convey, and so to her he would always be ugly. She could feel the waves of hatred coming from her brother from across the clearing, and Elle had to consciously try to close herself to those feelings. Since her magic had grown, those with especially strong emotions could hit her like a clap of thunder. The emotions coming from her brother were more intense than any she had ever experienced. The thunder clap was more like a full blown storm with strikes of lightning. Elle turned her magic to his companion and found only curiosity and appreciation for her beauty. She was startled by this and let it show before she masked her thoughts, something she was continually working on. She started across the clearing and Donnal proceeded towards her with her brother in tow.

Sir Devin caught the end of this exchange and quickly made his way to intercept Elle, having been charged with her wellbeing, before she came upon these newcomers that were unknown to them.

"Thank you for your help with the goblins," Devin addressed the men. "What good fortune brings your aid to us at this place and time, if I may ask?" It was more of a demand than a question.

Gustaf immediately became angered at being questioned and started to reply although he was interrupted by Donnal, "You are welcome for the help. My traveling companion, Gustaf of House Kar, was trying to reach his sister and I decided to accompany him since I have my own business to attend to further south. My name is Donnal, of no house, and I am pleased to meet you......?"

Sir Devin heard the open question and answered, "Sir Devin, Commander of the Knights of the Kingdom of Amjukar. You are welcome to join us when we stop to rest. I'm afraid we must finish the cleanup here before we settle down for the night."

Gustaf started to walk away when Donnal piped in, "We would be happy to assist in any way we can."

Gustaf glared at Donnal. He had no intention of participating in any cleanup and defiantly sat down on a log he found furthest from any work needing or being done. Donnal looked at Gustaf with thinly veiled disgust and went to work alongside the knights of Amjukar, joking and telling tales to everyone's amusement, including Elle's. Once the goblin funeral pyre was no more than a pile of hot ash and the family had been given sleeping blankets and a place by the camp's, fire everyone sat around and enjoyed a quiet evening of food, drink and talk as far away from the stench of battle and corpses as possible. Donnal explained that he had business that he could not speak of that was in the south and would very much like to join their group for his protection, as well as theirs, since he would be providing them with another seasoned fighter. Gustaf simply said that he had shown up at the capitol to see his sister, only to find that she had recently left on a training expedition. He stated, with no small amount of anger, that he had been refused entrance into the castle to await her arrival and then gone off somewhere to sleep. It was clearly obvious to everyone present that Elle's brother was brooding, to put it mildly, and although he had found his sister, it appeared that he could care less about the fact. Elle was worried. She knew her brother and she knew that if he had come all this way to see her, then it was for a reason not in her best interest, for he only did things in the best interest of himself. She then considered the hatred coming from Gustaf in waves that was so strong it literally hurt to feel them, and she became more worried still. She knew that he had become jealous when she became a Draconas, so she came to the conclusion that becoming one of The Seven of Amjukar was more than her brother could tolerate. She would need to discuss her concerns with Sirs' Devin and Borg and Draconas Akhena to make them aware of a potentially problematic situation. She hadn't formed an opinion of his companion as of yet. His emotions seemed to be what she would consider normal, and at least he made not only an effort to help but had done the work of two people. She was still leery of anyone that would acquaint themselves with her brother, and so she held off on welcoming him to their group.

Elle was contemplating what, if anything, she could do when Donnal spoke to her, "Draconas Ellindria of House Kar, one of The Seven, may I have a word?" He indicated an open area next to her at the fire.

"Only if that is the last time you use my entire title. Please call me Elle." she said with an easy smile.

Donnal sat beside her and looked at her fully as if studying her every feature in detail. She began to blush much to her horror, and in a voice that could only be heard by the two of them, he said, "Please accept my apologies. It was not my intention to embarrass you." He saw that his acknowledgement caused her to blush all the more and he apologized once again. "I am so sorry. I would walk away from this situation to save you further embarrassment, however, I need to speak with you in private and hope we can come to some agreement. I understand if you would feel more comfortable with someone you trust at your side. Will you meet with me tonight before retiring?" Donnal kept eye contact with Elle while waiting for her answer. Gustaf had told him of her ability to read the feelings of those around her. He believed that Elle was exquisite and he kept his thoughts along those lines while he watched her contemplate meeting with him. Elle looked at Donnal, looked past the handsome face and knew that he was hiding something. She didn't know if it was something to concern her or just something he kept hidden as all people had something that they preferred to keep to themselves. She did not feel anything malicious coming from him and that was what she based her decision on.

"l will meet with you and I will have Sir Devin in attendance as well. We shall meet you in Sir Devin's tent if that is satisfactory?" She asked.

He agreed and they continued with their meal in amicable silence.

Later that night, Sir Devin and Draconas Elle were waiting in Sir Devin's tent. The tent was slightly larger than Elle's or Akhena's because they also used it for planning and needed room for their portable table with which they could gather around. Donnal arrived at the tent in a timely manner and was shown inside. The table was large enough to seat six people, yet it was currently occupied only by Sir Devin and Draconas Elle. Donnal entered the tent and was directed to a seat directly across from Sir Devin. Elle could feel only concern coming from Donnal, not ill intent, and she visibly relaxed. Devin took his cue from her and relaxed a little in his seat as well.

"Donnal is it?" Sir Devin queried and at Donnal's nod continued, "to what do we owe this pleasure?"

Donnal replied, "I like a man that gets right to the point. I would like to start by saying that I greatly appreciate the courtesy shown me. That being said, I will get right to the point as well. I am on my way south for reasons of my own, as I previously stated. I have travelled with Gustaf, though I would very much like to continue with your group. Had Gustaf and I come across the goblin horde and not seen it in time to go around, we would have been in a bad way to say the least. I believe that we can help each other. However, the main reason I wished to speak to you is to warn you. "

Sir Devin bristled at the statement as though it were a threat. Donnal read the look on his face and held out his hand with his palm facing forward as though to stop Sir Devin's assumptions and said, "I am not threatening you." He paused and continued, "I am concerned for Draconas Ellindria." He turned to face her directly and continued, "I have travelled with your brother and have been subjected to his tirades about you. He has great hatred for you. I have never seen such jealousy. He feels slighted, or should I say he actually feels duped by you, and thinks that you did something to take what should have been his. When you became one of The Seven, he went to the Capitol to take advantage of your new status. The fact that you were not in the capitol when he arrived, was seen as yet another intentional slight.

I wanted to tell you this so you could be on guard. I realize that he's your brother, and I would understand if you didn't believe me. After all, we just met and you don't know me, but I would not put it past Gustaf to cause you harm. I could not in clear conscience keep this from you." Donnal finished his prepared speech and sat back in his seat for her reaction.

"I appreciate that you have brought this to my attention. I am aware of my brother's ill feelings towards me, although I did not know the extent of them. If you will please allow Sir Devin and me to discuss this amongst ourselves, I will speak with you again if the occasion arises tomorrow. In the meantime, please make yourself comfortable."

"Of course, my lady, and thank you." He gave a slight bow and left the tent.

Devin looked at Elle, "Did you know about your brother?"

"I was beyond shocked when I saw him today during the fight. My brother has always alienated himself from our family. He has always been rather arrogant, and when I became a Draconas, he became angrier than I had ever seen him, whereas my mother and sister were very happy for me. I felt his hatred, and I do mean hatred, coming from him when we saw each other today. I had every intention of telling you, Borg and Akhena at the first opportunity. Like Donnal, I was also concerned, more so that an innocent person may be harmed if they are in the way of anything my brother may decide to do to alleviate his anger."

"I will make all of those in positions of authority aware of the situation. Do you want me to force your brother to leave the camp?" Sir Devin inquired.

"I thought about doing just that, but think we are better off having him where we can keep an eye on his activities."

"And what of this man Donnal? What do you get from reading him?" Devin asked.

"I am undecided regarding Donnal. On the one hand he comes across as genuine. I also feel an underlying deceit which may have nothing to do with anything and may only be personal, considering our mission however, I'm not sure we can take a chance. Then again, as with my brother, at least in camp we can keep an eye on him as well."

"I am inclined to agree. At least for the time being, we will allow them to remain in camp as long as they do their share, although based on what I heard about your brother, he may be asked to leave the first day for that reason alone."

"Gustaf always felt he was entitled. If he doesn't do his share, then we will have to make him leave and deal with the consequences if they arise," she stated.

Donnal was close enough to pick up the conversation with his Draconas hearing without being obvious. He knew that by going to her regarding her brother he would gain some level of trust. He would have to continue to gain that trust because being on the inside was by far easier than traveling behind and trying to gleam information. Now all he had to do was convince Gustaf to play along. He knew that Gustaf would never be able to hide his anger, and he was banking on that to get closer to Elle. He thought about the emerald eyes that had searched his in the tent and felt a twinge of guilt that he was doing all of this to betray her. Donnal was the type of man who believed in "live and let live" and would not intentionally cause harm or deceive someone. However, he owed his allegiance to King Baldor and he would follow through as always. No pretty girl···or in Ellindria's case···a beautiful woman would cause him to forget his duty to his king. He would enjoy flirting with this elven Draconas just enough to pique her interest. Although he rarely used his talents, he was quite adept at wooing the fairer sex when it suited him. Let the games begin, and the gods help Gustaf if he gets in his way.

The next morning, Soros followed his sister Somara from the sky. Before the sun god Sol would make his appearance, the camp started coming to life. Everyone was busy getting their gear packed. Donnal watched Gustaf take care of his equipment only and he sat and waited for everyone else to finish with the tents and common areas. Disgusted with Gustaf's attitude, he decided that the best way to keep the peace was to do enough around the camp for both of them. His work ethic did not go unnoticed by those that were most important, and Elle found herself making her way to the handsome man that morning when all was ready to continue.

"I wanted to thank you for what you are so obviously doing. It was decided that if my brother did not do his share, that he would have to leave the camp and I'm afraid of the consequences of such an action. Thank you for your help in keeping the peace. I certainly don't expect you to continue to do so."

Donnal looked down at Elle and replied, "I am happy to do so. Please do not concern yourself."

"Again, you have my thanks." Elle turned on her heel and mounted the dapple gray waiting patiently for its rider.

The day proceeded without incident, allowing Elle to practice her magic while they continued on their journey. On occasion, she would accidentally pick up a stray thought and one of those thoughts was about someone killing her. She actually tried to tune out the thoughts of others, but was glad that she had been unable to when she turned in the direction of said thought and saw her brother's eyes boring into her back. Her brother knew that she could read feelings. She wondered if he would be so blatant in his thoughts if he knew to what extent that her power had grown. Elle was well aware that her brother hated her, but was still shocked by the random thoughts he was projecting on ways to eliminate her from his life. Elle knew that she was stronger than her brother in many ways and was not afraid of him. Unfortunately, anyone could get lucky, and someone who wanted you dead could find many opportunities to do so. One only had to know of her father's death to know that for a fact. Her father was known as the fastest and best all-around fighter in the kingdom of Valsara, if not the entire realm, yet he was killed by treachery and cowardice. She would need to stay alert and let the other members of the party know the extent of what was happening. Perhaps she should speak with Donnal as well to gain another set of eyes, since he seemed to care about her wellbeing. Once again, they made camp for the night with the hope that each day would be as uneventful as this one.

Chapter 9

King Baldor was in the suite of rooms he occupied at the castle. He had been amusing himself with a few of the girls he kept on hand for just such occasions. When he had had his fill, he simply told them to leave, which they did with all haste; all except one young woman who lingered slightly to both the anger and amusement of the king. He had to admit that of all the girls he had slept with, she was without a doubt the best in anticipating his wants and needs. Not only was she talented in the bedroom, to an extent, she also derived pleasure from her own pain. Her beauty was unmatched by few others in his kingdom as well, although there were others that he considered to be more beautiful. In many ways she mirrored him. Her long black hair fell below her waist, ending at her hips, drawing his attention to the soft roundness found there. Her dark brown eyes flashed with pleasure and mischief. Perhaps he may have found the right woman to bear him a male heir. He supposed he should inquire as to her name. He would think on this at a later date; right now he had more pressing matters. He turned to her with a hard look that said in no uncertain terms that she needed to leave with all haste. Any other woman would have run from the room and been thankful to do so but this one flashed a smile his way and sashayed from the room without a stitch of clothes on. Baldor was again both annoyed and amused, although he watched her leave nonetheless.

With the exception of the amulet around his neck, he was naked as he moved around in his rooms. Sweat glistened from his pores and anyone that might see him in this state would swear that power oozed from his pores as well. His body was muscular and tanned and he was magnificent to look at even though he was by far the cruelest man that existed in the realm. He continued pacing and thinking about what he had just learned. He had tracked down the man that brought the scroll to Draconas Callis and had him tortured and questioned. He was sure that no one could hold up under such torture and still hold back information. The man knew nothing other than the fact that the scroll was old and he believed it was written in Draconas. It also may or may not have been about a land. The man was unclear on this. That was little to go on, but he was sure that Donnal would prove to be resourceful enough to find out more. Once again he used the ever present amulet around his neck which never left his person and contacted his trusted servant and commander.

***

Donnal was making his way into the forest, following Cylas, when his amulet became warm signaling that his king was trying to reach him. The timing was awful, but he knew that he could not ignore it. Much like Cylas' use of the trees, Donnal could speak directly through the amulet. Baldor informed him of the man they broke and

130

asked if he had anything to add. Donnal told his king that he had been able to ingratiate himself into the "training party" and was building the confidence and trust of Draconas Ellindria. Additionally, he was currently keeping watch on someone on the inside with an apparent ulterior motive and he was trying to ascertain the nature of that motive and how best he could exploit that information. King Baldor was impressed with Donnal's progress although he would never say as much. Once his conversation was over, Donnal continued to the place Cylas had been approaching, only to find him already on his way back. He turned and proceeded to camp where he slipped quietly into his bedroll and was awake for quite some time considering what he had been told and what it could possibly mean before finally falling to sleep.

The next morning after they broke camp, they continued their journey south and noticed a gradual clearing of the trees in the forest that covered their passage. The further south they went, the warmer the climate and everyone found themselves wearing a little less armor to accommodate. Sir Borg was once again drilling the knights as though the very devil was on their tail, and the higher temperatures caused for higher tempers. Woe to the poor soul fool enough to complain within range of Sir Borg's hearing. His height may have been lacking, but his hearing was just fine. More than one knight found himself quivering in Sir Borg's presence after receiving a tongue lashing the likes of which they wouldn't soon forget. Sir Devin clucked his tongue and secretly smiled at the inability of some knights to learn to keep their mouths shut. He remembered when he was in training and he made a comment that was unfortunate enough to reach the ears of his commander. He learned his lesson well after the additional duty of cleaning the horses' stalls for a month. They would learn also. They had chosen well for this mission and he knew that eventually he would have to tell them the true nature of why and where they were heading. He couldn't disclose all and definitely not too soon. There were too many ways for the information to be leaked with that many people in the know. People talked, it was their nature and it was impossible to ensure that more than fifty men could all keep their peace.

Although the trip was going as well as could be expected, Sir Devin still worried. A foreboding was growing within Sir Devin's mind in direct relation to the incredible speed with which Elle's powers had been growing. He knew in his gut that the reason they were increasing in such a manner was because they would be needed in the days, weeks or months ahead. He knew that those who were called to The Seven were always called for a specific purpose. The fact that Elle had been called at this time is the reason he knew Draconas Markim insisted she be the one to go on the expedition. Considering her impressive powers, he knew that the leader of The Seven had chosen well. Sir Devin's concern stemmed from the need for so much power. He wondered if the incredible power Elle was coming into was by necessity for what lay ahead. If that was the case, how much power were they sure to come against? Sir Devin almost smiled when he considered his good friend Borg. Even Borg may think twice regarding his eagerness for what may come when he finally put the pieces together and came to the same conclusion as Devin had.

"You be thinkin' hard enough to hurt me head. Wanna share?" Sir Borg strolled up to him and shook him from his reverie.

"Nothing that I can speak of, unfortunately. How long do you estimate before we reach the foot of the Krull Mountains? Do you think any of your kin will be there when we arrive?"

"I wouldna think no more'n a few days and with the lookouts the clan's been postin', they'll be aware of us before we reach there; so, yes, I believe we'll be met by 'em. If we weren't in such a blasted hurry, I'd say we stay a day or two and indulge in the mead that flows freely in our halls. Mayhap we'll have time on the return trip."

Devin put aside his previous musings and said, "If all goes well and you would like to spend some time with your kin, we can make arrangements for you to stay a few days before returning to duty when all is said and done."

"I'll be holdin' you to that." Borg quipped.

At the same time Devin and Borg were discussing his stay with his clan, a runner from the advance party came up to Sir Devin to report. "There is a small group of people on their way to Elliston. They are happy to escort the family that we rescued from the goblins back to their home which, as luck would have it, is on their way. I told them I would confer with you and get back to them."

"I would be grateful not to have the responsibility since we are in no position to do so ourselves. Elle and I will meet with this group and decide."

Elle was requested to go with Devin to get a feel for the group in question. She agreed and they followed the runner back. After a brief conversation with the new group, as well as with the family now in their care, both Elle and Devin felt confident leaving the family in their hands. They provided them with sufficient rations to get them to their destination. Devin decided that this break in their routine was as good a time as any to rest both the men and the horses. A halt was called once they saw the others on their way.

Elle and Akhena sat side by side on an old log they claimed for themselves. They were speaking of ways in which they could improve their magic, when a shadow fell over them. They both looked up to find Donnal smiling sheepishly before asking if he could share their seat. Elle was delighted to have his company; she had been wanting to learn more about the stranger. Akhena, on the other hand, was less than pleased at the intrusion. This was the very reason that Donnal had decided not only to sit with the girls, but to also sit by Akhena and learn more about her. He knew that Akhena was leery of him and he was determined to change her mind. Everything he had to do would be that much easier if he was looked upon in a more favorable light. With that in mind,

Donnal took his seat and began to question Akhena about things she found of interest.

"I have had little time to get to know everyone. Akhena, I have found myself wondering if you think of yourself as a dwarf or a human," he asked.

Akhena gave him an appraising look to see if he was sincere in his request. When she saw no malice there, she replied, "I was raised by a human, though I feel closer to Borg than I ever felt to the woman that raised me. Does that mean I relate more to my dwarf side? I don't know. To be honest, I just want to be Akhena for now. Why do you ask?"

To which Donnal replied, "I, like you, am from no house." He thought on that and clarified, "...at least no house of import. Perhaps the need to belong to something or know one's self is more important to people such as ourselves. I look at you and I see a woman Draconas who is also one of The Seven. I don't see the dwarf or human, just a remarkable woman."

Akhena once again looked to the stranger that had joined their group, trying to determine if he was sincere or not. She turned to her good friend Elle and knew that she wasn't receiving any thoughts or feelings from Donnal that would indicate he was not being sincere. Donnal was not worried because he truly thought Akhena was a remarkable woman whom he admired.

"Thank you," Akhena said with a shy smile that caught both Donnal and Elle off guard and they both smiled in return. A smile from Akhena was rare indeed and transformed her into a very attractive woman.

Elle looked over to Donnal and said, "So, based on what you just told us, you have no house. Finally we know a little something about our new friend." She raised her cup in a mock toast then drank the water inside.

The party continued on and Donnal rode next to Elle whenever the opportunity arose. Since Elle spent most of her days practicing her magic with Akhena, those times were few and far between, but he knew that he was making progress with her. Although his tall frame, sandy hair and light brown eyes turned the heads of most women, Elle was not the type to fall for a handsome face. Donnal knew this and spent his time with her speaking of subjects dear to the hearts of most elves and watching out for her brother.

Gustaf, in the meantime, knew that Donnal was using him to get close to his sister even though he was unclear on Donnal's intentions. He decided that since his sister knew that he hated her, there was no point in fighting it. Perhaps Donnal could actually gain her confidence and they could both benefit. He also knew that everyone in camp disliked him, to put it mildly, and he didn't care. The stupid people did not realize he could choke them with a thought or at least cause a panic by making it very hard to breathe. He had been practicing his magic as well and had progressed to medium-sized animals, almost. It seemed that the angrier he allowed himself to be, the more powerful was his magic. The only problem with this scenario was that if he allowed his anger too much room, he made mistakes. He needed to be careful. He wished this stupid trip was over. How much training did these knights need? He wanted to get back to the capitol and find some way to make the castle his home. His sister was a fool and would give him the chance if he asked just to keep the peace. He daydreamed about the life he intended to have on his return and paid no attention to those around him, oblivious to the fact that his sister now heard his thoughts.

***

In the Kingdom of Amjukar, everything was proceeding in what had become the norm. Draconas Markim was overseeing the day to day administrations of the kingdom and delegated as necessary to the other members of the council still in attendance. He checked on the progress of their soldiers on a daily basis to make sure they were doing everything possible to get them in fighting form. He still had nothing definitive, only rumors, and he wanted the kingdom prepared. In addition, he had the castle drill daily on the defenses of the city proper. People were beginning to ask questions regarding this change in routine. Draconas Markim simply stated that it was time that the defenses of the Kingdom of Amjukar were taken seriously. He spoke of other times in history that their kingdom had been under attack and said that it was best to be prepared. The people began to calm when day after day of preparation became like a mantra. They did it without thinking and

Draconas Markim began to relax just a little. Although Markim was unaware of the progress of the "training party," the High Wizard Malek and Wizard Tannis were reasonably informed. They were, however, unaware of the fact that their daily reports were being overheard by Donnal. As a result, King Baldor was learning more due to the wizards' duplicity despite their good intentions. Cylas informed the wizards that once they were through the forest that the trees would be sparse, and communication would become irregular. Since nothing of import had been gleaned other than Elle's power, they were unconcerned at this time. If the Kingdom of Amjukar had been aware of the preparations being made by King Baldor, they would have worked that much harder on their own.

***

Inside the Krull Mountains, the dwarves were making their own preparations. They too were aware of the rumors coming from the Kingdom of Erewyth. The dwarves had a tendency to look out for their own. However, since Brock, the third prince of King Druek, was one of The Seven of the Kingdom of Amjukar, they decided that they would send a representative to Amjukar to speak with the council regarding the rumors. They wished to know if it was in their best interest to combine forces if and when an attack should arise. The dwarves were fierce fighters and as a result, goblins, humans and elves were outmanned on a one to one basis in hand to hand combat. However, some humans and all elves had magic which was

138

also a great asset in a time of war and could level the playing field or tip the balance altogether.

The King of Moe Din sat on his throne in the great hall that was placed in the middle of Krull Mountain to allow the different clans within the larger clan equal access to the extent that it was possible. The great hall was enormous with ceilings reaching a height of more than one hundred feet. Balconies surrounded the throne room on two separate levels as they went up to allow for additional seating during large gatherings. There were several doorways leading to various tunnels that served a multitude of purposes from all levels. Some were shortcuts to various parts of the mountain or to one of the four entrances that were used when leaving Krull Mountain. Some of the tunnels travelled deep into the underbelly of the mountain and further still. One tunnel, known to all dwarves, led to the furthest side of the mountain in the event of a tragedy that would require the women and children to be evacuated. No self-respecting male dwarf that has come of age would use the evacuation tunnel unless it was due to a natural disaster. In times of war they would fight to the death.

The throne was at one end of the room. The throne itself hid a doorway known only to the royal family, and it could access any major tunnel in the kingdom. Statues of the former kings were aligned behind the throne in the chronological order of their reigns. The details of the statues were exceptional in their realism, depicting what each king looked like, down to the last battle scar, and were at least twenty feet in height. Dwarves were renowned for their ability with stone and the likenesses had no equal. Thankfully, the average lifespan of a dwarf was long enough that there was still plenty of room for future kings to take their place alongside their ancestors before expanding the current room or starting a new one altogether. The chair of the throne itself was one of few items in the kingdom that was made of wood. The seat was made of velvet and was stuffed on a regular basis so as not to lose its regal appearance. It had been a gift by the Elves thousands of years ago, during a time of treaties and peace following the great wars of that time, to the dwarf King Krull, whom the mountains were named for. Opposite the throne rose a statue to the mountain god Knor. Knor's likeness was dwarven in appearance with a long beard and broad shoulders. He had an axe in one hand at his side and a war hammer in the other, raised to strike down his enemies. Like the other statues in the throne room, every detail was beautifully rendered.

The king looked upon his oldest son and heir Prince Karnuk. The prince was tall for a dwarf with a strong jaw, broad shoulders, long dark brown hair kept tied with a thong and a mustache and longer beard which he also kept tied just under his chin in a continuing pattern to the end. His dark eyes, which often appeared as though he was enjoying some private joke, showed no sign of that humor now. He stood there with a small contingent of dwarves whom he both liked and trusted and waited for his father's instructions.

"Karnuk, me son, I'm sure you've heard rumors of the buildup of the army in Erewyth. There are more rumors 'bout a group o' knights from Amjukar bein' sent south for what they be callin' a trainin' mission. They must think we're dumb as trolls cause a trainin' mission would'na be cause for travelin' with two o' The Seven. I want you and those you choose to go to Amjukar and speak with Draconas Markim 'bout these rumors. Since you are next in line, I want you to be represent'n me in this matter. I canno' go; I 'ave things to tend to 'ere. I'll also be sendin' a group of warriors to the south to intercept the group from Amjukar and join with em' whether they want us there or no. I'm sure me soldiers could use some trainin' too." The king said this last with more than a little sarcasm, then said, "May Knor guide your journey, my son." The king placed his hand on his son's shoulder and squeezed ever so slightly, a sign of love from a king and father to his son.

At this command, Prince Karnuk took his leave; the dwarves of his choice in attendance. They would spend a good part of their travel through the mountains that were so familiar to them and proceed northeast to the capitol. King Druek watched with trepidation, although he would die before showing his concern, as his first born son left the safety of the clan for the first time in his life. As with the Kingdom of Amjukar, the dwarves had seen peace for many years and the majority of the dwarves under his care had never seen a real fight, let alone a war. However, it was common knowledge that fighting was in the blood of every dwarf born, male and female alike, and unlike the humans, the dwarves trained as soldiers from the time they could hold an axe, again both male and female alike.

King Druek thought about the latest addition to The Seven. The elven kingdom of Valsara was far to the southeast. King Druek was well aware of who Ellindria of House Kar was. Her father had been a very good friend of King Druek's. Although Elle's family had once held the position as the royal family among the elves in Valsara and still had a claim to the throne, her family now resided near the southernmost section of the Kingdom of Amjukar. If this became an actual war, King Druek was curious to see if the elves would get involved. If the dwarves were ones to stay out of the affairs of others, the elves made the dwarves appear as the humanitarians of the realm. It would take a war that threatened the lives of the elves to gain their involvement. It had been longer than time could recall that war had come to the elves. Since the elves had not had cause to fight on their homeland, the elven kingdom had never been ravaged by war and was more than beautiful. The ability of elves to manipulate their environment without desecrating the forests and hills made it possible to create the most serene and breathtaking kingdom in all the realms. This fact, along with the ability of all elves to have some form of magic and to live long lives, attributed to the arrogance of the race. Elle had grown up in both kingdoms and was now one of The Seven of Amjukar with a right to the crown in Valsara. King Druek hoped that Elle had the ability to bridge the gap---if and when the need arose---based on this. Having placed the matter in his son's hands, the dwarf king commanded a group to leave immediately to seek the Amjukaran's and had his second son, Prince Strom, go as well. This decision was hard on the king, as Strom was not like most dwarves, but it couldn't be helped since his son Brock was now one of The Seven. The King shook his head as a display of clearing it and decided not to give the matter another thought. Instead, he turned towards internal affairs needing his attention until news arrived and decisions needed to be made.

***

Gustaf's anger had become a constant state of being. The scouts had started reporting an unusual number of deaths of smaller animals that were appearing in their path. They were concerned that perhaps some sickness was plaguing this section of the forest. Elle slightly calmed their fears when she explained her brother's abilities. Now the knights were no longer afraid of an illness, they were afraid of her brother, as well they should be. It became increasingly apparent that Elle had no choice but to confront him. When she felt that the people in her party had suffered long enough, she sought her brother out.

She found Gustaf towards the back of the group and pulled alongside his mount. As usual, the hatred coming from her brother was like a physical blow. Due to her increase in abilities, it caused her to bend over from the shock and pain of it until she could control her reaction. She was caught off guard and knew that this was something she needed to get under control sooner rather than later.

"Gustaf, I would speak with you privately," she stated.

Gustaf slowed his horse until they were travelling at the back of the group. Refusing to allow Elle out of their sight, especially when in the presence of her brother, Donnal and Sir Devin kept a watchful eye on Elle. They nodded to one another and fell back as well to stay in the shadows, while at the same time keeping brother and sister in sight. Donnal, with his Draconas senses, would be able to hear the conversation as well.

Gustaf glared at his sister. She sat tall on her horse and steeled her resolve. "I don't pretend to understand your hatred of me," she began, "and do not wish to address it at this time. The trail of dead animals that you are spreading around is creating much trepidation among the group. Is this intentional or no?"

Gustaf continued to glare at his sister and instead of answering her question he said, "What did you do to become a Draconas in my place? What magic did you use to also become one of the most powerful people in the kingdom? You may not want to speak of my hatred, but I have no such qualms. I should have been a Draconas, not you. I should be one of The Seven, not you. And more importantly, I should be sitting on the throne in Valsara right now, yet that has also been taken from me. I travelled to the capitol because I thought that at the very least my little sister could make arrangements to provide a suite of rooms that I could reside in. As for the animals, you will have to determine if I am killing them intentionally or not. Tell your new friends to stop acting like scared little girls and gather the ones I kill to add to our rations before the scavengers get to them first."

Before she became a Draconas, Elle would have cowed at her brother's fury and would have done what she could to appease him. That Elle was gone and was replaced by Draconas Ellindria of House Kar, one of The Seven of the Kingdom of Amjukar, and it was apparent to Gustaf when she spoke, "I am quite sure that you know that I had nothing to do with becoming a Draconas or one of The Seven. It is not something I thought about or aspired to. It simply happened. As for a residence in the castle, I would never subject the good people there to a man such as yourself, brother or no. We have allowed you the courtesy and safety of this group in your travels but your disruption of this camp will no longer be tolerated."

At this, she called for Sir Devin, Sir Borg and Draconas Akhena and declared: "My brother is no longer permitted to remain with our group. Can we arrange to give him extra rations before sending him on his way?"

Gustaf began to protest, and was stopped when Akhena stepped in front of him and changed into her Draconas form. Draconas Akhena was only a mid-sized Draconas, but even at that her presence dwarfed Gustaf atop his horse. Gustaf was not the smartest man when in an angered state, but even he knew that to protest further was futile. He turned to look at Donnal and knew that he was on his own. It occurred to him to spill Donnal's true reason for being there, though based on the looks he was getting, he doubted that anyone would believe him. Besides, he may be able to use the information at a later date. He knew that argument would do him no good at this time. Gustaf turned his horse to return in the direction they had come from, knowing that he would be followed for a time. Once they felt sure that he was heading back to the capitol, he would reverse course and catch up, for there was still time. *You will get yours, Donnal, you son of a bitch,* he repeated to himself over and over. Had it not been for Donnal's interference, he may have been able to talk his way into the castle to wait for his "dear" sister instead of traipsing across country. He could be enjoying the hospitality of the castle servants and drinking in the local taverns. He continued thinking on all that had been stolen from him and his anger continued to grow, keeping him warm in the cool air.

Elle watched her brother's retreating figure and knew that this wasn't over. The group sped up to make up for lost time and continued on their way.

Donnal pulled up beside Elle and gave her a sympathetic look. Although Donnal had never had any siblings, he still understood some of the inner workings of a family, for he had loved his mother very much. Elle could tell that the sympathy was genuine and so she continued to ride at his side.

After a while she spoke, "I did not think you would go with my brother when he was banished, though I was not sure. I am glad that you have decided to travel with us for now."

"I was never fond of your brother. I am afraid that I have a tremendous dislike for him now. I cannot fathom how he thinks or why he does the things he does. Brother or no, I would have taken his life if he had tried to cause you harm." Donnal stated this with a passion that surprised both Elle and Donnal himself.

"My brother has always felt as though he has been grievously wronged and has lived his life in hate. I cannot imagine what that could do to a soul over time. In some ways I feel sorry for him, although not enough to allow him to take advantage of my station."

"You are a good woman, Ellindria of House Kar. The Kingdom of Amjukar is lucky to have one such as you among their leaders."

Elle was pleased with Donnal's comment and had to try not to blush from the praise. If there was one thing she was trying hard to overcome it was the fact that her emotions were an open book for all to read. Despite her effort, Donnal knew that she was pleased and that in turn made him happy. Donnal enjoyed the camaraderie that they were sharing until he came to his senses and realized that it could only go so far. He was very attracted to the beautiful elf and needed to keep a balance between gaining her trust and maintaining a distance; he had a job still to do.

Chapter 10

The elven kingdom of Valsara was far to the south and east, nestled to one side on the Sea of Azulea. The kingdom boasted mountains with breathtaking waterfalls and trees that grew to widths and heights that allowed some of the elves to make their homes inside them. Magic was used to weave the trees into becoming both functional as well as beautiful. At the foot of the mountains were fields with many rivers, brooks and streams that allowed for all life···elvish, plant and animal··· to flourish. The Castle of Valsara and the great city it was part of was situated on the high cliffs by the Sea of Azulea. The only way to gain entrance into the city was by one of two gates that were magically reinforced and protected by elven archers. It was well known that the elves were by far the best archers in all the kingdoms. Of course, being an elf with a naturally long life span allowed more time to perfect their craft. The only other way to gain entrance to the city was if one was ambitious enough to scale the cliffs which were not as heavily guarded, the cliffs being a deterrent in and of themselves. No kingdom had considered attacking or laying siege to the elven kingdom in recent memory, knowing it to be suicide.

The queen stood in her room in the royal wing of the castle which had views of the distant mountains to one side and the sea on the other.

She had a letter in her hand that she had just received. She called for her advisor to be there when she reviewed, once again, the letter from one of her informants. The information it contained regarded the kingdoms of Amjukar and Erewyth. The informant worked in the castle in Amjukar and had been in the employ of the elven kingdom for many years. For the first time, however, he had real information to impart. He wrote the queen of the death of Draconas Callis, the subsequent calling of The Seven to Draconas Ellindria of House Kar, and the parting of the knights with Draconas Ellindria and Draconas Akhena among them. He had heard whispers of an important scroll in the hands of The Seven which was undoubtedly the reason behind the impromptu "training mission." When the queen and her advisor finished reading the letter, she placed it in the fire that burned continually day and night with the help of elven magic.

"What do you make of this?" she asked her advisor.

"Without more information, I cannot say. The contents of the scroll are unknown. We should send someone that is adept at getting things discreetly. We have a few that I can think of that would be able to obtain the information needed without the person realizing they had given anything away."

Queen Teserath gave it little thought and said, "We shall send Sakira. She is by far the one that I have the most confidence in to get close to one of The Seven. See to the arrangement. I wish her to leave as soon as possible."

The queen turned away to gaze into the fire as her advisor left the room.

Her twin brother, younger only by minutes, stepped from the shadows and asked, "What do you think of Ellindria becoming one of The Seven? Do you think that her new status will give her the confidence to claim your crown?"

The Queen resumed her musing while watching the fire, "I don't know Tomlin. Have I not been a good queen?" The last question was rhetorical and so her brother made no comment. "It has always been believed that Ellindria is a good and decent woman, which is one of the reasons her father favored her over Gustaf for the crown. Perhaps she will continue her role with The Seven and leave us be. However, you know as well as I that she can claim the throne whenever she so chooses. I, for one, do not wish for bloodshed and will acquiesce without incident if it comes to that."

Tomlin looked at his sister with barely concealed disgust. To give up the throne so easily after all he had done and sacrificed! He had been so patient for all of these years, and for what? He turned his back to her to compose himself; then turned back to her once again.

Queen Teserath had an idea that her brother was involved in their elevation in station although she did not know for certain. If she was truthful with herself, she knew that she didn't want to know if he was involved. She enjoyed her status as

Queen and was actually surprised that she still enjoyed that status. In the beginning, when she knew in her heart of her brother's involvement, she worried for her own welfare. Perhaps her brother would dispose of her to wear the crown himself. However, as the years had passed, Queen Teserath relaxed her guard. She came to the conclusion that as long as she included her brother in all things and he felt equal to her, that he was content with his lot. She may have relaxed her guard, although she knew better than to think herself safe. They were elves after all and could live for many, many years. Her brother may simply be biding his time, since they had so much more of it than the other races of the realm. That thought led her to another thought, which she voiced aloud, "Now that Ellindria is a Draconas, perhaps she will bide her time in claiming the throne if it even comes to that. After all, she will live much longer than even you or I, and time should have new meaning for her. What do you think?"

Prince Tomlin thought that regardless of time anyone that didn't want to claim the throne of Valsara, or any other kingdom for that matter, was a fool. By Tomlin's way of thinking, he could not conceive of anyone with ambitions not like his own. He assumed that everyone was like him and he would not have waited, present situation excepted, for which he had his reasons. He did not say this to his sister, of course; he said instead, "Right now Ellindria is one of The Seven and on a trek of some sort, so she is not an immediate threat. However, I think we need to make sure someone is in place to eliminate any threat she may pose if it comes to

152

that. We should send a guard of the Elven Elite to intercept them and inform us of their movements. We also need to know what they are up to and determine if or how it might affect Valsara."

Queen Teserath did not like the idea of "eliminating a threat" when the threat in question was her own cousin but she couldn't argue with the logic of what her brother said.

"Alright brother, I will leave it in your hands to make the arrangements." She preferred to keep her hands clean, staying as far away from any plans that may cause her cousin harm and was relieved to be leaving it to Tomlin.

Tomlin knew his sister did not have what was needed to make the tough decisions. This is why he knew that the day would come when it would be his turn to take the throne. All in good time he thought, all in good time.

***

Sakira was honored to be chosen for this mission. She packed lightly for her journey to the Kingdom of Amjukar. The woman looking back at her in the mirror was tall and slim with long white blonde hair and dark blue eyes. Her pointed ears, common to all elves, parted her hair so that a few strands fell in front and the rest cascaded down her back. She was beautiful by elf standards; to a human she would be nothing less than striking. She would change into her Draconas form to make faster work of the time it would take for her to reach her destination. As a thirty foot dragon, her scales were a pearly white with light blue at the extremities. When flying, she could easily blend in with the sky looking much like a passing cloud at a quick glance. However, if she used her magic, she could take on the appearance of her surroundings, making her all but invisible. Sakira was a young elf at just over 300 years and had spent almost half of that time as a Draconas. She also spent a good deal of her young life training to be one of the Elven Elite who were used to indoctrinate themselves into other cultures to learn their secrets and make known to the Kingdom of Valsara anything that could affect their elven way of life, be it good or bad. Others were used as a small specialized fighting force that was trained to work and fight together.

At the time she was preparing to leave, the "training party" from Amjukar had departed more than a week previously. Since there were several hours left in the day she was to get started immediately. Her queen was made aware of her departure and Sakira flew from her home in the elven kingdom.

She couldn't resist the urge to fly over the cliffs upon which the castle of her kingdom was placed. The castle shone brightly and looked quite large even from her current elevation. She was proud of her home, her kingdom and her place in it. She lived to serve and was elated that of all those that could have been chosen for this mission it had been she.

She allowed herself one more pass then turned west where not too long from now she would be following the setting sun. She practiced her magic and disappeared into the afternoon sky.

Chapter 11

Commander Andal stared at his reflection in the puddle on the training grounds and was once again taken aback at what he saw there. Andal had by no means been a small man, but what he was now he had trouble coming to terms with or just understanding. He had been taken separately from the other soldiers and given his own residence, and humble though it may be, it was still preferable to sleeping on a bunk with several other soldiers in the same room. The Wizard Balquin had taken him aside and placed his hand on Andal's head. After Andal drank the potion as directed, the wizard began chanting, his hand still atop Andal's head. Balquin's eyes rolled back into his head, showing only the whites, as his chanting became faster and faster, his voice rising to a crescendo. At first, Andal felt nothing and felt kind of silly standing there thus. After a minute or so, though, his body began to ache and then it began to hurt. Before much longer, he was screaming with pain. He both felt and saw his bones moving beneath his skin, his tendons stretching, detaching and reattaching. His joints were popping and reshaping themselves, causing agony the likes of which he never imagined could exist. Sweat covered his body and saturated his clothing which began to rip apart quite literally at the seams as his body became both larger and taller. He pulled off his boots before his feet pushed through the leather or his bones broke from lack of space. His blood felt like it was boiling in his body, and his screams were such that they were heard throughout the training camp. Just when he knew he could take no more and the pain would kill him, it suddenly stopped. The wizard's chanting had come to an end. Andal had closed his eyes toward the end in an effort to close out the pain, and it took several minutes before he was able to compose himself enough to open them. When he did, he looked at the wizard and he realized that his point of view had changed. When they had started, Andal and the wizard were looking at each other eye to eye. After the transformation, Andal was looking down at the top of the wizard's head and could see the bald patch that was just beginning to take shape. Having been put through a great deal of pain, he derived some satisfaction in pointing this fact out to the wizard. Over the next twenty four hours, he began to realize other changes, some small and some not so much. His teeth were sharp, though not quite as sharp as a canine's and he had a full set just as before. His senses were enhanced and were something he was still getting used to. He truly did not want to hear another soldier taking care of his needs, whether it be in the privy or the privacy of his own bedroll. He was not altogether happy with all of the changes that had taken place. He was, however, especially thrilled to have was his enhanced strength. He had been strong before and an excellent swordsman. Now Andal was almost without equal. He felt that perhaps only the king himself could best him in combat, and even then, he felt he could give King Baldor a run for his money. Andal was also intelligent, which was the reason he had been chosen in the first place, and so he knew that even with his magical enhancements he would be put to task sooner rather than later. He glanced once again at his reflection in the standing water before going to face the soldiers under his command.

The soldiers placed in his command had also been magically enhanced, although they were very different from Andal. He shuddered slightly at the sight of them and gave thanks once again to the king for his promotion. The soldiers before him were more animal than human. Their faces had taken on the appearance of a wolf. Their eyes still looked human, giving them an odd and unsettling appearance. Although they had elongated snouts they could still speak though it sounded as if they were barking the words. Their upper bodies were large and appeared to be a melding of both human and wolf. The arms and legs were more wolf-like, complete with claws. They too had enhanced senses and strength, yet they had lost some of the intelligence that they were born with, making them more malleable. The one thing that they had over Andal was their speed. Due to their wolf-like legs, they were much faster and could cover a good deal of terrain without tiring. They could still carry and use a sword and other weapons to some extent, yet they were now more deadly with their teeth and claws. Andal was tasked with training them to be versatile, at least as much as you could train a slightly smarter than average dog. He knew that they would be leaving in a couple of days to go south past the Krull mountains to catch up with the party out of Amjukar and determine what they were up to. He was to stop the party at all costs and he had no intention of letting his king down. He would be riding one of the dragons and the others would go on foot. He had been practicing riding the magnificent beasts and he could tell that they were allowing it against their will. He didn't like depending on anything or anyone that was not doing something of its own free will. Unfortunately, he knew that he had no choice in such matters. The dragon he was to ride was a large royal blue drake, a prince in the dragon hierarchy, named Quintos, and approximately eighty feet from snout to tail. Andal had read anything and everything he could get his hands on regarding the dragons and knew that, unlike the Draconas' of his world, the dragons would grow until death, and would not be expected for thousands and thousands of years. Quintos was an average size dragon; some of his bloodline was as large as one hundred feet or more. Another difference was, of course, the fact that dragons were born fully able to defend themselves, fire breathing and all, from the moment of hatching from their eggs. A Draconas was not as large, was born as a human, elf or dwarf, and did not grow beyond sixty or seventy feet regardless of their expanded lifespan. Additionally, a dragon's magic was different from a Draconas' magic, something that over the years they had learned to accept and respect of each other for the most part. Under normal circumstances, dragons and Draconas' were allies.

Quintos was quite sure that no Draconas' were aware of their plight and the plight of their eggs. He believed that if he could only communicate with one of them, he could gain their assistance in retrieving the eggs. Dragons placed all of their eggs in one area for incubation until they hatched. This had advantages and disadvantages. Those in charge of the dragon eggs could regulate the temperature to ensure the hatching of an appropriate number of male and female dragons, based on the needs at that time. Once hatched, the dragons had a honing ability to return to their homes for their upbringing. The disadvantage is that it made the theft of the next generation of dragons much easier, which is exactly what had happened. Like the rest of the realm, peace had caused even the dragons to become complacent in their security.

Prince Quintos continued to think on his predicament. The Draconas' ability to blend by taking their natural form could be advantageous in any rescue attempt if he could convince his distant cousins, as he thought of them, to risk their own lives for the dragons. He would keep alert for any chance that might present itself to gain their help. Although Draconas' were small in number, he kept his thoughts on the possibility to keep him from lamenting his current situation.

Commander Andal waited for Quintos to lower himself so that he could climb onto his back without too much trouble. Andal knew that Quintos found this to be humiliating, both as a dragon and a royal. Quintos had no choice, however, so long as the dragon eggs were in the hands of King Baldor. Once seated, Andal gave the command and the beautiful drake took to the sky.

***

Sakira pushed herself to her limits, stopping only long enough to rest herself and eat the occasional deer, boar or any other animal large enough to satisfy her appetite, her Draconas form requiring much more nourishment. She was on an important mission and knew that time was a luxury she did not have. Not only could she tell by the message sent by the Queen, she could also feel it in her bones. Sakira was an intelligent woman and had learned long ago to trust her instincts and act on them always.

After leaving the elven kingdom of Valsara, she noticed a rapid decline in the country around her. She had left the kingdom before on other quests for her realm, though she could not recall having noticed such dramatic changes previously. Whether that was because it was actually less appealing than before, or was a reflection on her mood, she did not know. Her orders were to go to the Kingdom of Amjukar and learn any information she could by any means necessary. Her instincts, however, were telling her to head for Fallon Forest. The last thing she wanted was to defy her queen. However, she felt that if she denied her instincts the consequences would be dire, and that feeling was strong. She made the necessary adjustment to her current course and headed in the direction of the forest where she believed she would be able to meet up with the party from Amjukar. Sakira was unaware that the Queen had already put into motion a contingent of Elven Elite to intercept the Amjukarans, so Sakira travelled on unaware of the additional soldiers to follow. Had she known, she would have followed her original orders regardless of any instincts she may have had. Whether or not this would make a difference in the end, only time would tell.

***

Elle found herself constantly looking over her shoulder, literally, for her brother to turn up. Concerned for her welfare Donnal, Sir Devin, Sir Borg and Akhena all took it upon themselves to keep an eye on both her and the woods around her. The forest had thinned dramatically, and it would take an excellent hunter or someone with the magical ability to camouflage to make their way through without being seen. Gustaf was no such hunter, and as it cleared more and more everyone began to let down their guard somewhat, though continuing to remain vigilant.

The further south they travelled, the more it felt like summer rather than the spring they knew it to be. Sir Borg, being a dwarf and used to the forges that were a constant source of intense heat used in the making of weapons, was the only person, other than the elves, that appeared unaffected by the heat. There were only a few elves on the expedition, to include Elle, so for the most part the knights were miserable and grumbled about having to wear armor during a simple training mission, although most were beginning to realize this was anything but a simple training exercise. Once again, Borg was forced to put a few in their place. He told them that the training had been extended to the desert wasteland and if they thought they were hot now, the gods help them when they reached the desert. There were more than a few moans at this revelation, and Sir Borg rewarded them by making them march in full armor, although not for as long as they would have expected from the grumpy dwarf.

Elle found herself riding alongside Donnal and took the time to try and read his emotions once again. He was always guarded in his thoughts, and this disturbed her, although it could simply be one person trying to keep personal secrets that were none of her concern. She could also tell that he enjoyed her company, and for the time being, that was sufficient to make her feel comfortable in his presence. Donnal glanced at Elle and was once again awed by her. She was truly stunning he thought, a beautiful woman both inside and out. He smiled at her and relaxed in the saddle. She had that effect on him. As soon as he realized this, he chastised himself and closed down his thoughts and feelings. Elle was caught off guard by all that she had sensed and seen by this man of mystery. She knew that Donnal was attracted to her, as she was to him, but every time they had a "moment," he would pull away and close himself off to her. She didn't understand why, but did not feel that this was the time or place to pursue it. There were matters of importance that she needed to keep focused on. She turned her head forward and picked up her speed.

Donnal watched her pull ahead of him and felt like a fool for being caught off guard. He had a mission, and the feelings he was developing for this woman were compromising him. He had never had an experience like this before. Donnal knew he was handsome and never had trouble finding a woman to warm his bed when the urge struck him. He always chose women that were solely looking for some company or money or both to keep it simple. A man in his position would never be able to have a family without constant fear for their safety, so he intentionally avoided getting to know any one woman. This thing with Elle was becoming a problem. Perhaps he should have stayed away and followed from a distance, as he had originally. It was too late for that now. He would need to keep his distance as much as he was able.

Although Elle had pulled ahead, she could feel his emotions in turmoil and wondered at the cause. Perhaps he was married with children. Perhaps he was promised to another. She didn't know. She decided that if what was developing between them was causing him this much conflict, she would keep her distance.

Elle's pace brought her alongside Akhena. Elle brought up the fact that additional training in their Draconas forms was something that she felt was necessary. Akhena agreed so they caught up with Sir Devin who was leading their party. Sir Borg was watching the rear.

"Akhena and I feel that practice in our Draconas forms···both flying and using our magic··· is of the utmost importance. We can do this while we travel and would appreciate it if you would have our horses tended to while we are in the air." Elle requested.

"I would be happy to help, ladies." He turned to the nearest knight and directed him to find Cylas and Kyle. When the knights arrived, he instructed them on what was needed. They took the proffered reins from Elle and Akhena and promised to treat the horses with the utmost care. Elle thanked the men and turned to Akhena whose face revealed the excitement Elle was feeling herself.

Donnal was lost in his thoughts when he saw a shadow cross his path from overhead. He looked up to see Elle and Akhena in their Draconas forms flying low across the tree tops. Donnal was quietly upset. He loved being in his Draconas form and would like nothing more than to join them. Circumstances being what they were, the opportunity had not presented itself to make them aware that he was one of them. At this point in time, he wasn't sure that it would be welcome or not. How could he explain why he had kept it secret? Then it came to him. He had been in the habit of keeping it a secret because of Gustaf's anger at his sister. For that reason, he had decided to keep the peace by not letting him know that he also was a Draconas. When he would have to explain to Elle, she would know it to be true because it was. He had withheld the information from Gustaf when he realized the elf's jealousy of his sister. Elated, he found the nearest knight and handed over the reins of his horse, much to the knight's surprise. No sooner had he stepped off than he changed and took to the sky.

Always on the alert, Sir Devin took immediate action. Once the knights were over their initial shock of seeing an unknown Draconas among their ranks, they formed up to deal with the potential threat. Elle was practicing banking when the flurry of activity caught her attention. She flew towards Devin, but turned back when she heard a familiar voice in her head. A rather large Draconas was flying towards her. Draconas Akhena took a defensive position in front of Elle.

"Elle, it's me, Donnal. There is no reason to fear me. I mean you no harm."

Elle nodded to Akhena to let her know she was ok and asked her to speak with Devin and to ensure that no one was harmed. She then turned her attention to Donnal and spoke to him in his mind as was a common form of communication among the Draconas'.

"You are a Draconas, yet you never told us. Why?"

Donnal could hear the betrayal she felt in her question and it tore at him.

"I was not intentionally trying to deceive you or anyone in your party. When I first met your brother and we agreed to travel together, it did not come up. As time passed and I learned of his hatred for you and his jealousy that you had become a Draconas, I decided that it was in my best interest to keep my Draconas form to myself. After

166

he was made to leave, it just never came up until today when I saw you take flight."

Elle listened carefully and could find no deceit in his answer. She spoke with Akhena who shifted and asked Devin to stand down. Everyone took this opportunity of a break in routine to take a short rest. Donnal and Elle landed near Sir Devin who took his time asking his own questions to satisfy himself that Donnal was sincere. This time, when the party was once again underway, it was with three Draconas' flying overhead.

The Draconas' practiced flying with Donnal in the lead and Elle and Akhena to either side. They made a V formation much like a flock of birds. Flying was liberating, and the Draconas' flew all day while practicing simple battle tactics. They allowed Donnal the lead since he appeared to know much regarding battle as a Draconas. Both Elle and Akhena felt both fortunate and leery of this fact. The Draconas training sessions would continue and become more complex in the days that followed.

Chapter 12

Prince Karnuk and his party had spent the majority of their journey travelling through the Krull mountains and exiting from a hidden door in the mountain known, to very few which placed them within a reasonable distance from the capitol of Amjukar. Spring had arrived in earnest. Once they left the protection of the mountain, their journey seemed to be hit by one rain shower followed by another. Fortunately for the dwarves, their garments were made to resist the sparks from the iron forge. Additionally, the process used also acted as a deterrent to water, and so they stayed relatively dry as the raindrops could gain no purchase and rolled right off. It didn't matter what came their way. The dwarves were taught to deal with pain, torture, exhaustion, the elements and whatever else the gods sent to test them. Such were the traits of the hard bodied, hard headed dwarves.

They arrived outside the capitol of Amjukar. Word had already reached the castle regarding their arrival, since a party of dwarves parading through the countryside was more than unusual and caused local tongues to wag at an alarming rate. Before making their presence known to The Seven, they decided that some local refreshment was in order and headed to one of the local watering holes. They entered The Three Headed Dragon and ordered a round of drinks for all, much to the amusement of the locals and the thrill of the tavern's owner whose daily income had received a much welcome boost. Perhaps his wife could buy the dress she had wanted after all. The tavern owner whistled a happy tune as he collected payment for yet another round. Dwarves were known for their ability to out drink any other race in the realm despite their shorter stature. Prince Karnuk bought round after round for his people and any locals lucky enough to have been there that day. Large platters of meats, bread and cheese were brought out by the tavern owner's wife and the dwarves had their fill. Since the tavern was not large enough to provide them all rooms for the night, they finally made their way to the castle despite their inebriated state.

The party of dwarves were met at the gate by Draconas Markim himself despite the lateness of the hour. He had been told that the first Prince of Krull was on his way with a small contingent. Having assumed that the party would require accommodations, Draconas Markim had a suite of rooms readied for the occasion and the dwarves were shown to their rooms with the promise of a meeting with The Seven in the morning.

The following day was a rare sunny day during this spring season in Amjukar. The beauty of the countryside and the castle gardens, still wet from the previous day's rain, was lost on the dwarves. They appreciated their mountain homes, but gems were their beauty of choice and those that were mined in their mountain allowed them the ability to trade with their neighboring kingdoms and keep them fat and happy.

The prince and his party were invited to break their fast with The Seven still in attendance at the castle. The meal, which would normally be a loud and boisterous affair in the dwarven kingdom, was subdued with all parties sizing each other up prior to the meeting that was to follow. Shortly after the morning meal, Prince Karnuk and his two closest friends, acting in the capacity of his captains, were shown to the Seven's meeting room.

Draconas Markim, as the leader of the Seven, took his seat at the head of the table while Prince Karnuk was seated at the opposite end. Everyone else sat three to each side of the table with Draconas Brock seated on the side with his family next to his brother Prince Karnuk. The brothers had always gotten along well together and acknowledged one another with a grunt and a nod, which was the same as a hug and a kiss in other cultures to show great affection. Drinks were poured and the meeting was underway.

"Draconas Markim," on behalf of King Druek of the Kingdom of MoeDin o' the Krull Mountains, I thank you for the courtesy shown to me and my fellow dwarves."

"Of course," Draconas Markim smiled, "We are honored to have you. I know that my dear friend Brock is especially glad of your arrival. Knowing your brother as I do, I'm sure you would prefer to get straight to the point. How can we be of service?"

The prince directed his query at Draconas Markim while looking at his brother, for any reaction.

"My father sent me to find out about the rumors that are spreading far and wide. One of those rumors is about King Baldor using magic on his soldiers to make them stronger or alter them in some way. The other is about a scroll which was found and a training mission that was dispatched at the same time with two of your own councilmembers. Do you care to shed some light on these rumors?"

Prince Karnuk continued to look at his brother, and despite Brock's best efforts, it was apparent that he was feeling torn in his loyalties ⋯ his loyalty to his father's kingdom ⋯ and the kingdom he was charged to protect. The prince knew that his brother was loyal to his family and also had a duty to the Kingdom of Amjukar as one of The Seven, and he wondered what Brock would reveal in private if The Seven were less than forthright with information. The Seven in attendance exchanged glances; then Draconas Markim addressed the Prince.

"We also have heard rumors regarding King Baldor and his soldiers. We have taken precautions and are stepping up training to include running emergency drills for the city proper in the event of a possible siege, although we do not have any definitive information or reason to believe our

171

kingdom will be attacked. As for the other, it is a matter of importance to all the kingdoms that it be kept secret. Too many people already know more than we consider desirable. I promise you that what we are about is in the best interest of both of our kingdoms, and I am sure that your brother will attest to that fact."

"With all due respect, Draconas Markim, my father and I will decide what is in the best interest of my people." Prince Karnuk stated with irritation evident in his voice.

"I meant no offense." Draconas Markim replied, "Would it be possible to speak privately, just the two of us?"

Prince Karnuk looked long and hard into the Leader of The Seven's eyes. He then looked to his brother who gave him a nod of approval so slight that only a brother would know it for what it was. The Prince looked back at Draconas Markim and asked his acting captains to step outside. Taking that as his cue, Draconas Markim dismissed the other members of the council. They each nodded respectfully to Prince Karnuk as they left the room. It had been decided prior to the meeting what would take place if the prince was insistent, and so the other councilmembers left without protest. Draconas Brock was last to leave and gave his brother a long look before making his exit.

The Prince of the Krull Mountains and the Leader of The Seven sat across from each other in the council chamber.

Draconas Markim looked at Prince Karnuk and sighed in resignation of what had to be done. "I have sent some of our knights and two of our councilmembers on a mission based on a scroll that was found in the home of Draconas Callis who was a member of The Seven, as I am sure you are aware." Markim paused here, the death of his friend still an open wound, "Draconas Callis was tortured for the scroll. Fortunately, the person or persons were unsuccessful in acquiring it. If I disclose the contents of the scroll, I must have your word that what I tell you never leaves this room with the only exception being your father King Druek." Here Markim stopped and looked hard at the prince to bring his point home. "Do I have your word?"

"You have my word." Prince Karnuk placed his fist over his heart with a resounding thump.

"We are in the possession of a scroll that speaks of a land known as Desne Mar," he began.

"I have not heard of this land," Prince Karnuk interrupted.

Draconas Markim continued, "Some people that have heard of it believe it to be a child's story. Some people believe the land to be real and some do not believe in it at all. The land is supposed to be magic and will increase the magical powers of those that claim it. The scroll gives a basic description of the whereabouts of Desne Mar. The exact location is unknown. Supposedly, someone with magical abilities will be able to feel the change in their magic and will know when they have found it. It is also written that the land will undergo some kind of transformation, although what that entails we honestly do not know. We have sent a party of knights with two commanding officers, one of which is Sir Borg from your kingdom, whom we have had the good fortune of having as a training officer. We also sent two of the councilmembers as well. Draconas Akhena, who is half human and half dwarf, is accompanying Draconas Ellindria of House Kar who is an elf, although she has lived in the Kingdom of Amjukar for the majority of her life. Draconas Elle is, I believe, the key to unlocking the magic of Desne Mar. She is strong magically as both an elf and a Draconas. Her calling to The Seven feels fortuitous. It is my hope and the hope of the Seven that she will be able to claim Desne Mar for the Kingdom of Amjukar and by association, the Kingdom of Moe Din on behalf of the dwarves."

"I am not so naïve," Prince Karnuk stated, "as to think that you had our kingdom's best interest at heart when you sent your expedition. Dwarves are not magical by nature; however, we do have Draconas' and wizards that could represent our interest in this 'expedition.' Also, what do you know of the elves? Are they aware of what is taking place?"

Draconas Markim ran his hand through his hair and stood up from the table to begin his routine of pacing when thinking or addressing others.

"Please understand, Prince Karnuk, when we came into this information it was with the death of a fellow member of The Seven and we felt that we must take immediate action. Our main concern at that point was King Baldor. What if we had taken the time to speak with the other Kingdoms? The more time that passed greatly increased the chance that our true mission would be found out. Had that happened, the Kingdom of Erewyth would have made a run for the land and could have very well claimed the land before us. What then? Think of the consequences if King Baldor, who is arguably the strongest Draconas in the realm as well as the cruelest, were to acquire the additional power of this land of magic. We were acting in good faith based on the information we had at that time. We proceeded on the assumption that the land is real and in danger of being claimed by someone without the best of intentions." He concluded and sat down heavily upon his seat.

The prince thought on what he had just been told and addressed Draconas Markim, "I understand the position you found yourself in, and if the roles were reversed, I am sure that we would have done the same. However, I am also quite sure that my father would demand that we be an active participant in this quest to include helping to remove any obstacles that may arise and to share equally in the rewards when completed. I will advise him to send a Draconas from one of our clans to try and catch up with the party you sent, before they reach this land of magic. I am not sure how any of this works. I am sure that the king will want one of our own there to represent our kingdom's interests."

"I understand and respectfully request that this person you send be someone that you trust with your life. This secret must be kept at all costs. It could cost many innocent lives. To be honest, I fear that too many people are in the know already, and with each day that passes, the chance of losing Desne Mar to King Baldor becomes that much greater. I will give you the direction for your Draconas to head and a general idea of the location of the land. It will be up to your Draconas to arrive in time."

"I am glad that we have been able to come to an agreement," the Prince responded. "I have much to prepare in very little time. I will leave you to your responsibilities and may the gods grant us success."

Prince Karnuk joined his group and preparations were made to leave immediately. The prince's closest friend and advisor was a Draconas who's magical ability was about to be put to the test. Under normal circumstances, King Druek would appoint the champion that would represent their kingdom. Due to the limited time at his disposal, he felt it prudent to make a fast decision and get Corvus underway. He pulled Corvus aside and explained what was expected of him. As with any dwarf, Corvus was honored to be chosen and within the hour he was on his way with rations, supplies and a letter provided by Draconas Markim himself. The letter indicated the purpose for Corvus' addition to the party, without which he would stand little to no chance of being welcomed into the fold. The Prince knew that he must make all haste back to his father and report on what he had learned. In addition to sending Corvus to try and reach the party sent by the Kingdom of Amjukar, he knew that they must also make preparations in the event that the Kingdom of Erewyth, or more specifically King Baldor himself, was planning to put an end to the many years of peace the kingdoms had enjoyed. Prince Karnuk enjoyed a good fight, probably more so than the average dwarf, though even he was more than concerned about the possibility of a war with the Kingdom of Erewyth lying just beyond his mountain home.

The Draconas Corvus was a dwarf that for some unknown reason had become a Draconas a decade earlier. It was rare for a dwarf to become a Draconas and a little less so to be born a wizard. Currently, the dwarven kingdom was host to thirteen Draconas' including himself and Draconas Brock of the Seven. If he included Draconas Akhena, then that number was increased to fourteen. He did not know her and was unsure if she considered herself a dwarf or a human and whether her Draconas form was from her dwarf or human side. Corvus felt that his magic as a Draconas was pretty basic as far as magical abilities were concerned. Although he was an average size dwarf, not tall like his friend the Prince, Corvus was a stocky dwarf and broad through the shoulders. His burgundy hair was well kept for a dwarf and his beard was neatly trimmed, going against a tradition he didn't care. He was his own person, and for this very reason Prince Karnuk called him his best friend. Corvus' Draconas magic enhanced his already strong body. He could see well at night and his hearing was greatly enhanced as was the case for all Draconas'. He also had the ability to wield any weapon in his dwarf form with deadly accuracy and apparent ease. He may have had additional abilities, although being a dwarf first and a Draconas second had not allowed him much time to test those abilities. As a Draconas, he knew that he would live for several thousand years and as such he had not felt an urgency to learn more about his Draconas self before now. He resigned himself to the new direction his life had taken and he realized that he would be gaining lots of experience with his Draconas magic during the time it would take to reach the knights of Amjukar and the journey from there.

The sister moon Somara began her journey into the sky while the sun god Sol was still visible on the horizon. Corvus was flying in his dragon form and headed in a southerly direction. He was exhilarated from the flying, for he had not flown in many months. The life of a dwarf is lived mostly underground and few opportunities presented themselves to take to the sky. He was a rather thick Draconas, as well as relatively short, measuring at twenty-five feet from nose to tail. He had dark brown scales fading to burgundy. His dark brown eyes were focused on the terrain ahead scouting a good place to set down to rest. Although Draconas' were very strong and could fly for miles at a stretch, they still needed sustenance and sleep like any other animal or person. In fact, they required more for the energy spent in flight. Unlike a bird whose bones were hollow to lighten the amount of weight the wings needed to lift, a Draconas was built like a dragon with hard scales, strong bones and thick muscled legs, and these attributes required a significant amount of energy. He spotted a small herd of deer and changed direction to come up behind them. Using his sharp claws, he grabbed the hind quarters of a yearling in the back of the herd and sunk his teeth into him before he knew what was happening. With little effort, he lifted the yearling into the air and flew away before the herd was any the wiser.

Corvus flew to a nice secluded area, and with the equivalent of a yawn, he roasted the deer before eating it. The nights were chilly, so Corvus used his fire to warm the rocks in the area and promptly fell asleep maintaining his Draconas form for protection. The brother moon Soros followed his sister across the sky and before Soros set, Corvus was up and once again on his way.

Chapter 13

King Baldor called for his wizard and asked for an update on the "Baldoran Horde," as he was so fond of calling them. The High Wizard Balquin had them line up by the designations as he had instructed them before. The commander Andal sat atop Quintos at the front of his magically altered soldiers.

The King looked over his horde and was pleased. The alterations to their physique would make them much harder to kill and allow them to travel longer distances without tiring as quickly. He was ready to send them to back up his loyal commander Donnal who had integrated himself into the party as only Donnal could have done. Whatever the final answer was to what the Kingdom of Amjukar was up to would soon be known and then he would be able to thwart their plans. Of this he had no doubt. Originally, King Baldor had decided to leave this to his Commander Donnal, Lt. Commander Andal and his soldiers. However, after hearing more and more rumors coming from Amjukar, as well as the other kingdoms, King Baldor decided that he had best see to this personally. He did not like the idea of leaving the kingdom in the hands of anyone else, although it could not be helped. He would send for Princess Lira to attend him straight away. Once he gave her detailed instructions, then he could be underway.

The princess Lira walked into the king's chambers with an air of someone used to being observed as well as obeyed. Like her father King Baldor, Lira was tall with long black hair. Their difference was in the eyes. Where his eyes were green, hers were a dark blue, a reminder of her mother who had died in childbirth. Her nose was straight, her lips soft and full. Due to her daily training sessions with weapons as well as tai'ka training, her body was strong with a small waist, perfect bosom and round hips. Although she was his daughter, he could appreciate her womanly attributes.

"You sent for me father?" She asked in a bored tone.

"Indeed," he replied, "I will be leaving on the morrow and will leave the kingdom in your capable hands." It was said with the hint of a question.

She looked around his chamber and asked, "What of Donnal?" "Can he not do this? He has always done so before." She crossed her arms over her chest and waited for his reply.

Irritation showed on Baldor's face; only his daughter could get away with questioning him although he would have never allowed it in public. "Donnal was sent ahead a while ago. I am surprised that you hadn't noticed." He looked at her with what was now irritation replaced by amusement and awaited her answer.

"I have better things to do than keep an eye on the comings and goings of your commander," she quipped.

King Baldor smiled inwardly for he knew that his daughter had wanted Donnal from the time she was a young girl.

"I am quite sure that you do. On another matter, I will be taking Lt. Commander Andal and the soldiers placed in his charge as well. I want you to oversee the wizards I will be leaving behind that are overseeing the dragon project. The High Wizard Balquin will be with me. Additionally, have the Captain continue to train and drill the soldiers that are not otherwise engaged in my project. Do you have your amulet?" At her nod he continued, "If you need to contact me, do so with the amulet and be sure to wear it at all times without exception. I have requested that the adjoining suite be prepared for you. I wish you to be more centrally located while acting on my behalf. Do you have any questions?"

"Yes, of course. Where are you going and why? I have never known you to handle something personally, so it is apparent that whatever you are up to is of the utmost importance."

"My reasons are of no concern to you. I expect you to run this kingdom in my absence and keep me posted on anything that you deem to be important. If you wish to rule this kingdom in the future, you would do well to just make sure that I arrive to the same kingdom that I left. Am I clear, daughter?"

"I have no doubt that you will succeed, father, in whatever it is you are not telling me. I will bide my time while I await your return and keep you informed of any news that I deem important, as you have requested."

"I expect no less from you Lira. If anything that you believe may be even remotely important, I want you to contact me immediately. I will tolerate nothing less than complete obedience in this. I have many things set in motion that must continue to go smoothly. Make sure they do."

"Of course, father."

King Baldor left by way of the balcony in his Draconas form. At one time, Lira would have looked on with envy. However, unbeknownst to her father, she had come into her Draconas form during the past year. She was not sure why she had held it from him, but she enjoyed her secret too much to give it up just yet. It was not uncommon for Draconas' to recur in a family. Usually it skipped a generation or more which was one of the reasons that they were so few and far between. She would of course have to tell him eventually. It would not be this day. She smiled to herself and called for refreshments and one of the informants that she knew spoke with her father on a regular basis. She wanted to make sure she knew all there was to know.

***

Sakira hid behind a rather large oak and looked out at the goblins dressing a buck for the fire. Despite popular opinion, goblins preferred to prepare their meat, although they would eat it raw if necessary. It had been many years since she had seen a goblin and here she was looking at a group of about fifty or more. She spoke some goblin due to her training with the Elvin Elite. Based on what she heard, the goblins were out looking for their comrades that had not returned to their home. Goblins were not known for caring about the welfare of others, even if the "others" were one of their own, so the group they were looking for must have been special indeed to have warranted a search party. The reason for their presence was of no concern to her. Sakira just wanted to get around the goblins undetected. She could change to her Draconas form and fly over them. However, she would probably be pursued and possibly hurt before gaining enough altitude. A goblin could throw a spear far with enough strength to penetrate her hide if it hit the right spot, whether intentionally or no. Normally she would wait until they moved, on but she was in a hurry. Staying in her elf form, she used her magic to blend into the environment making her virtually invisible. She looked for the path of least resistance through the goblin party and started on her way. The goblins were spread out, some lying down, some taking a nap and others arguing with one another or helping in the meal preparation. Sakira was making her way at a good pace until one of the goblins that she passed a little too close to was obviously alerted to her presence. He sat up straight and began to sniff the air. Unfortunately, becoming invisible did not extend to scent and sound. As an elf, being quiet was an easy accomplishment. Masking her natural scent was a different matter altogether and this is what had gained the goblin's attention. The goblin's sudden change in his demeanor got the attention of those nearest him. Using the grunts, whistles and hand signals goblins used to communicate, he let those near him know of the smell close by that was unfamiliar. They began to make their way towards Sakira, who decided that holding still would only aid in her capture. She slowly made her way back from the oncoming goblins, whose numbers had swollen, as each goblin became aware that something of interest was going on. She continued to maintain her ability to blend with her surroundings, much like a chameleon, as opposed to actual invisibility. The slower she moved, the better the camouflage worked. Unfortunately the fact that several goblins were literally sniffing her out caused her to move faster than her camouflage could keep up with. Because of this fact, there were fluctuations in her camouflage that became visible to the eye. Additionally, her normal grace as an elf would normally allow her to traverse the forest floor with barely a whisper of her passing. Instead, her hasty retreat had begun to show visible signs of her passage in the leaves and pine needles that blanketed the forest floor. Realizing this, she gave up all pretense of stealth and ran as fast as her legs would carry her to the nearest opening in the trees to change into her Draconas form. Goblins are tall and fast, but elves are naturally faster and given enough space and time could outrun most species, be they animal or human. This speed kept Sakira just out of their reach. Once she reached the gap, she began to shift into her Draconas form. It was at this exact time that a well-placed spear caught her deep in her right thigh. Sakira cried out and with more effort than usual, she completed changing into her Draconas form. She whipped her head around and blew fire at those closest to her, causing them to slow their pursuit as she took to the sky and gained altitude as quickly as possible to avoid any other lucky throws.

She continued in the direction she had been headed and did not stop to tend to her wound until she felt she had placed enough distance between herself and the band of goblins. She found an outcropping of rocks in a small clearing that was just large enough to set down in her current form. She touched down, and before she changed back, she used her maw to push the spear through the front of her thigh. Once she had completed that task, she changed back to her elf form and sank to the ground. Sakira rummaged through her pack for the medicinal herbs she kept on hand to place in the wound to stave off infection. She then dug out the strips of cloth used to keep the herbs in place and stop the bleeding. Since she hadn't maintained her Draconas form for long, she was able to placate her appetite with the rations she had on hand. After eating and drinking her fill, she settled under the boulder outcrop to rest for a while in the shade it provided.

The sun was getting low in the sky when she resumed her journey. She enjoyed this part of being a Draconas more than any other ability...flight! As an elf she would live a long life

186

and have some form of magical abilities. This was different. She was flying just over the treetops when the sun was making its final descent from the sky, causing the horizon to explode in a myriad of colors. Reds, purples, oranges and more were playing across the sky. The fading warmth of the spring day turned into a cooler evening. Despite the beauty and the lightness in her heart, she knew she needed to rest some more very soon. She was tired and her leg was aching more than it should. Although it was throbbing where the arrow had pierced her thigh, Sakira continued to make good time and it wasn't until exhaustion began to cause a disruption in the rhythm of her flight that she gave in to both the exhaustion and the pain and decided it was time for another break. Before she could take the time to rest, she knew that she would need to find dinner for her ravenous Draconas self. She scanned the area with her exceptional eyesight for the better part of an hour before spotting a wild pig. Sakira maneuvered her way through the dense trees and grabbed the squealing omnivore with her claws. She would be eating pork that night.

Once an acceptable place was located, she set down with the squealing pig and put it out of its misery. After making quick work of her supper, she returned to her elven form and removed the bandage from her thigh. Much to her dismay and despite her best efforts, the wound had begun to fester. She cleaned the wound once again and redressed it. She knew that she had done a good job of dressing her wound before and wondered what had been on the tip of the spear that hit her.

Sakira would have preferred to continue on until she found sufficient cover for the night. Her body refused to cooperate, for it was sapped of its energy and a fever had taken hold. Perhaps if she rested for just a bit, she could feel sufficiently well enough to continue on until adequate shelter had been found or she could change to her Draconas form to feel less vulnerable. As soon as she laid her head down on her pack, she fell into a fitful sleep.

Chapter 14

When the scouts sent to spy on Gustaf's whereabouts finally stopped following him, he turned around and continued in the direction he knew that his sister Elle and the rest were travelling. His anger had become a tangible thing that stayed strong and kept him warm. He was angry at Elle for so many reasons, and now his anger towards Donnal was almost as great. He had no doubt that he had been used by Donnal, and that did not sit well with him. He was the one to use people, not the other way around. He had almost decided to head back to Amjukar and forget this whole thing. The more he brooded, the more he knew that it wasn't in his nature to let things go. He would double back and travel night and day, if need be, to catch up with the group. He was somewhat concerned about traveling alone, but he had abilities as an elf to help aid him in a crisis. Although Gustaf abhorred work of any kind, he put all he had into catching up with them, his hatred and anger acting as a source of energy. He slept little and ate while in the saddle. He didn't care that he was putting his horse through too much; it was there to serve him and he felt no attachment to the animal otherwise. The problem with travelling alone was that he had only himself to converse with. He agitated himself to the point that he spoke aloud to himself and agreed heartily with everything he said. If one were to come upon him without him being aware, they would most likely think he had gone mad...and perhaps he had. Being mad, however, did not stop him from his current course. He didn't have a specific plan; he just knew that he wanted to be close enough to find out what was going on. He kicked the horse once again to quicken his pace and continued on.

***

While Prince Karnuk was making his way back to his kingdom, his friend and confidant the Draconas Corvus was making his way south to catch up with the party from Amjukar. The sky was lightening as the sun began to make its ascent and the air was warming up after a somewhat chilly night. Corvus was making good time by flying for long periods, stopping just long enough to hunt, eat and catch a few hours' sleep. He flew over the gap in the forest where the Su River flowed, following the same course taken by the knights of Amjukar. Although travel had picked up on this route, the game was still plentiful. It was fortunate that a meal was easy to come by because maintaining his Draconas form for long periods of time caused his appetite to increase substantially. Corvus had always felt comfortable in his role as a friend, companion and advisor to Prince Kornuk. Now, however, he felt as though he was over his head with this assignment and was afraid of letting down King Druek, Prince Karnuk and the entire dwarf kingdom. He understood what was at stake here, though he was unclear as to what his role was to be. Corvus was deep in thought when he spotted a woman alone tucked into a small outcropping of rocks in the forest. If not for his enhanced sight, she would have gone unnoticed. He started to fly over her when something gave him pause and he banked towards her instead. Corvus landed a few dozen feet from her. The alarmed woman tried to stand and draw her sword. She staggered instead and slumped back onto the forest floor, the rocks acting to hold her in a sitting position.

"I didn't mean to startle you. I saw you from the air and stopped to see if you were alright," Corvus stated after transforming back to his dwarf form.

Although Corvus had spoken in his own language, Sakira understood it perfectly because she had mastered the dwarf language years ago, as well as many other languages of the realm. She had woken that morning feeling extremely ill and she knew it was from the gash in her leg. Something had caused the wound to fester and she felt as though a poison was slowly making its way through her body and would kill her in a manner of days; if she had that much time. She had let down her queen and could not think of a worse way to die. Dying during battle for her kingdom was one thing, but this···this was no warrior's death. This was her body being too weak to fight the poison that must have tipped the spear. In addition to that, she had changed direction to follow the party sent from Amjukar so no one would look for her in the direction she had taken. She had certainly made a mess of things. With much effort, Sakira lifted her head to look at the dwarf in front of her and was shocked to see that he appeared to be genuinely concerned for her wellbeing.

Despite his obvious concern, Sakira was a loner and an elf and as such she was brought up believing she was of a superior race. Her first instinct was to ignore the dwarf. Her current state was such that, she could not afford to send him on his way. Although it went against her nature, she had little choice but to try and enlist his aid in possibly getting a message to her queen so that another might be sent in her place. With this thought in mind, she answered him.

"I was travelling and ran into a band of goblins. Unfortunately, I was not quick enough and I was hit with a spear which I am quite sure was tipped with poison. I'm afraid that there is nothing anyone can do."

Corvus stepped to her side, and despite the fact that she was sitting, he only needed to bend slightly at the waist to have eye contact with the tall elf. Although Corvus was a dwarf, it didn't take another elf to know that the woman in front of him was beautiful and probably more beautiful than any woman he had seen in his lifetime thus far. He introduced himself and after hesitating a moment, she gave her name in return.

"I never tried before, but maybe I could carry you while I fly an' try to get you to a healer," he offered.

"That is very kind, though I doubt I have that much time. Perhaps you could get a message to Queen Teserath instead?" she inquired.

"I have a very important mission an' cannot deviate from it, yet the offer to fly you somewhere still stands." He saw her doubt and said, "We won't know unless we try," he coaxed, "Let's give it a try. The worse that can 'appen is you die on the way, but you an' me both know you will die if I leave you here anyway."

Her first thought was an aversion to sitting on this dwarf's back. Her second thought was that she had become quite arrogant to think in such a way, especially given her present circumstance.

Sakira thought on it more and realized that what he said was true and she was not ready to just lie down without a fight. She agreed, and Corvus took her hand to help her to her feet. As soon as their hands clasped one another, a strange feeling flowed between them and neither could pull their hand away. Their Draconas marks flared to life on their faces. When the energy flow, which is what it felt like, finally ceased, Sakira was standing strong and feeling healthy while Corvus slumped to the ground in exhaustion, effectively changing their places. He looked at Sakira with a dumbfounded expression and saw the slight smile that tugged at the corner of her mouth.

"You were unaware of your ability to heal I assume?" Sakira smiled down at him.

"I had no idea," he replied in a voice made hoarse by exhaustion.

"I am familiar with the powers of a healer, and I know that the first few times the power is used, it can drain the person of most of their energy as it has done to you. It will get much easier with the passage of time and practice. Soon you will be able to heal many before tiring yourself as you are now. I am also on a quest for my kingdom that, thanks to you, I can now complete. However, I now owe you a blood debt. You have saved my life, and in doing so, you have saved my mission and by association, perhaps my kingdom as well. I would be honored to attend you while you regain your strength. I have elven wine in my sack. A sip or two should help to rejuvenate you nicely. Between the wine, some food and some rest you should be good as new in no time." Sakira pulled some rations from her sack and poured the wine.

During the few hours it took for Draconas Corvus to regain his strength Draconas Sakira found herself enjoying his company and opening up to him much to her surprise. It was an extremely different experience than any she could have imagined. Sakira was amused by the dwarf. Most dwarves that she had ever met or known were gruff or rough, and they all seemed to be downright grumpy. Draconas Corvus did not fit the standard she had become accustomed to. She wondered if he was the only one, or if there were more dwarves that were "sociable." She told herself that when all was done, she would take the time to think on all that she had learned.

Corvus had similar thoughts as well. Dwarves typically only tolerated other races out of necessity. There were exceptions to this, for he was aware that the dwarves that lived in the Kingdom of Amjukar instead of their mountain home had developed friendships with both humans and elves. He had always known that elves were arrogant due to their magic and longevity. He now knew that they could be quite likable as well. If not for his current responsibility, he might have liked to spend more time learning more about them. Certainly, at the very least, the elven wine needed more consideration.

Within a few hours, Corvus found himself ready to proceed with his journey, and realized that he was reluctant to do so. Sakira was not only a beautiful woman she could be quite humorous as well. He would have been surprised to learn that she was reluctant to be on her way as well.

"Thank you for the food an' drink, and now I must be on my way," he said in a tone that let her know he wished it were not so.

"I too must be on my way and you have made that possible. For that you have my gratitude as well as blood debt, and if there is anything I can do, you need only ask. If it is within my ability to do so, it will be done."

Simultaneously the two changed into their Draconas forms, one slim and light the other dark and stocky and headed south once again. Upon realizing that they were going in the same direction, they began to speak to each other as all Draconas' were capable of.

"Are you by chance trying to reach a party going south out of the Kingdom of Amjukar?" Sakira asked in his mind.

"I am," was his simple reply.

195

Sakira put aside her preconceived notions of dwarves and made a decision based solely on her instinct and the time they shared and said, "Since we are obviously headed in the same direction for the same reason, perhaps we should travel together for safety."

"I would enjoy your company very much," Corvus replied with a grin evident in his voice.

The two Draconas' continued on their way, gaining on the group from Amjukar with every mile they flew.

***

As he had done thousands of times before, Draconas Markim paced in his suite. He had no contact with the group he sent out, having been in too much of a hurry to make the necessary arrangements for a speaking amulet. He was hearing from his informants that not only did the dwarven kingdom know what was happening, the elves were aware that something was amiss as well. In addition, he had heard of a contingent of soldiers currently making their way from the Kingdom of Erewyth, headed by King Baldor no less. He could only assume that they were making their way to intercept his "training party." This was now a great concern and he had called a meeting of the councilmembers still in attendance to review the situation and decide what they could do, if anything. The meeting was to start shortly, and he began to make his way to the council chamber.

He was the first to arrive and he sat heavily in his chair, the weight of his responsibilities feeling as though they had a physical substance. What he wouldn't give to be able to turn the reins over to someone else, yet it was not to be. One by one, the other members arrived and the meeting was called to order.

Draconas Markim looked around the table and then addressed them: "I called this meeting to order due to new developments that have been brought to my attention. As you are already aware, the dwarves are aware of our plans regarding Desne Mar. I understand their stand on sending their own advisor on this mission, although what will become of it is unknown. I have also heard that the elven Kingdom of Valsara and the Kingdom of Erewyth are also aware that something is going on, however, unlike the dwarves, they do not know what we are trying to accomplish, only that we are looking for a land. The elves have sent some of their Elite to intercept our people. King Baldor himself is leading a contingent of soldiers to intercept as well. It doesn't take a wizard to realize that this is coming to a head, and we have no way of reaching our people to warn them to take the additional precautions that have become so very necessary." He started to continue, then stopped when he noticed the silent exchange between the High Wizard Malek and Wizard Tannis. He said nothing, just gave them a look that said, "I assume this has something to do with your newfound friendship? Out with it."

"Forgive me, Draconas Markim, but there is a way we can get a message to the group," Tannis stated.

Markim and the others looked at Tannis for clarification.

"Malek and I were deeply concerned when we sent a new member of The Seven, not to mention she is also new to being a Draconas. Then we also sent yet another woman who is still relatively new to The Seven. A mission of this potential importance, keeping in mind we still are not sure of the validity of this mission, should have been handled by those with more experience in these matters...in our opinion, of course. We discussed our concerns with each other and I approached my brother Cylas, who is one of the knights with the party that was sent, and requested that he keep us informed on a regular basis. Cylas was not told of the actual reason that they were going on their "training mission," although he does realize that there is something else going on. We have received regular reports from Cylas indicating that they are close to the end of the Fallon Forest and that Draconas Ellindria is making significant progress with her magic to the point that she may soon be the most powerful Draconas in the realm, with the possible exception of King Baldor. We are truly sorry for the deception. We felt that we were acting in the best interest of the realm." Tannis stopped and looked to Markim for a reaction.

Draconas Markim sat quietly contemplating what he had just learned. At least this explained the reason for the sudden friendship between the wizards. There was a look of disapproval from Draconas Brock, for he believed that no one had the right to go behind their leader's back. The meeting was quiet while everyone waited for Markim's reaction.

Draconas Markim sighed and spoke, "I admit that I am disappointed that you felt it necessary to take this action without talking to me first. There was ample opportunity in the meeting for this to be addressed. However, in light of the fact that we have no other way to reach the group, I will just be thankful that we now have a way to do so. We are The Seven. It takes all of us to run this kingdom and protect the people within it. Although I am your leader, it does not mean that my voice alone holds sway over all decisions. Can you reach this Cylas and have him take a message to Sir Devin for those involved?"

"I cannot reach him at will. He contacts me at the end of each day by using the trees. We are limited in the amount of time that will occur, perhaps another day or so, and then it will be sporadic because there will be little-to-no trees which was our source for communication. He usually calls to me in the evening during their meal."

The High Wizard Malek spoke up then. "I have also been trying to 'read' the situation to try and learn more; unfortunately my sight has been closed to me. I don't know if a force is at work but I feel as though my ability to foresee has left me, at least for the time being. I don't know what this means, although I do know that it makes me very nervous...to say the least."

Draconas Markim thought about this but knew that there was nothing he could do. He turned his attention back to Tannis.

"I wish for you to tell Cylus the following: Others are in the know. Dwarves, elves and Baldor are working to intercept. Beware." Markim continued, "Before we adjourn, I want to emphasize that a contingent of King Baldor's soldiers have been magically enhanced. According to our sources, they look more like large wolves than men. They are strong and very fast. This has been confirmed by more than one source lending to its authenticity. Additionally it is said that a dragon carries their commander. I have never known a dragon that would voluntarily commit to any kingdom and allow someone to use them as one would use a horse. Only in the direst of circumstances, and for those to whom they had allied themselves, would this be done. And even then it would be a rare occasion. I must assume that something is causing this drake to act against his will, and I want someone looking into this immediately. I know in my gut that this is important, as I knew that Draconas Ellindria of House Kar was important to our mission despite the reservations held by some of you. We need to make sure that we do everything within our power to keep Desne Mar out of the hands of King Baldor. Are there any suggestions on who we should send for the information regarding the dragon? We need it as soon as possible."

"I hate to cut our council down by another member but don't you think that a Draconas is needed for this as well as someone that we all trust with our very lives? Draconas Lias would be ideal if he is willing to take on this monumental task. He would need to enter the Kingdom of Erewyth if he wishes to find out what has happened." The High Wizard Malek emphatically stated.

"How do you feel about this, Lias?" Markim asked.

"How would anyone feel about travelling alone into the kingdom of Erewyth?" he tried to joke, which was unusual for Lias to say the least. "However, since King Baldor is no longer there it makes it an easier proposition. I do agree that no dragon would willingly act as someone's horse, and if Baldor has more dragons at his call for some unknown reason, then we need to find out. If a battle for this land, if it exists, becomes imminent due to this mission, dragons on either side could tip the balance considerably. I will leave immediately."

"Does anyone have anything to add?" Draconas Markim pointedly directed his question to the wizards when he asked the question. The wizards looked appropriately ashamed and shook their heads in the negative.

When no one spoke up, the meeting was adjourned and Markim walked with Lias back to his rooms to discuss his upcoming journey and make sure that they had a means of communication available to them. He was not about to make the same mistake again.

Chapter 15

Prince Karnuk and his contingent of dwarves had arrived at the first door in the Krull Mountains entering into the Kingdom of MoeDin. The door was used only by those of royal blood and those trusted by the king. The door was indiscernible from the face of the mountain and only a dwarf would be able to locate it. Prince Karnuk felt eyes upon him, and after looking around, he finally looked up. There···several hundred feet in the air···was Draconas Lias, one of The Seven. The prince waved to Lias and contemplated his reason for being there, though he did not have time to pursue the question. He turned his attention back to the door and pulled the invisible lever that set into motion a series of unseen pulleys and wheels, and before long, the door disappeared into the mountain itself. Once inside, a different lever was tripped and the door slid to a close, once again becoming invisible in the mountain face. The tunnels in the Krull Mountains were many and extensive for a variety of reasons, not least of which was eluding an enemy. There were times over the years that a breach was attempted on the dwarf mountain for the riches within. Each and every time, the enemy was defeated due to the tunnels. Once the attackers became lost, they were killed or simply starved to death. A secret known only to a very few was the fact that several of the tunnels had false walls that could be added or removed with little effort, effectively causing confusion and panic in any that believed they had discovered the secret to the tunnel system within. When walls could so easily be moved, it was impossible for invaders to master the tunnels; however this was not common knowledge. The tunnel they currently followed was a main tunnel used for quick access to the throne room. The mountains were vast though, and it still took a good deal of time to go from the invisible door to the throne room. The prince then made his way to his father's study to await his arrival.

***

King Baldor was in bad spirits which meant he was his usual self. He was by no means a "soft man" although he did appreciate the finer things in life, many of which he was unable to partake of on their journey. He had considered bringing a girl or two to warm his bed and had decided against it at the last minute. His sexual appetite was enormous and he was already regretting his decision. He decided that the in next town they went through he would alleviate his problem.

The Kingdom of Erewyth was on the western side of the Krull Mountains and towards the southern end. Baldor decided that they would go around the mountains, as opposed to over them, to allow his soldiers the opportunity to raid any towns or villages they passed for supplies and anything else that was needed. He realized that by doing this he had sent a message to the Kingdom of Amjukar and the others saying: "I am here, beware!"...giving them an opportunity to try and waylay his soldiers. He had it on good authority that the Kingdom of Amjukar had become soft over the years and he expected little or no resistance from the small party that was sent. The soldiers he had at his command were larger, faster and meaner than any in the realm, and he knew that if necessary he could call on the dragons to come to his aid. All the eggs were in his basket, so to speak, with one exception. He still did not know the purpose of the land that was being sought. Nevertheless, he thought, he would find out soon enough. They would intercept the group from Amjukar and beat it out of one of them. In fact, he was looking forward to it and hoped that whomever they caught would not give in to torture too soon and spoil all of his fun. He had not spoken to Donnal in a few days and decided that tonight he would reach out to him for their current whereabouts, allowing him to direct his horde accordingly.

They were an afternoon's march from the end of the Krull Mountains where they would pass through a small town at the foot. Being that it was a small town he hoped that it was possible to find a girl that was attractive enough for his bed. They were making excellent time due to the enhancements to the soldiers and his ability to fly with the dragon Quintos at his wing, carrying Lt. Commander Andal. It amused him to see the prince drake humiliated so.

The day was turning to dusk when King Baldor and his soldiers reached the foot of the Krull Mountains and the town that was nestled there.

There had been workers in the field, finishing their chores for the day, who had seen the soldiers at a distance. They had run back to their family and friends to try and hide or flee from the coming danger. Unfortunately, the Erewyth soldiers were too fast and some of the workers never made it back. Since the soldiers were more wolf than human, killing and eating the people in the town came naturally to them. Baldor encouraged them to eat their fill, for that was less he need worry about feeding them later. Screams could be heard for what was probably miles as the Baldoran Horde tore through the residents of the town with little or no resistance. Strict instructions were given that all females were to be brought directly to the king. They could torture or eat any males they desired. Lt. Commander Andal had no stomach for the cuisine on his soldier's menu, and so he took it upon himself to find the girls for King Baldor's bed. High Wizard Balquin watched his creations with a critical eye to see if there were some ways in which he could improve upon them the next time.

Because Andal had also been magically enhanced he was able to pry the girls from even the largest of the men's hands, leaving the fathers and husbands to the others for their food or sport. Girls, women and wives, it made no difference···he brought them all to Baldor. They were presented to him one by one. The ones he turned away were allowed to be made into the soldiers' whores before they were killed or devoured, for even wolves had a longing for the fairer sex. In the end, there were three girls chosen to warm the king's bed. Two were of the age when they were becoming young women, and the other was just a few years older. The woman was married with a small boy and was forced to watch as both her son and husband were killed by the wolf-like soldiers who tore into them, their canines ripping the flesh from their bones. Her cries and screams could be heard above the din until she finally broke down and sobbed uncontrollably. All of this was witnessed by Baldor, who took great pleasure and fed off the horror of it all. In ways even he didn't understand, his magic was fed by the misery of others and he was more than happy to tuck in to supper.

Under normal circumstances, they would have continued for many hours more before calling a rest, but the King was ready for some entertainment. When the females were brought to his tent, only two were in attendance.

"Where is the other girl?" Baldor demanded.

"She grabbed a knife from one of the soldiers and slit her own throat, my liege." The unfortunate soldier answered with a husky bark due to his canines and elongated snout.

"Bring that soldier to me!" the king commanded with barely concealed rage.

The soldier in question was brought before the king. He knew that his life was to end on this day and that it was useless to try to change it.

"Your liege," he said with resignation.

"You allowed a woman to take a knife from your person. You are a fool. Under any other circumstance, I would kill you on the spot, however, given the nature of our business, I wish to maintain as many of my soldiers as possible for anything that may come our way. If you are lucky, you will die in battle fighting for me. If you are unlucky, I will kill you myself when this is over. If you try to escape, you will be hunted down and tortured for what I assure you will feel no less than an eternity. Is that understood?"

"Yes your liege, thank you," he replied, and he was truly thankful, for to die in battle was without a doubt better than to die at the hand of his king whose imagination on ways to make one suffer and bleed was legendary.

"That was very kind of you." High Wizard Balquin said.

"Yes, yes it was..." Baldor replied as though he had been most generous and perhaps for Baldor he had.

Once the town had been stripped of anything useful, King Baldor himself and the drake Quintos under Baldor's orders, torched what was left of the town. The flames could be seen for miles and the dwarves living closest to the foot of the Krull mountains made haste in getting a message to their king regarding the town's demise.

***

The party from Amjukar was at that time unaware of all that was taking place in the kingdoms around them. They were a day outside of the end of the forest and the beginning of the plains leading into the desert wasteland. Donnal found it harder and harder to keep his objectivity where Elle was concerned. He had never met a woman quite like her. She was very beautiful, although he knew some women that were perhaps more beautiful. It was more than her beauty; it was her passion for life and her personality, which had shown itself once she was comfortable with the people around her, that made him want to spend time with her and keep her close. To protect her even. She had gotten under his skin when he had thought it impossible. In Donnal's opinion, King Baldor's daughter Lira was more beautiful than Elle. She had been the exotic offspring of the mating of a human and an elf. According to stories, Lira's mother was the most beautiful elf of her age and she was forced into marriage with his king. Some say she was fortunate to die in childbirth. Regardless, Lira was the result of that marriage and he could have had her if he cared to. Regrettably, she had never made his breath catch the way Elle did. There was something about Lira that made her unappealing to him, much to his king's dismay. King Baldor had been accepting of a match between the two of them, yet it was Lira that had made the request not Donnal. His king had not forced the issue, though he felt that it was not beyond the realm of possibility and would worry about it if and when the time came.

Donnal knew he was in a bad place. He knew that his king was cruel but he owed him. How do you turn on the person that gave you a life with purpose? Had he lived through his childhood beatings, he would have amounted to nothing more than a street beggar. Perhaps he could have achieved more, since he did become a Draconas, then again maybe his Draconas side would never have shown itself. King Baldor had raised him as a son. Although in his own way Baldor was just as bad a father as Donnal's own father was he at least had something to offer. Regardless, Donnal knew what he had to do and what was expected of him. Unfortunately for the first time in his life he was having a hard time doing it. He continued to pull back from Elle when his emotions became overwhelming and he could tell that she was confused by his actions. Donnal knew he was sending her mixed signals, yet couldn't seem to help himself. He was aware that she was attracted to him as well. He also knew that if she found out his actual agenda, her attraction would most likely become hatred at his betrayal. He forced himself to quell his current thoughts and watched as Cylas made his daily trip to one of the trees in the forest. The forest had almost come to an end, and the trees were scarce, causing Cylas to walk further to keep from being seen. As usual, Donnal followed Cylas, although he did not expect to learn more than he had already. He was almost lazy in his attendance when he realized that Cylas was being *given* a message instead of the other way around and almost missed what was said. "Others are in the know. Dwarves, Elves and Baldor are working to intercept. Beware." Not understanding the reason behind the message, Cylas silently repeated it to himself one more time and raced back to the camp. Donnal made his way back to camp shortly thereafter and stood outside the tent that Cylas entered to hear the conversation within. When Cylas left the tent, Devin, Borg, Elle and Akhena conferred on the meaning of the message. The longer he listened, the more he understood. The last piece was in place. Desne Mar, the Magic Land. If Donnal had been confused regarding his loyalties before, he was even more so now. Just the thought of King Baldor reaching and claiming a land that enhances magic caused Donnal more than a little concern. If he was honest with himself, he was probably scared. Donnal was not naïve. He knew that that much power in his king's hands was less than ideal, to put it mildly. Before he could think on it further, he felt the warmth of his amulet and he answered the call of his king.

"King Baldor, it is good to hear from you."

"Donnal, my Commander and most trusted servant. How do you fare?" King Baldor queried.

It was not a good sign that his king asked how he was. Baldor never made small talk, preferring to get straight to the point or more to the point; Baldor simply didn't care. Donnal answered, "I am well my King, and how are things in Erewyth?"

"I would not know. I am not there. I have left Lira in charge and sincerely hope she is equal to the task," the king replied. "I am leading my special new soldiers to intercept the party you are with and must know their proximity and where you expect them to be by the time we arrive. Keep in mind that I am flying and the soldiers have been changed to allow for more strength as well as speed."

Donnal was not prepared for this and he took a moment to gather his thoughts. "We are closing in on the edge of the forest that has been our path thus far. We should be entering the beginning of the plains that are between our location and the desert in a day or so. I am not yet sure of our direction once we reach that destination."

"You disappoint me," Baldor growled. "I would have assumed that with your way with the fairer sex and your abilities that you would have easily obtained this information by now. The desert is vast, and I need a close estimate of the whereabouts of the land they are searching for and I am still waiting for the reason behind this. Have you yet to determine that as well?"

Donnal struggled with his inner self and could not bring himself to disclose what he knew just yet. Perhaps he was holding out hope that all of this was for naught. He shook himself from his reverie when Baldor barked his name to get his attention. "I am sorry," he thought quickly, "I thought I heard someone and could not take the chance of being overheard. I believe that only the leaders of this group are aware of the actual mission and they have yet to speak of it even to each other in private. I am sorry and will endeavor to learn more."

"I expect no less and I expect it soon. Do not let me down Donnal. Do not forget all I have done for you."

"For which I am eternally grateful my King."

"I want results not your gratitude."

Donnal hung his head and wondered how things had become so damn complicated. It was not long ago that he would have done his king's bidding without question. He was not sure what had changed that. Was it Elle? Or the fact that his king···with the power of the land behind him··· was too terrifying for even him to comprehend. Perhaps it was both. He went back to the camp with only his conscience for company.

Chapter 16

Draconas Lias had taken to the sky and was watching the castle and the capitol pass beneath him. Although it was cooler the higher he flew, in his Draconas form it was easy to keep warm. He had a natural ability to stay warm, and if additional warmth was needed, he simply blew a little fire that swept back over him, warming his scales. A dragon or Draconas' scales were designed to be strong enough to protect them from most weapons and also acted to absorb heat and maintain it for several hours. Since he had been called to The Seven approximately six hundred years ago, Lias had little time for just flying in his Draconas form for the pure pleasure of it and so he was enjoying his newfound freedom immensely. The clouds had parted for a while, and Lias dipped lower and watched as his shadow crossed the ground beneath him so quickly that those it passed over went unnoticed by all. Ahead of him the clouds were starting to gather and take on an ominous look. A good rain would not deter him from his task, whereas thunder and lightning would ground him for the duration. He was hopeful that if it was the latter, that it would pass quickly. He was closing in on the Krull Mountains when he looked down and saw Prince Karnuk and his contingent of dwarves making their way to the northern face of the mountain to gain access through the door known only to a few. The Prince felt eyes upon him and finally looked up to see the Draconas flying west. He knew who the white and silver Draconas was and waved in acknowledgement. Lias tipped a wing in response.

Draconas Lias had not spoken with an actual dragon in over a hundred years. He was both concerned and honored to be chosen for this quest. He could not understand the reason any dragon would ally itself with Baldor, but he was fairly certain it was because they had no choice. The question was what, if anything, had convinced the dragons to align themselves with the most notorious King in the realm's history, and what could be done to change things? King Baldor had been the King of Erewyth for more than a thousand years and it was unknown how old he was. Baldor had shown up over a thousand years ago and no one knew from where he hailed. He was handsome, charismatic and extremely powerful and it took little time for Baldor to overthrow the royal family at that time and take their rightful place on the throne. Lias still remembered the tales of the mutilation that was wrought upon the royal family and the display he formed with their mangled bodies, discouraging anyone from opposing him in an attempt to take back the crown. Also, since he made an effort to leave no living member of the royal line alive, there was none to challenge him that had a true claim to the throne. He had apparently been successful since none had come forward since that time to stake a claim. Then again, as far as Lias knew, there was no one strong enough to challenge the self-proclaimed king.

The trip to Erewyth by horse was rather long with a mountain to traverse but in his Draconas form he could make it to their capitol in just a few days. Normally they would not send an elf for a mission such as this since elves were extremely rare in the kingdom of Erewyth. An unfamiliar elf such as himself would stand out. Fortunately, one of Lias' abilities was to be able to change his appearance to others. He didn't actually change his appearance, just other people's concept of how he looked. If he wanted to appear a beggar, anyone looking at him would think him so, although his physical appearance never actually changed.

Lias had forgotten, yet soon remembered, that his appetite in his Draconas form was in direct proportion to his size and therefore he would need to eat in the same form before resting or he would not take in enough sustenance to maintain his current pace. Had he forgotten about this part, or had he just not spent that much time in his Draconas form to find it out? He didn't have a clue. It had been so long.

As he had expected, the clouds darkened, the winds picked up, whipping in several directions seemingly at once, and within a few minutes the thunder, lightning and rain made their appearance as well. Lias made his way down and found sufficient shelter in a cliff face which had just enough room in a shallow cave for his elf form to lie down and have a small fire. He flew to the mouth of the cave and turned into his elf form while in midflight, which he was proud of accomplishing despite his stumble on the landing. He was hungry and becoming more so with the passage of time. It was imperative, however, that he wait out the weather to hunt. Once the storm passed, he would make that his first priority before continuing on. In the meantime, a little sleep while he waited out the storm was in order.

***

The party from Amjukar had reached the end of Fallon Forest and had begun the trek to the desert wastelands. The transition between forest and desert had them riding through the open grassland plains with the sparsely scattered stand of trees providing shelter from the occasional downpour so common this time of year or for the sole purpose of stopping for nourishment and a short reprieve from their quickened pace.

Elle had realized earlier on that the extent of her magical prowess was far above the norm. She had actually begun to hold back around people for fear of what her companions would think. Her ability to manipulate animals was so incredibly easy that she finally allowed herself to try a simple command on a person. She chose one of the rookies in their party and caused him to walk, turn, bring his horse to a halt, as well as other small movements that would in no way harm the young man though she still felt guilty at having done so. When she let control of his mind return to him, he appeared puzzled with little or no memory of what had transpired. Whether or not she could command someone who knew what she was doing, or whether she could make someone do something against their very nature, she did not know for she would not allow herself to experiment to that extent. Her ability to sense what others felt was now combined with their actual thoughts and she put much time into learning how not to hear them without wanting to do so. She was embarrassed by her accidental invasion of their privacy, although she was still amused by some of the inner thoughts she had heard before she gained control. She knew the rain was beneficial to the land and so she rarely used her ability to manipulate the elements. Also, as with any magic, the more she used the more tired she felt. Magic was not without its limitations. Again, not wanting to scare her friends, she would gradually change a rainy day to sun to allow for easier passage and without their knowledge. Then she would allow the elements to resume back to normal when her party was out of sight. Her ability to grow things at a phenomenal rate allowed her to build shelter in the plains when the trees were not in abundance, and most thought it was a normal ability of all elves. All elves could grow plants; it was one of only a few abilities that they all had in common. However, only Elle could grow a seedling into a tree for shelter with little effort and time. She usually dragged it out to at least an hour so as not to appear too easy. The fact was that Elle was becoming a power unlike any known, besides King Baldor, and if anyone knew the extent of her powers, they would believe her to be more than an even match for the cruel Draconas of legend.

She had flown off far enough to gain privacy to practice her magic on this day. She took one of the seedlings she had harvested during their trek through the forest and held it in the palm of her hand. She tipped her hand and allowed the seedling to fall, lost in the tall grass of the plains. She brought the image of a well rooted sapling to mind. When she felt the warmth of the magic fill her, she opened her eyes and smiled at the little tree before her. She then walked several feet away and dropped yet another seed. This time she pictured a large tree shaped in such a way as to have a hollowed out trunk large enough for a person to sit comfortably inside and read a good book, something she would have very much enjoyed doing herself. She was amused to find that when she opened her eyes, the tree stood majestically before her. The hollow in the trunk actually had an area resembling a seat. Taking it as a sign, she sat inside the hollow and pulled a book from the pack slung across her back which she had conjured from the castle library. She had recently discovered that if she had the ability to see something clearly in her mind's eye, that she could conjure said object for a brief period of time. The larger and more complex the object, the harder it was to obtain and the more it drained her of her strength. This ability, above all others, both excited and frightened her at the same time. She had practiced with this ability to discover more of its limitations. She had so far been able to conjure most anything she tried with the exception of prepared food or drink. She had yet to try and conjure a person or other living creature, the consequences if it went wrong was simply not worth it. It would be so easy to conjure whatever she had want or need of, within her limitations, although the ability to do so with relative ease led her to believe that this particular gift should only be used when the need was great indeed. She did not feel that the conjuring of a favorite book, however, would be an abuse of her ability, and so she sat back and allowed herself to enjoy a few moments in the lives of the book's characters and their trials and tribulations, forgetting for just a while, her own. She had flown ahead of the party and would rejoin them when they caught up to her, allowing her that precious time to indulge herself.

The other leaders of the group were acutely aware of the race they found themselves in. However, they also knew that the development of Elle's magical gifts could be the difference in their ability to take that which they sought and maintain it as well. It quickly became obvious to the leaders of the group why Elle, who was so new to it all, had been chosen by Draconas Markim. He must have known or had some inkling of the magic within her that had been untapped.

Once Elle practiced a while longer she flew back to her group which had been making their way in her direction so as not to lose precious time. The day was nearing its end, and they would be readying themselves for supper and the night's rest before long. They had been travelling as far as possible without injuring the horses and themselves. They pushed harder each day to test their limits by travelling later and breaking camp earlier. It would soon take its toll on everyone involved. Elle was hopeful that they would be able to lose those on their way to intercept them in the vast desert they were headed to, if not before. She spoke with Sir Devin about the direction they were travelling. The scroll that Draconas Callis had come into possession of, the scroll that had put all of this into motion, gave only a vague reference to where Desne Mar was located. It indicated that when the land recognized the magic necessary to claim it, that it would make itself known. That was all. During their travels, Elle had followed where the group led, yet for some reason she began to feel a great desire to travel south with a slight reckoning to the east. She relayed this feeling to Devin, who immediately implemented the change in direction without question. Having no specific directions to follow, he was happy to make a course adjustment even if it was based on a "hunch."

They made camp for the night. Elle sat down beside Donnal at the cooking fire and accepted the offered drink. It did not take a seer to realize the difference in Elle since the beginning of the trip. He could not help but admire the woman she had grown into in so short a time. She had gone from an overwhelmed young elf maiden to a confident Draconas and member of The Seven. He had also stopped trying to hide his affection for her. He told himself that it was to gain her trust, so he could follow through with his orders from his king. Donnal knew in his heart that he was only lying to himself.

Devin watched from across the fire, always keeping an eye on the man that he still did not trust. Donnal was holding something back from them, and until he knew what it was, he was going to keep an eye on his charge. Borg sat to his right and Akhena next to Borg's other side, listening with rapt attention to yet another tale from the dwarf's repertoire of what seemed to be an unlimited supply.

"Me brothers an' me got ahold o' some elf wine and made our way to a place we found in the mountain tunnels when we was explorin'. We were thinkin' that there is no way any elf could out drink a dwarf, so we took turns with that wine…passin' it aroun' between us. Next thing we know, it's three days later and we're standin' in front o' me father. We'd drunk a whole bottle o' that wine and we were told we were lucky to be alive. Lucky they found us, too, cause we were wanderin' the tunnels for who knows what reason and for how long. We didn't remember anythin' an' for the first time we were lost in our own mountain. Me brothers an' me got the worse arse whoopin' on top o' the worse headache anybody ever had. I was sure there was someone holed up inside me brain with a war hammer just walin' away. I swore never to touch that shit again."

It was at that time that Borg removed the lid from his flask and took a healthy swallow of the elven wine inside. Akhena and Devin both laughed at the dwarf's sheepish expression and took a swig of their own when he offered.

When Akhena laughed it lit up her entire face. She was growing to love the old dwarf like a father and considered herself very lucky to call him friend. Akhena was also thankful for this time that she had to get to know him because it was the first time a situation like this had presented itself. She glanced over at her other new friend and frowned slightly at the sight of her sitting with Donnal once again. She had to admit that Donnal was a handsome man and quite the warrior, though she also had reservations. She knew that of all people, Elle could read him, and if she was satisfied then they should all be. However, Akhena felt that perhaps Elle was jaded in her perception due to the fact that she was attracted to him. Akhena made a mental note to speak of this to Elle when next they were alone and returned her attention to the next tale in progress from the dwarf seated beside her.

***

Draconas Corvus and Draconas Sakira continued in the direction that the Amjukar party had passed. They had made good time flying over the treetops of Fallon Forest, stopping only to rest and eat. Since it was just the two of them, they were able to leave at a moment's notice. Everything they had with them fit in the packs they carried which magically became a part of their Draconas forms, allowing them to fly with ease. Corvus felt a nagging guilt that he did not disclose the exact nature of the purpose of the mission. Then again, he knew it was not his place to do so. Still, he felt worse as time went by and he learned more about her. During their flight, they spent much time telling each other of their respective homes and traditions, closing the gap between them. All in all, the two both came to the realization that they had more in common than not.

Corvus was impressed with the magical ability of her people and especially so with the elves' ability with both sword and bow in battle. A lot was due to the longevity of her people, allowing them to perfect the arts of swordsmanship and archery. Other forms of battle included the ancient form of tai'ka which required a flexibility and ease beyond the capability of a stocky dwarf. He also listened to her description of her homeland and the castle. Dwarves were not ones for making their surroundings beautiful, so he was surprised to realize that he actually found himself wanting to see the Kingdom of Valsara with his own eyes.

Sakira was amazed at the ability of dwarves to manipulate stone, and their carving abilities with said material were well known. The ability to cut gemstones in such a way as to make each one unique and bring out the best possible color and clarity was unmatched by any other race in the realm. She was also impressed that a race so short in stature could be so feared on the battlefield. The dwarves had taken their short and stocky bodies, what some would consider to be a detriment, and made it one of their greatest assets in battle. They were able to bring a man down by slicing the tendons in the back of the legs and using their broad girth to knock them down. Oftentimes a dwarf would use his powerful upper body to strike the enemy a killing blow with this hammer or ax without the need of bringing them down first, regardless of the difference in size.

More years ago than they could remember, the elves and dwarves worked hand in hand to create some of the most beautiful objects of art ever known. Jewelry, elaborate boxes, swords, knives and more had at one time been available to those who could afford them. The most beautiful and powerful magical artifacts had been the result of the combined efforts of those two races as well. Many of the objects, magical or no, had been lost or stolen over the years. Most went missing during times of war. If one were to purchase some of the items from that time, it could cost the equivalent of buying a small kingdom, or at the very least, a small palace.

They woke from their slumber while the sky was still dark. It was too early for the promise of day, yet they set out just the same. Before the light broke over the horizon, they had travelled to the end of the forest and were making their way across the plains. When the sun began to make its appearance, they came upon a camp just coming to life.

.***

In the morning, the camp was beginning to stir when one of their designated lookouts came riding back to camp to tell of two Draconas' headed their way. The camp readied itself for anything and stood alert as the two Draconas' dropped into the middle of their group. Corvus and Sakira immediately changed into their elf and dwarf forms and held their hands up palms facing out in a gesture of good will. Sir Devin and Sir Borg strode forth, followed by the Draconas' Elle, Akhena and Donnal. The knights formed a circle around the newcomers, bows at the ready, their constant training paying off when their reflexes spurred them into action. Sir Borg was secretly proud of them, although he would never say so.

"Who are you and what brings you to our camp?" Sir Devin asked without preamble.

"I am Draconas Corvus of the Kingdom of MoeDin of the Krull Mountains. My travelling companion and friend is Draconas Sakira of the Kingdom of Valsara. I have a letter from Draconas Markim, Leader of The Seven, explaining my purpose here. I request that I may show you the letter and speak with you in private."

Sakira did not speak, for she had no such letter and hoped to become a party to what was going on by staying by his side and trying to look as though she belonged. Sir Borg looked Corvus over and nodded in recognition. Corvus was happy to see a face he knew and nodded back. Devin looked to Elle and waited for her decision. She looked the two over while reading their emotions and agreed to the meeting. They made their way to the command tent which had been in the process of being torn down for their day of travel and pulled the curtain shut. Once they all took seats around the table which had been hastily reconstructed, Akhena placed a dampening spell around the group. As usual, however, Donnal was not in attendance, for in all truth, he was still a stranger. They were still unaware of Donnal's basic knowledge of the events taking place.

Refreshments were served and Devin started the impromptu meeting.

"I ask again, what brings you to our camp?" Devin leveled his most commanding look at the dwarf, demanding a response of nothing less than the truth.

"Before I speak, it would save some time if you first read the letter sent by Draconas Markim," Corvus answered.

Corvus handed the letter to Devin who read it in silence and then read it aloud for the others: "I, Draconas Markim, Leader of The Seven of the Kingdom of Amjukar, request that Draconas Corvus of the Kingdom of MoeDin of the Krull Mountains be shown every courtesy and be given a place at the command table alongside Draconas Ellindria of House Kar, and all others as she so designates. He is aware of the full extent of our mission and has been sent to represent his kingdom. Please keep him informed in all matters and those that have already come to pass. In this I speak for the majority of The Seven of the Kingdom of Amjukar. May the gods guide your journey." It was signed and sealed by Draconas Markim, Leader of The Seven, the Kingdom of Amjukar.

Devin placed the letter on the table and squared off on the dwarf. "This letter says nothing of an elf; yet, here she sits."

Draconas Corvus had not prepared for this obvious question and he kicked himself for not having done so. He thought on how best to proceed when Elle prompted him, "It's best to just begin with how you came to be travelling with this elf and go from there."

"I was on me way to find you when I happened to see Sakira alone in the forest. Something about the way she was sittin' made me go to her and see what was wrong. She was feelin' very poorly and was unable to rise of her own accord. I convinced her into lettin' me help, and when I grabbed her hand to help her stand, well, I healed her." He paused at this moment, and it was obvious to everyone that he was still amazed by this fact. "It took most of me strength, and she helped me get back on me feet. When we realized that we were goin' in the same direction, we decided to stay together for protection. We travelled quickly with little time for rest to catch up with you before we lost you in the wastelands." He looked embarrassed, not being used to speaking with anyone other than his own kind and now Sakira. His role as Prince Karnuk's advisor was really no more than friends with an official title needed for formal occasions. They had grown up together and were like brothers. However, Corvus was quite capable and his title which had been just a formality before was in earnest now.

Elle felt with all her being that Corvus was telling the truth in its entirety and thought it sweet that he would be embarrassed so easily. She tried reading Sakira, and found a wall that masked most of what she was feeling. Elves were taught to protect their thoughts at an early age to become instinctual, so this did not concern Elle. However, if she did indeed have nothing to hide, then she would allow Elle to take a peek. Elle could discern much from a few moments' time.

"Draconas Sakira of the Kingdom of Valsara," she began, "for the sake of this group I request permission to have you lower your defenses that I may read of your intentions."

Sakira had spent a good portion of her young life learning to construct a wall from anyone trying to gain access to her thoughts or feelings. They were drilled on this repeatedly in the Elven Elite and so it took a while to remove what she had learned to keep up without conscious thought. Once it was done, Elle gently probed her mind and saw the quick flashes of what had occurred and knew that Corvus was truthful. She also knew that Corvus was aware of the actual reason for their journey, and Sakira did not. Elle knew that she could not make a decision to tell her on her own, and so using the mindspeak of the Draconas, directed only at those she wished, she asked the others if it was futile to keep it secret any longer. Once they got over their initial shock of being spoken to in their mind and actually being able to speak back, they considered their options. Obviously the entire realm knew that something was amiss, and those in their party could better prepare themselves if they were in the know. It was decided, after much debate, to also bring in Donnal at this point, however the knights would still be kept in the dark until they believed they were very close to the land they sought. The dampening spell was lifted long enough to call for Donnal and was replaced once he joined the group. Donnal was surprised to be included and showed no signs of having already known what they told him. Once again, he wrestled with his conscience. His king was counting on him, but he was no fool and realized that the power in Baldor's hands could only result in destruction of the realm. There was a time that he would not have been so concerned about those around him, only concerned that he pleased the man who saved him. That had changed. He cared about these people, not just Elle, the knights themselves. He was also humbled by the faith shown him when they finally brought him into their circle. Donnal was both elated to be trusted in such a manner and distraught to know that he was supposed to be the one to thwart their plans. He needed to make a decision soon because for the first time in his life he did not know his path.

Sakira sat stunned when she listened to Elle relay the story and events leading up to this day. Having grown up in the elven kingdom of Valsara, she had also heard the story of Desne Mar and like the others of her kind, believed it to be a tale made up for the amusement of children. She was not sure how she felt. Did she believe the land existed? If it did, what did this mean for her people? Would she be able to claim a part for the elves? She understood the need for secrecy concerning King Baldor and the Kingdom of Erewyth. For many years the people of the realm had waited with bated breath to see what Baldor would do next after conquering the kingdom of Erewyth, and when nothing happened for several hundred years, everyone let down their guard. She shuddered to think what would happen if the land was real and Baldor knew. She looked at their small group and hoped beyond all hope that if the land was real that they would be able to claim it quickly before anyone was the wiser.

Once the meeting was over, everyone went their separate ways. Elle took Donnal aside and said, "I sincerely hope that I have not misplaced my trust in you, Donnal. I know that you are hiding something, and for now I will let it go. If at any point in time I feel that what you are keeping from me will in any way harm the members of this group, we will take action."

Donnal looked Elle in the eyes and knew that one day soon he would need to make his decision, and he hoped that it was a decision he could live with.

Chapter 17

King Baldor and his horde were making their way south of the Krull Mountains towards the vast desert beyond the plains. They were heading in the same direction as the party from Amjukar, although they were coming from the west as opposed to from the forest in the east. The king was growing bored once again and was actually looking forward to a run in with the goblins who called the cavernous hills several miles south of the Krull Mountains their home. Baldor decided that since they did not have a specific direction, he would take his soldiers through those hills and enjoy hunting the pathetic beasts. He made his thoughts known and a slight adjustment was made in their heading. His decision inadvertently caused them to miss crossing paths with the Dwarves sent to intercept the knights of Amjukar, missing them by less than a day.

The Baldoran horde made their way to the goblins hills, and for once, one of the goblins sent to scout out their area actually was doing what he had been told. Unfortunately, the fact that he was alert and ready to warn his leader made absolutely no difference. King Baldor was flying in his Draconas form alongside Quintos and they both spotted the goblin lookout before the lookout saw the mutated soldiers. Baldor dispatched him in short order. Several of the goblins were not present at their home site, having left to hunt. Those left behind consisted mostly of women, children and the elderly, or those too sick to participate. There was no fun in the taking of easy prey for Baldor. His soldiers had no such qualms. The mutated soldiers happily chased down those that were unable to hide and began to have their fun. Like the villagers, no one was immune to their hunger. As before, they caught their prey and devoured them alive. The royal drake Prince Quintos watched on with pity for those unable to defend themselves. Dragons had no love for goblins any more than for any other race, however, there was no honor, no sport in preying on the weak and innocent regardless of who or what they may be. Lt. Commander Andal shared his dragon's views, and so they turned away and made themselves busy elsewhere without showing their disdain for what was happening. If it became obvious to Baldor, he would most likely ensure that they would not only be onlookers, but participants as well. Baldor enjoyed watching people squirm.

King Baldor watched from on high and then decided to get a closer look at the activities, landing himself on the closest hill in the area with the best view. Quintos landed beside him at his command with Andal sitting atop his back. Life was sacred to a dragon and Baldor's treatment of it a sacrilege. Quintos would have liked nothing more than to feed the king to the goblins as he was allowing them to be eaten.

The King of Erewyth became bored quickly as usual. It was like watching his soldiers eat at a banquet with all of the food laid out for their enjoyment. There was little fighting back, so the king called a halt to the feast, having received no enjoyment from it himself.

Those that were spared ran, if they could, to join their brethren in hiding for the duration of Baldor's stay. Those that did not die from their wounds lay as quietly as possible. They quickly learned that any noise they made brought a soldier to torture them some more. All they could do was try and remain still and silent until they were gone.

Tents were erected for King Baldor and Lt. Commander Andal. The mutated soldiers curled up by the fire to sleep as any dog would do. King Baldor sat inside his tent and glanced at the girls that lay atop his bed. They were scared, and their scent filled his nostrils, making them flare in anticipation. Baldor fed on the fear of others and these two were making him very strong. One of the magical gifts he had been blessed with was the ability to literally feed on fear. It was an addictive thing to be sure, and he gloried in it. Sitting atop the hill during the killing of the goblins had provided him with more magical energy, though it did not compare with that which he had gained in the human village. He had been living on small doses of it for quite some time and had forgotten the incredible surge of magical energy provided by a large group in fear for their lives. Of course he ate food to fuel his body, but this was different; it fueled his magic and right now he felt more powerful than he had in a long time. The fear of the villagers, combined with the fear of the goblins, made him feel invincible and he wanted, no needed, to show his dominance over others. He knew that if he took the girls into his bed that night that he would probably kill, them which bothered him only in the sense that he would need to find more. He finally came to the conclusion that he would wait a day and then he informed them that their services were not needed that night. He laughed out loud at their more than apparent relief and hasty retreat.

***

Queen Teserath paced in her rooms while Draconas Markim paced in his. Had they been a witness to each other's actions, they would have felt as kindred spirits. Both leaders of their kingdoms were growing more worrisome with each day. Queen Teserath had received additional information on the comings and goings of the other kingdoms, and the movement of King Baldor was more than a little unsettling. Andres' father had been king during the uprising when Baldor stole the throne of Erewyth, and Queen Teserath was well versed on the stories. It was said that every single member of the royal line had been eradicated to the smallest infant, regardless of how tenuous the blood line might be. Baldor was taking no chances. Baldor was strong both physically and magically and made for a terrifying opponent. If he was involved in this, then it must be important indeed. Queen Teserath was unaware of the exact nature of what was transpiring, although she knew with every fiber of her being that it was big and her kingdom would play a part in whatever it was. She requested her brother's presence to see if he had heard anything of importance but was disappointed to learn that he had not.

Unfortunately, her faith in her brother was misplaced. Had he known anything he would have kept it to himself.

***

At the same time, Draconas Markim was pacing and worrying about the news of the Erewyth Kingdom's forces and wondering if he should send more soldiers. If he did send more, would they make it in time to make a difference? The party that had been sent originally had begun at a pace that was set so as not to alert anyone. Unfortunately, those days were long gone. He could only hope that Elle would be ready when the time came. It was becoming increasingly clear that they may have to fight for the land they sought. He was comforted in the fact that he had sent some of his best and brightest and was now happy for the additional Draconas sent by the dwarves, as well as the additional soldiers that he had it on good authority were well underway.

***

Draconas Lias decided that his best bet was to spend as much time flying over the Krull Mountains until such time that he would need to leave his cover and approach the capitol of Erewyth. He was hoping to find one or more of the dragons that resided in the mountain's caves that were prevalent throughout the range in its highest peaks. Any information obtained from them would be invaluable. It was not to be, for it was as though all dragons had fled the territory. Lias was becoming greatly concerned. Normally the peaks were home to many dragons, which for the most part, kept to themselves, yet he wasn't finding any. It was as if the entire dragon kingdom had left the area.

Lias had almost given up all hope of ever making contact with the majestic beasts. He decided to make a final pass over an area that was riddled with caves, both large and small, when he spotted what appeared to be a small dragon. It disappeared so quickly, he questioned whether he had actually seen the dragon or wished it to be so. Deciding that a quick look could cause no harm, he alighted onto the overhang of the cave and remained in his Draconas form. Tufts of grass and small rocks, made loose by his talons, fell to the ground, announcing his arrival. He dropped down to the mouth of the cave under the assumption that perhaps the small dragon had taken refuge within. He entered the opening and his Draconas hearing picked up on the frightened dragon's breathing before he was able to see him. Using the Draconas mindspeak he addressed the dragon.

"I am Draconas Lias of the Kingdom of Amjukar. I only wish to speak with you for but a moment and then I will be on my way."

After a brief hesitation, the dragon slowly made his way to the front of the cave. Staying in the shadows, he remained just inside the caves entrance. Lias may be a Draconas, but he was not a dragon and therefore the small drake was not inclined to trust him fully; especially considering recent events.

"Speak and be on your way." The dragon said in what he hoped was a forceful tone.

Lias recognized the false bravado and tried to sound as unassuming as possible. "As I said, my name is Draconas Lias; and you are?"

"I am none of your concern," he replied, "What do you want, Draconas?"

"I am searching for the dragons that usually reside in this mountain. So far, you are the only one I have seen, so to speak, since you are in shadow. I wish to converse with someone in a position of authority that can answer my questions."

"My kin have gone missing, though I know little of what has transpired regarding their disappearance. Unfortunately, I cannot point you in the direction of someone to help either. All I can tell you is that over the past year, my mother, father, and sisters have disappeared. There are rumors to the effect that dragons are being pressed into service by the Erewyth king. I can only assume that it is true, since I have no way of knowing for certain. Occasionally, a Draconas from the Erewyth kingdom comes searching for more of my kin. Much to my dismay, I believe I am all that is left on this mountain. My father has always told us that although the Draconas' were different that we were to treat them with the same courtesy shown to our own kind. It has always been a mutual courtesy according to my father's teaching, until recently. I only speak to you of this because you are from Amjukar, and I am an excellent judge of character. Had you been from Erewyth, I would have killed you where you stand." At this he exited from the cover of the cave. Although the dragon was a young male, he was almost as large as Lias. His scales were forest green, which probably had aided in his ability to hide within the Krull Mountains. His eyes were amber and regarded Lias with an intelligence he did not expect in one as young as he. After sizing up the elven Draconas, he spoke aloud this time in a gravelly voice, "I am Torik. Why do you wish to find my kind?"

"We have received information indicating that one or more of the dragons are working for King Baldor. What we don't know is if it is willingly or coerced? In all the years we have never known a dragon to subjugate himself to anyone, yet there are reports of humans riding atop the dragons like a horse. Do you know of any of this and the reason behind it?"

"I have heard rumors, though I have not witnessed this myself. However, as I told you earlier my family has been taken from me; to what end I know not. I have been in hiding, waiting and hoping to learn more," Torik replied.

Lias continued, "I am travelling to the Kingdom of Erewyth and the mountains just beyond that, which are home to the largest clan of dragons in the realm headed by Prince Quintos. I am hopeful that I might find answers there and perhaps be in a position to help if needed. I thank you for your time, Torik. I recommend you continue to stay out of sight and let no one know of my plans, or it could ruin any chance I may have to be able to help your family."

"I am going with you," Torik said. "Hiding out in these mountains is no longer an option. I will be of help to you, making it easier for you to gain the trust of the other dragons. Not all dragons have my ability to know when someone is genuine and being truthful. I can ease the way for you."

"What I am about to undertake is very dangerous," Lias countered, "and I do not wish to bring you to harm."

"I am coming with you." He was adamant, "I can travel as your partner or follow you. Either way I will be coming." The young dragon was determined and Lias knew there would be no changing his mind.

Lias sighed in resignation, "I see I have no choice. I need to eat and rest and we can be on our way."

The dragon and Draconas took flight and found their meal. They took their bounty back to the cave and once the meal was finished they fell asleep. Lias maintained his elven form making him appear very small in comparison lying next to Torik. They woke at sunset and began their journey across the mountains and into the kingdom of Erewyth. They would travel towards the mountain range where the dragon's royal line kept residence in the network of caves that would make the dwarves envious.

Flying at night was a good idea for the most part, but Lias' white and silver stood out boldly in the night sky. Torik, on the other hand, with his forest green scales blended into the night beautifully. Much to their mutual embarrassment, it was decided that Lias would wear a dark cloak and ride on Torik's back when travelling at night. They found that the added benefit was that they required less food. In Lias' Draconas form he required meals the size of the dragons', yet in his elven form he could manage on much less. Relying on nuts and berries allowed them more time for flying and less time for finding sufficient game to satisfy them both.

The two became very adept at communicating whether it be with the Draconas mindspeak or the dragon's ability to project thoughts and images and soon they began to move and think as one. Before long, they entered the kingdom of Erewyth. They passed the training grounds for the Erewyth soldiers and both became very aware of the distinctive smell of dragons in the area, although none were present at that time of night. They went in search of an area close by to hide out until the following day. They would take what they could get and be thankful for it. In the morning, Draconas Lias would disguise himself as a commoner to see what, if anything, he could learn about the missing dragons. Because of the dragon's scent in the area he hoped to see them and speak to them directly instead of relying on local gossip. A few miles outside of the training grounds they came upon an abandoned farm. After making a few changes to provide themselves with an easily defensible position, they settled in for what was left of the night and fell quickly to sleep.

***

Prince Karnuk stood alone in his father's study, awaiting his arrival. He looked around at the sparsely furnished room which was typical for dwarves who felt that most embellishment was frivolous and should be saved for important things like armor and beautifully rendered statues or gemstones. He had been waiting for quite a while and had decided to take a seat, when his father strode purposefully into the room and shut the door to enunciate his arrival. He looked his son over to see that he was no worse for the journey taken and motioned him to continue to sit. Although King Druek was his father, Prince Karnuk was still in awe of the man and he always felt more child prince in his presence.

"I am sorry to take so long. The matters o' the kingdom go on regardless of what is happenin'. One day you will bear the responsibility and you'll see." His father sat behind his desk of oak and marble on a large exquisitely chiseled chair of unknown age. Both were crafted from the materials found in their mountain home. "Well, lad, don't be keepin' me waitin'. What did you find out?"

"I spoke with the council an' I spoke to the leader Draconas Markim in private as well. It would seem that they are in possession of a scroll that talks about a land called Desne Mar which is supposed to be in the desert wasteland. It is said that the land will enhance the magic of those that claim it. They sent a party to try an' locate the land before anyone else hears about it. They were worried about King Baldor and his spies. No one knows if the land actually exists, although they believe it does. I demanded that our kingdom be a part of this an' they allowed that we send someone to catch up with those that had already been sent. Since we had no time to waste, I took it upon myself to send Draconas Corvus, as he had the best chance of doing so. "Prince Karnuk stopped, feeling as though he were rambling and looked expectantly at his father.

"I am glad you sent Corvus; it was a good choice. I heard more rumors that caused me some alarm, and so I sent your brother to lead a group of soldiers to make their way south with all haste. We have also heard disturbing stories about that damn King Baldor and his mutated soldiers; that information came first hand from our own people."

"You sent Strom? Is he ready for this? Father, we both know that Strom is more interested in crafting the gems found in these mountains than in fightin'. Is he in charge, or did you send Commander Lorn?" The Prince asked with much concern.

"Do you question me boy?" The King was angered. "You were gone; your other brother is One of The Seven, and I needed to make sure that one o' me boys was there. Would I rather it 'ad been you?

Of course I would but you weren't here." He calmed himself at the look on his son's face and continued, "Yes, I did send Commander Lorn to be in charge. Your brother is more of a figurehead. If I could, I would be sendin' you as well but I need you here. Things seem to be coming to a head, and I want my son to be at me side for anything that may come our way."

"Yes father. What did our people have to say regardin' King Baldor?"

"Tales that would make the hardest man weep, my son. His mutated soldiers set upon the small town south of our mountain and destroyed every living creature whether for sport or..." here the king had a hard time continuing which frightened his son since his father was the strongest man he had ever known. The king collected himself and looked at his son directly, "...His soldiers ate many of the villagers alive."

The prince was glad that he had not yet eaten for the look on his father's face and the idea behind what he had heard made him nauseous, a first for him since he was sick as a child.

King Druek walked to his son and placed both hands on his shoulders as he touched his forehead to his son's head. It was the most affection that he had ever shown, and it caused the prince to leave the throne room quickly before he was brought to tears, which would have been yet another first.

The king watched his son leave, returned to his chair and sat back down heavily. He was indeed concerned for his 2nd son Strom who was unlike most dwarfs. He had had mixed emotions when he sent him. His sons were all good honest dwarves, yet only Karnuk had the ability to take the throne when the time came and he died or stood down due to health reasons. His son Draconas Brock would have been a natural for the mission had he not been called to The Seven. And even Druek knew better than to force his hand on a magic that had been part of their realm for longer than any could remember. When it came right down to it, he needed Karnuk safely at his side learning to rule the kingdom, not charging about the countryside looking for the Knights of Amjukar.

As for the townspeople, King Druek whispered a prayer to his god on their behalf. That was all he could do.

***

Draconas Markim called upon the High Wizard Malek for an informal meeting. They met in the small room adjoining the larger meeting chamber and waited until the servants provided drinks with cheese and bread for a light snack. Markim partook of the wine and cheese and looked to Malek before he spoke.

"What was once a small expedition has turned into so much more. I feel that it is necessary to be able to contact our people at any time, not just when your man Cylas is able. When they enter the desert, we will lose contact with them altogether unless we have a contingency plan. We have magic within ourselves and within these

245

walls in tomes that fill several rooms. You are a great wizard of magical talent. There must be some way to open the lines of communication so that we may be aware of what is going on. Had we the time before they departed, a speaking amulet would have been ideal. We need other options and we need them soon. Erewyth, MoeDin and Valsara have all sent soldiers to intercept our party, who until this time, had been travelling at a normal pace so as not to arouse suspicion. We know how well that worked." He rolled his eyes and continued, "I am more than concerned that King Baldor will intercept and torture our people until he has the answers he needs. Is there a way we can speak with them using what we have?"

The High Wizard Malek took a sip of his wine before answering, "I have projected my soul out of my body though I am not learned enough to do so without a specific place in mind that I have already been to. I am not sure if the Wizard Tannis has this ability or no. We have abilities that are the same as well as different. Even if he cannot, perhaps between the three of us we can come up with something that will suffice."

Draconas Markim called for the attending servant and requested that he see to it that the Wizard Tannis join them right away. After several minutes Tannis arrived and made his way to the table looking expectantly at the two of them. Draconas Markim repeated what he had asked of Malek and waited for Tannis to reply.

"I have also travelled by soul and much in the same manner as Malek. However, perhaps I will have a chance of finding our party and speaking through Cylas who is related by blood. It is always easier if one has something to "tether" to, and blood is one of the strongest bonds of all. I would prefer that if I do this, that Malek is there to help bring me home in the event it does not work and my soul becomes lost."

"Are you sure that you should do this if the possibility of your soul becoming lost is an option?" Markim asked with concern.

"I believe that in lieu of what has been happening throughout the realm that the risk must be taken. We are guardians of this kingdom after all and if this is what is required to help in this quest then who am I to say no."

Draconas Markim could think of no other alternative and so he agreed and asked that they take every precaution, requesting of him anything that would be needed. They agreed to meet later that night, as it would be easier for his soul to travel while the world slept.

***

The night was clear and cool. No rain was evident and the moons were high in the sky. Cylas slept soundly, for they were travelling much longer days and at a quicker pace causing most to fall in a dreamless sleep as soon as they laid down for the night. He swatted at the annoying thing that kept irritating his face while he slept. It was common for the occasional insect to annoy one even at night, and it was not something that would normally wake one used to the outdoors.

"CYLAS..."

He heard his name in his sleep and automatically said, "Yes?" while continuing to sleep on.

"CYLAS!!!"

The voice was more insistent and the sleepy Cylas opened one eye at the intrusion. What he saw at first startled him awake and then his beating heart slowed when he realized who it was and what was happening.

"Tannis?" He asked the faint apparition in front of him.

Tannis nodded his head and spoke quickly while he could: "We want to establish a link that will keep us in touch so that we can be kept informed of your movements and we can keep you informed as well. I do not know how long I can maintain this, but I see that you are in good stead for the time being. As you know, there are several groups of soldiers headed towards your party and you must be diligent in looking out for them, especially Baldor..." Tannis began to fade and pushed his soul harder into the world. "I will be trying this as often as I am able, usually at night so the next time be more open to my call." Tannis disappeared into the night and Cylas resumed his slumber.

Back in the Kingdom of Amjukar in the Wizard Tannis' room the High Wizard Malek and Draconas Markim used their combined magic to ensure that Tannis' soul made it safely back to his body. It was unfortunate that they had lacked the time necessary to create the magic speaking stones for the journey, for the magic used to project his soul tired him considerably and greatly reduced his ability to perform more than simple magic until he recovered. Thankfully, the elven wine kept for just such an occasion helped the healing take place within hours instead of the days it would normally have taken. Even so, it was realized that to speak with them on a daily basis would be difficult for all involved, if not impossible, making every other day or so more suitable given the circumstances.

The next morning, Cylas requested a meeting with the camp leaders and relayed what had happened. It was decided that Cylas should be brought into the fold and using the excuse of a promotion, Lieutenant Cylas' quarters were placed within easy access of Sir Devin and Sir Borg.

The Knights of Amjukar were aware that they were on a very important mission for their kingdom. The exact nature of said mission was so important as to be kept secret until such time as it would inevitably need to be revealed. The fact that they did not know the real reason for the secrecy meant that if any of them were captured and tortured, they would be unable to reveal the information and put the others in jeopardy. They all understood; even the young cadets that were being trained now respected the training more after their encounter with the goblins. They were also aware of the convergence of the other kingdoms seeking to find what they were about. The knights had grown up with stories of the King of Erewyth, none, however, could truly appreciate the man's ability to make one wish they were dead and his absolute joy at doing so. Sirs' Devin and Borg drilled them daily on what it was to fall under a tyrant such as Baldor; however, they knew it was hopeless until they were actual witnesses to the cruelty the man was capable of. The knights had picked up their pace in light of all that was happening and the party made their way closer to the north eastern edge of the desert.

Chapter 18

There was a small town on the outskirts of the barren land that for the most part its' citizens made their living on the trade of goods between Erewyth and the southern kingdom known to most as Horarti-Sol. It wasn't a kingdom per se because the ruler was self-appointed and ran the territory based on fear and threats. He referred to himself as Lord Matris and commanded a small army that saw to his personal interests. For the most part, the other kingdoms had nothing to do with this southern "Lord" and did not interfere in their affairs. Only the Kingdom of Erewyth traded openly with the man; some merchants of Amjukar did so as well if they required goods found nowhere else. The small border town served as a way station between the kingdoms and the navigation of the desert wasteland they wished to traverse. It was decided that they would stable their horses and pay for the use of lacallas which were more suitable to the desert climate. Most people travelled directly southwest on a well-established route to the opposite town which worked in tangent with the one in the north where the lacallas would be available for those on the return trip. Sir Devin spoke with the other leaders of their group and decided that they would acquire the animals, based on the assumption that they were also travelling the established route. Allowing anyone to know that their direction was further to the southeast and that they had no idea of the length of time they would require the lacallas would give away more of their intentions to those they wished to avoid. It was only a matter of time before their trail was picked up and they had no intention of making it easier for those on their way to intercept them. The lacallas' were large beasts of burden. Each one had two large humps that in some way allowed them to store the nourishment needed to traverse the desert for weeks without water and very little food. The neck was long and the head resembled a cross between a horse and a cow. Their legs were long and sturdy. The animals are the same color as the sand and are extremely difficult to see at any distance without the addition of a rider and their belongings perched atop. Each lacalla bore two people, and so they all paired off for the trip through the desert. The knights paired off as they saw fit, it being decided that if they had to stay in such close proximity of each other that it should be with someone with whom they already had a connection or friendship. Draconas' Elle, Akhena, Donnal, Corvus and Sakira and the commanders Devin, Borg and now Cylas each had their own lacalla, allowing for easier maneuverability for defense. Before they left the hard-looking town, they purchased additional supplies for the trip. Every lacalla was made to carry that which was reasonable without overtaxing the animal, drawing a few raised eyebrows from the shopkeepers when they realized that the supplies were over and above those needed for the average person crossing the desert to the town of Gardwell where fresh supplies could be had. However, although it raised a few unanswered questions, to the shopkeepers in the end it mattered not since the gold that traded hands was all that they really cared about. Once the group had their supplies, they began their trek in the direction they were expected to go. They would continue on the main route until such time that they deemed it an acceptable risk to deviate and follow Elle's "hunch."

***

Gustaf had originally wanted to go back to the castle and try to gain entrance once again using his sister's name, but it wasn't enough. He wanted revenge and the best way to obtain that had accidentally fallen right into his lap. Gustaf stood behind a small tree that actually managed to hide his slim and wiry form. He had narrowly avoided being seen by a group of soldiers from the dwarf kingdom of MoeDin and was now staring at the Draconas he knew to be King Baldor. Gustaf was in awe. What a magnificent Draconas King Baldor made. He had never known a Draconas of that size and obvious strength. In addition, not far from the king was a semi-human riding atop a dragon even larger than the Draconas King himself. He was green with envy at the sight, and all he could think of was how to get himself in that position. Now *that* was what he wanted. He was no Draconas, but he could learn to command a dragon to head a military campaign or use for his own personal reasons, it mattered not. What he would not give to ride a dragon and have that dragon put his sister in her place. Hell, the one before him was more than twice the size of his sister Elle. She would have no chance, no chance at all. He was practically giddy with all of the possibilities.

He knew better than to get ahead of himself. That being said, he needed to be quite sure that the king of Erewyth would find his information and insight into the party sent from Amjukar invaluable. Perhaps, dare he hope, that it would be enough to earn him a dragon and dare he hope again to earn a place at the king's side? He found the magically enhanced soldiers that he saw from a distance to be fascinating. He hid for more than an hour watching them. After gathering his courage, he made his presence known and held his hands out palms up in supplication. Two of the magically enhanced soldiers were ordered to retrieve Gustaf and bring him before their king. Being the simple beasts that they now were, they did just that. Racing across the ground faster than Gustaf could fathom, they were on him in a flash. They each grabbed an arm and proceeded to drag the elf through the brush to their king. Brambles and thorns attached to his clothing, making his presentation to King Baldor less than ideal when he was brought face to face with the king who had just landed in his Draconas form. Gustaf, never one for reigning in his temper, even if it was in his best interest, screamed at the two wolf soldiers to unhand him immediately. Baldor watched on with some amusement and after Gustaf finally began to wear himself out, the king then gave the command to drop the elf, which again they did quite literally, causing Gustaf to land on his backside in the mud underfoot. Gustaf, still enraged at the mistreatment he had received, scrambled to his feet and was about to voice a complaint when one look at Baldor stopped him in his tracks. The King of Erewyth had changed into his human form, which was no less intimidating, and walked slowly towards Gustaf while eyeing him as if he was nothing more than a bug to be squashed beneath his boot. It was the first time in Gustaf's existence that he was rendered speechless by fear.

Baldor took his time looking over this apparent solitary elf and wondered why he hadn't fed him to his soldiers yet. Baldor, however, had not gained his current station by acting hastily and without all the facts at hand. He could tell that the man in front of him was afraid, as well he should be. He was also a man with hatred in his heart and for this reason alone Baldor had forestalled ringing the dinner bell for is soldiers.

Baldor smiled without a hint of it making its way to his eyes and with more than a little sarcasm he asked, "With whom do I have the pleasure of meeting?"

Gustaf's mouth had gone dry, and it took a few tries before he was able to reply, "My name is Gustaf of the House of Kar and rightful heir to the Kingdom of Valsara..." He added the last part without thinking. I have come searching for you because I believe that I have information that you may need. I also wish to join you."

"Really?" Baldor raised an eyebrow. "And what makes you think you know anything of consequence? And why would I wish you to join me?"

"I was involved, to some extent, in an expedition party from Amjukar. My sister is one of their leaders, the Draconas that is also the newest member of The Seven. Does this interest you?" Gustaf was warming to his topic and relaxed slightly.

Baldor was intrigued by this and sent for Andal to join them in the command tent for food, refreshments and conversation. His first instinct was to bleed the information from this self-important elf, yet the more he thought on it, the more he believed that Gustaf could be put to good use. If he turned out to be just another upstart, he would indeed feed him to his soldiers and happily watch as they dined on the screaming elf. The King of Erewyth enjoyed the obvious discomfort that his soldiers caused and actually went out of his way to see to it that one or more soldiers was within arm's reach of the elf just to keep him on edge. People were right, King Baldor mused, it was the little things in life that made it worth living. He laughed aloud at the thought and laughed harder when Gustaf squirmed even more.

Night was approaching as they finished their meal and drink. Gustaf drank more than he would normally, due to his uneasiness around the wolf-like soldiers and the King of Erewyth's relentless appraisal of him. It seemed that every time he took a chance to look at the king, the king was looking directly at him. He was constantly on edge, feeling as though the king could see right through him. It was more unsettling than his sister's ability of reading emotions. He was unaware of her ability to pick up thoughts as well, or perhaps she may have been more of a concern to him than she was.

Baldor couldn't read feelings or thoughts; though he could read people and he had not made up his mind where Gustaf was concerned. He began to question his new "ally."

"I am going to ask you some questions, and I strongly suggest that you tell me the truth in its entirety. In addition, it would be in your best interest not to hold anything back. I assure you, I will know in either case." He paused and then looked Gustaf in the eye only to have Gustaf avoid his stare out of fear. "Where are they going and why?"

Gustaf looked deflated, "That is one question I do not know the answer to. I was only told that they were on a training expedition through Fallon Forest that may continue further south, and that was all. I was not part of the inner circle."

"What good are you to me if you cannot answer my questions? What could you possibly have to offer me?

Gustaf scrambled for the right words and blurted out, "I can tell you anything you want to know about my sister and her traveling companions."

"Go on then," the king commanded.

It was obvious that Gustaf spoke of his sister with obvious disdain and more than a little envy, though he would never admit to such a thing, "My sister is Draconas Ellindria of House Kar, One of The Seven of the Kingdom of Amjukar. She is a new Draconas and new to The Seven. She is young and inexperienced. There is nothing noteworthy about her magical power, although she can read emotions."

King Baldor listened to Gustaf and knew that he was downplaying her abilities somewhat for the simple fact that he refused to acknowledge her abilities as greater than his own. He also knew from reports by Donnal, that the elf maiden's powers were growing and new ones were coming to light. He frowned at that thought, realizing that a report from Donnal was overdue. Obviously, this moron in front of him was not as informed as he believed. Baldor continued with his questioning.

"What of her companions? What can you tell me of them?"

Gustaf could see that this was not going as he had hoped. If he gave all he knew, he would have nothing left to offer other than his own magic, and he did not think it would be enough. If he wished to bargain, he needed to do it now.

"I am at your service, my king, and will gladly supply you with all that you request." Gustaf licked his dry lips and continued, "I would, however, like to know where I stand if I may be so bold." One look at the king made him realize that he had overstepped his bounds and he immediately backpedaled, "Of course it makes no difference, and I will answer any questions you ask of me." He rambled on quickly as if to stay an execution. "Her companions consist of a Draconas which is also a member of The Seven. Her name is Akhena, and she is a half breed, human and dwarf. She has very little magic." He drank some more to calm his nerves and continued, "Sir Devin and Sir Borg are in charge of the knights. They are both handy in a fight, but have no magic. And then there is a man I met and travelled with to catch up with them, named Donnal, who is good with a sword." At the mention of Donnal's name, King Baldor sat straighter. "Donnal was looking to get information on my sister and the others. He did not share who he was working for and I did not ask. My sister and I argued and I left them. Donnal decided to stay. I personally think he cares for Elle, and he stayed for her, although he would lead you to believe otherwise." Gustaf finished and finally looked up at King Baldor. Baldor sat in thought and worried about Donnal. He had felt that the last time they spoke Donnal was holding something back. He was angered to hear that his right hand may be vacillating and for a damn woman no less. Women were easy to come by, and Donnal could have whomever he chose, including the King's own daughter. The more Baldor thought on it, the more he felt personally rebuffed. Did Donnal not think his daughter to be good enough? Baldor stopped this chain of thoughts for he had other things to contend with. He viewed Gustaf with open hostility, he was the bearer of bad news, and Baldor had no qualms about killing the messenger. He started to kill the elf himself, but decided that perhaps he could be useful later on. He commanded Andal to take Gustaf prisoner, and the elf that had had such illustrious hopes and visions of himself in the Erewyth kingdom were dashed to dust with the sound of the manacles closing tightly on his wrists, suppressing his magical abilities. He started to protest though one look at King Baldor's countenance closed his lips and with eyes wide with fright he was led away in chains.

King Baldor pulled his stone from under his shirt and called for Donnal.

**

The dwarves had been on the march for several days, making good time in their quest to catch up with the party from Amjukar. Dwarves had incredible endurance and could walk day and night at a relatively fast pace especially considering their short stature. They had seen the soldiers from Erewyth, as well as the Draconas King Baldor, and had called a halt in a covered area to both rest and keep out of sight. The dwarf commander shook his head at the corruption of the natural order of things and nature itself when he looked at the soldiers that had been transformed. Dwarves were very rarely afraid. This was different. The "soldiers" they were watching made each and every dwarf more alert and wary. Prince Strom looked to Commander Lorn who used hand gestures and asked that they all be silent. The dwarves were actually very close. They had the ability to blend into their surroundings and so they watched and listened to what was taking place between Baldor and the elf Gustaf who is apparently kin to one of The Seven. Lorn could not believe the stupidity of the elf. Did he honestly believe that Baldor would reward him for turning on his sister? It was obvious from Baldor's reaction that the man, Donnal, was one of his own. That being the case, Baldor had someone on the inside, unless his man's allegiance had changed as was in question. Considering the nature of the business at hand, Lorn felt that it was imperative that his small group of dwarves make haste to relay what they had learned. The commander's biggest concern was the ability of King Baldor and the soldier riding a dragon to see them from a great distance, posing a problem that he hoped the wizard he brought along could provide an answer for. He motioned to the nearest dwarf to bring the wizard to him right away.

The dwarf Wizard Harkel silently made his way to Prince Strom and Commander Lorn's side. The commander explained the situation and was told by Wizard Harkel that he needed some time to prepare, though he promised to come up with something that would work to hide their group but would have no effect on the noise they made, so they would need to be as quiet as possible. Normally he would also invoke a dampening spell. Unfortunately, he had never worked one on such a large group that would also be travelling and could not attest to its effectiveness. He indicated that it would be best, however, to wait until the soldiers from Erewyth moved on. It was easier to bypass the enemy while they were both on the move since the noise of Erewyth's soldiers would cover up what little noise the dwarves would make. Had they realized how fast the "wolf soldiers" were capable of moving, they probably would have thrown caution to the wind and set out immediately.

***

The party from Amjukar had entered the beginning of the desert just that morning. The sun was currently high in the sky, beating down on their heads. Any thoughts of spring were now nothing more than a fleeting memory and the rains they had endured were looking beatific with each passing minute. Most had donned the clothing provided to them to deflect the rays of the sun as much as possible. The heat was oppressive and yet they were only in the beginning of the desert where flora still abounded and here and there the occasional tree offered a small amount of shade. They knew that the further they traversed the arid landscape the worse it would get, and not one of them was happy about it. As usual, the dwarves and elves tolerated the heat better than the humans, although even they were more than slightly uncomfortable. The elves came from a kingdom further south with hot and humid summers that they had learned to tolerate and protect themselves from over time. The dwarves spent a good portion of their time in the cool earth. The majority of the dwarves, however, spent more of their time near the fire forges making weapons and armor building their resistance to the heat throughout the centuries.

Although the chance of the party encountering resistance in their quest became greater with each passing day, it was no longer feasible for the knights to wear their armor. They would roast inside as surely as though they had crawled into a large oven. Had they been fortunate enough to have obtained elf-made armor they would have been able to wear it in any weather and the armor would maintain the same easy temperature. Elf-made armor was also extremely light, another advantage they would have very much liked at that time. As it was, their armor was packed inside the saddle bags which hung to each side of the lacallas, gently swaying with each step, any loose armament clanking together noisily until the rider adjusted the packing inside.

Due to their exposed nature, they were much more alert despite the heat. Everyone knew to be on the lookout. Not only for those in pursuit, but also for the beasts of the desert that can easily take the life of even the greatest of fighters. Had they stayed on the well-travelled route, the chances of encountering one of the desert beasts would have been very small. However, since they would soon be deviating off the beaten path, it was an unknown.

Donnal sat atop his lacalla in an almost trancelike state when he felt a warmth against his chest. It took him a moment to realize what it was. He was in a bad position to be speaking with his king when Elle was so close and could read his thoughts if she tried. He decided that he had little choice and hoped to keep his conversation with Baldor to a minimum, since he would need to cast a dampening spell in the hopes that no one noticed. Once all was in order, he answered the call.

"Yes, my king, how may I be of service?"

King Baldor was already in a mood based on the information obtained by Gustaf and he barked at his commander. "I have not heard from you in more days than I can remember, and I have been told that you are developing feelings for this elf Draconas. What in the name of the gods is going on? I want answers and I want them now!"

Donnal was taken aback by his king's attack. He quickly regained his composure and said, "I have not called upon you because there was nothing new to report. Additionally, it is harder to find an area to call from without being overheard. I am at this time using a dampening spell in the hopes that I am not discovered. As you are aware, Draconas Elle can read feelings and now thoughts as well, so I must be diligent. As for having feelings for the elf, I have indeed led her to believe so, which has brought me one step closer to the inner circle of these people. Did you not tell me to use my ability with the fairer sex? We have just entered the desert and are following the main course, to what end I do not yet know but soon hope to find out." He paused and asked, "Where are you getting your information?"

Although the king had raised Donnal, he saw him as a means to an end, not a son, though Donnal had always thought so, and as such did not like to be questioned. "I ask the questions and do not again forget your place. I have a bad feeling and hope beyond all hope that your loyalty is not in question. I will kill you if I feel otherwise." With that the king broke communication and Donnal quickly lifted the dampening spell.

He was afraid to look in Elle's direction yet he needed to know if she had noticed. He slowed his lacalla to look at her without being direct and did not see anything unusual in her manner.

Elle abruptly looked up to see Donnal visibly tense and quickly looked away before he saw her. She had been practicing and had schooled the look upon her face before she felt Donnal's eyes upon her. She had been open to all of the people in their group and lamented at their misery, knowing it would only become worse. At that time, she had felt the total disappearance of Donnal in her mind, which made her realize that she now felt all those in her party at all times. She was very concerned about the nature of what had just happened. It had felt like the dampening spell that had been used at the Council Meetings, though she was not sure. What was he thinking that he would go to such an extreme to keep her out? She kept her concerns to herself but watched the handsome Draconas more closely thereafter.

They located a watering hole that was indicated on the map provided by the shop keep where they had purchased the majority of their supplies. They took a break from the desert sun under the trees that grew in the arid climate. The hole was more of a small spring fed pond surrounded by water loving plants and mid-size thorny trees with large purple flowers in full bloom. The flowers were known to aid in the reduction of both headaches and fever. The healers took Corvus under their tutelage and instructed him in the collection of the delicate flowers and their proper care and storage. Corvus felt completely out of place at first. He soon realized, however, that he had a natural gift for the craft. Sakira laughed at his surprise, explaining that the gods would not have blessed him with such a talent if not the case. This simple statement gave Corvus the confidence that he hadn't fully embraced until that time.

Small lizards, frogs and insects called the watering hole their home. They all disappeared at the approach of the lacallas. Everyone alighted from their mounts and drank deeply of the spring and filled any and all empty vessels with the water. Shade was hard to find for this many people so everyone bunched together in groups to enjoy the brief respite and eat their share of the rations. They were warned that the heat would make them feel as though they were not hungry. Despite this feeling, they were to force themselves to take some nourishment although it would be less than the norm. Drinking plenty of water was the difference between life and death and they needed to hydrate on a regular basis. By now they all wore long flowing white robes that covered them from head to foot. The skeptics learned quickly that long robes did not mean 'keep in the heat' as they had originally thought and hastily attired themselves in the same manner as the nomads that called the desert their home.

Once they had collected the natural resources available to them and had their fill, they reluctantly left what little shade the watering hole provided and moved on. Scorpions skittered across the desert in the path of the lacallas to keep from being stepped on. The occasional desert snake hissed from its place in the small rock formations found throughout the area. They slowed only briefly to allow the collection of additional medicinal plants when found to augment their supplies. Under normal circumstances, they would have passed them by, but no one knew how long their trek would be and it was better to be overly prepared than not.

Elle guided her lacalla closer to Donnal and spoke as though nothing had transpired earlier.

"I sincerely hope that our journey is not overly long. I am afraid that the heat is already getting to those more used to the northern temperatures and would be better suited to a colder clime instead."

Donnal continued to look straight ahead and said, "I am sure you are right. However, these knights are proving to be stronger in mind and body than I would have originally given them credit for. They will adapt; they may not like it, but they will do so and make you proud."

Elle was surprised by his statement. She could tell that he meant what he was saying and it made her more comfortable regarding their situation. She was taken aback that the man who keeps her most on guard would also be the same one to make her relax her guard. He was a perplexing man and one that she was becoming more determined to know. Whatever secret he was keeping was the only thing keeping her from being so bold as to make the first move, since he clearly was not about to do so himself. She glanced briefly into his thoughts while appraising his profile. He was almost too pretty with his gold flecked eyes, however, his heavy brow and strong jaw made him handsome. She found only the emotional turmoil that seemed to have become a part of him, just as anger and hatred had become a part of her brother. They rode on in silence.

Sir Borg brought up the rear as he normally did, and by doing so, he was privy to much, having it all take place right in front of him. He was aware of Elle's feelings for the human Draconas. He was not convinced that Donnal could be trusted, so he kept him in his sights as much as possible. Something about him made the dwarf worry for Elle and he took his intuition seriously. It had never let him down before. Akhena rode beside him often and he knew that she shared his concern. He had grown very fond of the half breed and was considering going to his clan for permission to adopt her into his family and give her a name. She no longer needed a family name now that she was one of The Seven. But, he knew, as well as anyone else that knew her; that it would mean everything to her if she did. He respected her and would consider it an honor to count her as a daughter. He did not mention this to her in the event that it would not be allowed, though he would fight for her nonetheless. Perhaps he could solicit the help of Draconas Corvus who he was told had a close personal relationship with Prince Kornuk of the dwarves.

Draconas Sakira and Draconas Corvus spent a good deal of time talking to each other when Corvus was not busy elsewhere learning his new craft. Sakira was fast becoming a good friend. In any other place or time, their friendship may be frowned upon. This was not the case among their current companions.

When Sakira and Corvus first met, they were both of the opinion that the other race was not worth their time to get to know. This had been a fact in their lives that neither of them had ever thought to question before. Now, however, the two Draconas' could not understand the animosity between their two races and had agreed that when their mission was complete that they would do all they could to change that. Yes, they were different. But it was their very differences that made them compatible as races. What the elves were best at, the dwarves were not, and vice versa. If they were to work together, they would be able to create the most wondrous art, arms and more that the world had ever known, just as they had in the past. The possibilities were endless. Obviously, whatever had changed their ability to work together had happened a very long time ago and needed to be put aside. Some things that once were the norm no longer make sense in this new day and age. It was time to make a change.

Sir Devin led the party and called a halt as they approached an odd formation in the sand ahead. There were four humps under the sand, and unless his eyes were playing tricks on him due to the heat, the sand was undulating where they were. Everyone came to a complete stop and silence permeated the air. The expectation of the unknown was felt by all. They were all new to the experiences to come and it gave a feeling of both excitement and wariness which had them all on edge. The sand began to undulate even more and Devin knew he was not imagining things.

Donnal spoke up, "I have never seen one, although based on what I have heard over the years, I believe that we are looking at a desert worm making its way through the sand. I understand that they are harmless unless attacked. I suggest we move around it in the direction it is coming from so we don't cross its path."

Devin watched the motion and saw that it was moving to the left of their position. He changed their direction slightly and moved to the right to come behind it. Once everyone was past the path of the worm they all breathed a sigh of relief. It seemed funny to be afraid of a worm, but these 'worms' were approximately forty feet long with a girth larger than a barrel at their greatest width.

Akhena rode up beside Elle and asked, "What do you think they eat?"

It was Donnal, once again, that answered, "It is my understanding that they scoop up the sand and filter out the smaller worms, bugs, scorpions, etc. that live there. The filtered sand passes through and comes back out at the end of its digestive track."

"Are you saying what I think you are?" Akhena asked with a frown.

"Yes, we are basically walking through its shit." He laughed at the look on her face.

Elle watched the man as he let his guard down if only briefly. This was the man she knew was hiding inside there. The man she wanted to know. She smiled somewhat shyly at him and he smiled back. It warmed Elle to her core for the smile that he returned was real and genuine. Elle knew one thing for sure; she wanted to see that smile directed at her again and again.

Chapter 19

Commander Lorn and Prince Torik were talking with Wizard Harkel regarding the invisibility spell for their group. The wizard was confident in what he had though was still not sure about the ability of the dampening spell working on a larger group. He did, however, work the two into the same spell in the hopes that they would work together. When everyone was gathered, Wizard Harkel concentrated on clearing his mind and focusing on the combination spell he created. The dwarves looked on and were mesmerized at the changes taking place to the wizard during the spell. The wizard's eyes went wide before rolling back in his head. A small glow was visible surrounding the wizard and his hair crackled with static. Under normal circumstances the evidence of the magic would be nominal, if at all, but he had created a new spell to encompass a large group of people and the elements were changing to accommodate. When the wizard was done, he began to fall but was caught by those closest to him. A few sips of elven wine had him strong enough for them to be on their way within the hour. Much to their delight the spell worked, and as long as the sound was kept to a minimum, the spell was able to compensate for the noise as well as cloak them in invisibility. The dwarves did need to stay in relatively close proximity to each other, for if they stepped outside the spells range they would no longer be unseen or unheard. If enough dwarves stepped outside the spells range, the spell would collapse altogether. One of the dwarves in their group was a Draconas and he added his strength to help keep the spell in place.

King Baldor and his "men" were still camped within close proximity to where the dwarves had hidden themselves. The dwarves each coated themselves in the mud and dirt of the area to help hide their smell; something the spell could not do. Once they were ready and their enemy had settled for the night, they began their trek through the woods.

Although the Prince was the official leader of the expedition he was intelligent enough to know that the commander was in charge and he followed his lead in all things. He knew the purpose for which he had been sent was that of a figurehead only and would have done the same in his father's shoes. He followed closely behind the wizard and commander, making sure to keep them both in sight at all times. The Draconas stayed in the back to keep a lookout for anyone or anything trying to ambush them from behind. Despite the fact that they were under a magical enchantment, they were told to act as though they were not and the dwarves walked quietly and spoke not at all. A few of the wolf-like soldiers lifted their heads and sniffed in their direction. They had all eaten well that day and none were in a hurry to check out what they may or may not have smelled. Had their change not taken away some of their intelligence, they may have become curious enough to investigate whether they were hungry or not.

The dwarves slipped past the soldiers and picked up the pace once they were several hundred yards south. Each and every one of them could not stop thinking about what they had seen the enhanced soldiers do. Eating live goblins for sport more than fuel made them sick. No matter what would come, one thing was very clear: King Baldor's soldiers must be killed as well as the wizard who created them. Once they caught up with those from Amjukar, they would have much to tell. Since the dwarven group had been sent before the return of Prince Karnuk, they were unaware of the exact nature of what was to occur. It mattered not; they just needed to reach them as soon as possible.

They avoided goblins that were getting further away from what had taken place with relative ease. The goblins were in a panic and did not pay attention to anything other than their flight to another area with which to gather and regroup.

The dwarves continued for a day and a night stopping only long enough to eat and be on their way. They would stop shortly for a brief sleep and continue at the same pace until they reached the town of Horarti-Sol and continue from there.

***

On the other side of Fallon Forest, the Elven Elite of Valsara were making their way to the plains leading to the desert wasteland. They knew of the town of Horarti-Sol and had no intention of going there. The elves sent by Queen Teserath were among the most magically gifted in the kingdom. It was a small group, only twenty in all; however, one well trained elf was worth five dwarves or 10 soldiers. They were formidable in combat. Their magical talent spanned the spectrum from a healer to a conjurer. The horses that they travelled on were magically enhanced and could survive any climate, so there would be no need to obtain lacallas from a town they deemed to be unworthy of their gold. They were aware of the "Lord" that governed the town, and had they been pressed, they would have removed him long ago. The town was not needed by the elves, which was lucky for the "Lord" of Horarti-Sol.

The elves were led by Farris of House SeKar, a lineage of the House of Kar and Elle's kin though she did not know of him. Farris was approximately eight hundred years old. He was highly regarded as both a warrior and a wizard. As both an elf and a wizard, he could live for thousands of years···not unlike a Draconas. His magic had been honed over the years so that he could cast a spell with but a thought. He was gifted with both the sword and the bow, making him a formidable opponent up close or at a distance. He was the ideal leader for the mission they were on.

At the pace they had set they would arrive at the closest crossing into the desert, while avoiding the border town, in two days. They could magically conjure most of what they would need, though even that had its limitations and took a toll on the elf.

They would need to make sure that they had sufficient supplies to augment what they obtained by their magic. Farris called upon his second-in-charge to see that it was done. Also, if they had had the time, they would have investigated the reason for an unusual number of goblin sightings in their area. Unfortunately the mystery would have to wait for another day.

The horse that he rode atop was the fastest in the stable. He was a beautiful chestnut stallion with a black mane and tail and one white sock on his front right hoof. Farris was a tall elf and broader than was the norm. Not the most handsome by elf standards, but he was the most formidable. He, like his horse of choice, also had chestnut brown hair which fell to the middle of his back and was kept tied in a leather thong at all times. He had dark green eyes that spoke of intelligence and fairness. He was a good man. His second-in-charge was both his wife and best friend. Corrine was small in stature and big in heart. Her strawberry blonde hair and gray eyes had captivated him many years before. She was light of foot and quick with a bow and was the Elven Elite's conjurer. Their difference in size made them an amusing couple to behold. Although they were husband and wife, the circumstances dictated that they would be acting in accordance to their rank and responsibilities. There would be no open signs of affection or lovemaking while they were on their mission. The two had been on missions before and looked forward to the time they would make up once it was over. In the meantime, however, a modicum of decorum must be observed.

The other elves were all gifted in their own way and those chosen worked well as a team. They proceeded across the grasslands towards their goal, having no concept of what they would soon be facing, yet having every confidence that they would prevail.

***

King Baldor flew over the grasslands towards the desert wasteland. Coming from the west they were furthest from the area that the party from Amjukar crossed and Baldor wanted to be able to pick up their trail from there. It would take a day longer to begin at that point, though he deemed it necessary in the event that Donnal did not come through. He was unaware, but at that time he passed over the dwarves making their way to the same starting point on the assumption that they would have had to resupply in Horarti-Sol before continuing on. Prince Torik and Commander Lorn watched with mouths agape at the Erewyth soldiers overtaking their current position. They had run day and night to ensure outpacing the mutant soldiers for nothing. They watched as the king and another dragon with rider flew overhead and his soldiers loped by on all fours. There was nothing for it, they had to proceed as best they could and hope that the gods would see to favor them in some other way.

Baldor flew ahead to find the best dinner option. He came upon a pack of wild dogs, and despite his dislike of the furry food, he swooped down and grabbed one of them with his talons. He proceeded to one of the few trees offering shade in the grasslands and tortured the dog for a bit before his hunger overtook him and he finished the animal in one bite.

Like every other day, Andal flew atop Quintos who would have enjoyed nothing more than to roll onto his back and dump him from his saddle. Still, as far as it went, Andal was not an abusive rider and, in fact, went out of his way to ensure that Quintos ate well and was as comfortable as possible under the circumstances. Every day also took the prince drake further from his home and the brood of eggs currently under the control of Baldor. This was yet another reason to hate mankind. Typically, his kind tolerated the Draconas', which was how Baldor got close to the eggs in the first place. He vowed that if he made it through this and regained his freedom that the safety of the kingdom's eggs would be his number one priority over all others. Without the baby dragons to carry on the race, they would eventually die out, for even dragons did not live forever. Quintos did not know, nor did he care, where they were going and why. He just wanted to escape and return to his kingdom. His father had died and Quintos was to accept the mantle of king when this had happened. Now his kingdom was without a king or prince and the leadership was in question. Had there been someone to lead them, perhaps a rescue attempt would have been made. As it was, he was sure that his kingdom was in turmoil and he could not help but to worry about those he was supposed to keep safe. King Baldor may be the largest Draconas in the realm, but dragons were larger and all were magical as well. A united front should be able to unseat the thief of the crown of Erewyth. Unfortunately, he was in no position to start things in motion. He would still bide his time and hope an opportunity presented itself.

Lt. Commander Andal was not privy to the thoughts of the dragon beneath him. Had he been so, he would have been more leery of riding the beast. His newfound senses and increased strength notwithstanding, he was still the same man he once was. He was in awe of the handsome dragon and smartly feared him as well. He was awed by the power of the beast and enjoyed flying so much that for the first time in his life he wished to be a Draconas so he could fly of his own accord. More than once he wondered if his transformation may have hindered or completely eliminated any chance he may have had of becoming one. After all, there had been a Draconas in his family in the not too distant past according to his mother. The more he thought about it, the more he began to believe that he no longer had that chance. He consoled himself with the knowledge that more than likely he would have never changed, and if he hadn't been chosen for his current position, he would definitely be one of the Baldoran horde, not much more than a trained dog. He decided that he had made the right decision and put any fantasy of becoming a Draconas to the back of his mind. All in all, he was content with his lot and considered himself to be extremely lucky.

Baldor, as per the norm, was once again in a foul mood. He had sent for Gustaf to be brought before him. The elf was led to him in chains which bound both his wrists and ankles. Gustaf had been slim to begin with, yet after only a short period of time he appeared emaciated. The handsome face appeared gaunt and haunted. His usual cocky demeanor was nowhere to be seen. His chin touched his chest as he averted the king's gaze.

Baldor looked him over and felt nothing but disgust. That being the case, he also needed someone that he could control who had a chance of gaining information from the inside. He had an idea to be put in place once they reached the group from Amjukar. If he rushed in with his horde, a key person or element may be lost in the process and nothing would be gained. He needed to find out the precise nature of the business at hand to determine how best to proceed. It required patience which he had not had to use in a thousand years. He knew that, if necessary, he could exercise that patience once again. Gustaf could play a role in this if he believed that he could gain something in the end. Baldor, of course, would not follow through with any promises made to someone who would turn on their own blood; although if he was being honest with himself, Baldor would turn on his own mother. Nevertheless, the elf was bad news and could never be trusted.

"Look at me, elf," he commanded.

Gustaf raised his head and looked at the king that had placed him in chains.

"Do you wish to prove your loyalty to me and have your chains removed?" he asked, already knowing the answer.

"Yes your liege. If I had but a chance, I promise you would not regret it," he stated emphatically while his head bobbed up and down in his eagerness.

"I will explain what I want when it is time. In the meantime, the manacles will be removed and you will have the opportunity to bathe. If you are to be near me, I insist that you do not offend my senses." Gustaf almost lost what he had just gained due to his anger, for it was the conditions he was forced to live in that caused his current state of uncleanliness. With much effort he held himself in check. Baldor continued, "Once you are appropriately attired and have eaten we will talk further."

The soldiers unchained him and led him to an area where he could follow through with the king's orders. Gustaf did not care what the king requested of him so long as the chains were gone. He bathed, dressed and made his way to the cook fire. After eating his fill, he began to feel more like himself. He strode through the camp and found that his fascination with the mutated soldiers had changed to revulsion. They were little more than animals and beneath him in every way. Later that night, he met Andal, for whom he had some respect, although he still felt that the Lt. was beneath him as well. It did not take long for Gustaf to become his usual arrogant self. The time spent in chains did not affect him for longer than a few hours.

Later that night, Andal came for Gustaf and led him to the King's tent. He was led inside the opulent structure and found himself to be envious. The king did not sleep on a bedroll. He had a large bed that was carried, assembled and removed each and every day. In that bed were the naked forms of two young women huddled together in fear. The close proximity of the fear emanating from them caused a spike in power for the king and delight in the eyes of Gustaf who enjoyed their fear almost as much as the king and this did not go unnoticed by Baldor.

The king stared at Gustaf until the elf began to squirm. Only then did he invite him to sit. Once Gustaf sat down the king spoke.

"I trust that you have everything you need for your comfort?"

"Yes your liege, I am most comfortable," he knew to respond.

"Good. It is my intention that you will play an integral part in the gathering of information in the not too distant future. In the meantime, you will do as Andal commands and prove your loyalty to me, as well as your usefulness in other areas as well. Everyone will pull their weight without exception."

Gustaf had heard this once before, in the camp of the Amjukar knights. He did not pull his weight there because he knew he could get away with it. This camp was another story altogether. Gustaf was lazy by nature and would do the bare minimum to get by and keep from ending up back in chains.

"Now leave me," Baldor said, "I am eagerly awaited in bed." As he said this the girls began to weep...followed by the king's laugh as Andal and Gustaf exited the tent.

Chapter 20

Draconas Markim was addressing the everyday events of running a kingdom when Draconas Brock entered the room.

Markim smiled at his friend and gestured to a chair across from him. Draconas Brock took the seat and sank back into it as if he had the weight of the world upon him.

Markim noticed and asked what was wrong.

"I just got word that me brother Strom was sent with some of the dwarves to intercept our group. They were sent before Karnuk got back and do not know the reason they were sent. Me brother Strom is a good dwarf, but he is not made for battle. Most dwarves live for the opportunity to prove themselves in battle···or better yet···to die with honor and earn their place at the war god's table. Strom is not a battle dwarf. He has a natural ability when it comes to the finding of gems and cutting them to best show their fire and brilliance. There is no dwarf better at what he does. He's an honorable dwarf for sure. Unfortunately, he is not a fighter. I feel as though I should have been the one to lead my people. For the first time since being called to The Seven, I feel torn between the duty to my people and my duty to Amjukar. I love me life here. I also love and miss me family. "

"Brock, my friend, you know that I rely heavily on your counsel. That being said, you also know that you have a choice in this matter if you so choose to invoke it. I will support any decision you make. I would rather you be by my side, although I do understand your feelings."

"I did not come to you to talk of leaving. In truth it never occurred to me; I was just upset about me brother Strom. Me father is still king and hearty as a warhorse. Me brother Karnuk is well suited to step in to his place when the time comes. I just feel guilty that I was not available for me father in his time of need. Although, I admit, it is good to know that in the event that I ever did decide to step down, that you would stand behind my decision."

They sat in companionable silence, each wrapped in their own thoughts when Markim asked Brock to join him for dinner.

That evening Draconas' Markim and Brock made their way to the Wizard Tannis' chamber where they met both Tannis and Malek to attempt contact once again with their people.

The Wizard Tannis laid back on the chaise in his room and obtained the relaxed state required to send his essence out into the world. Both he and the High Wizard Malek invoked the spell required with Malek helping to guide his soul towards their goal. Markim and Brock were there to help reverse the spell if anything went wrong.

Tannis found himself floating above sand, sand was everywhere and he knew that they were in the desert. He searched out his cousin and found Cylas settling down for the evening.

"Hello, Cylas."

"Tannis, it is good to see you. Well, what I can see of you anyway."

"How does the party fair?"

"It is hot and will get hotter from what we are told. So far, though, everyone is in good spirits considering. We feel that we could travel more easily at night and will be doing more of our sleeping during the hottest part of the day. The nights are cold. It is easier to warm ourselves during our travels, however, than try to remain cool."

"Cylas, several groups are headed your way as you are aware." Tannis faded out then back in again and continued, "You may need to join forces with the dwarves and elves if what we hear about Baldor's soldiers is true." Tannis faded in and out before stabilizing once again. "Do not underestimate him. Tales of his soldiers eating both people and goblins alive have been substantiated."

Cylas grimaced and looked at his cousin as Tannis faded out for a final time...like a dream that seems so clear when you first wake but quickly loses cohesion until it's gone completely.

When Tannis made his way back to his body he was exhausted. The further away they were, the harder it became and the longer it took to recover. It would be at least a few days before he attempted to contact them again.

***

Draconas Lias and Torik woke quickly with the rise of the sun and discussed how best to proceed. Lias felt that it was necessary to get a layout of the area where the scent of dragons had been most prevalent. The last thing they needed was to have Torik captured, so it was agreed that he would stay behind in relative safety while Lias worked his way there using his magical ability to conceal himself as someone else. After much debate, they both felt it was best to be as unobtrusive as possible during the initial reconnaissance. Lias disguised himself as an elderly woman going about her morning chores. It was doubtful that anyone would question an elderly woman and almost certain that no one would pay attention to her comings and goings. Lias would fly low in his Draconas form to get closer to the destination to keep from spending a good portion of his morning walking there. Torik knew to stay put. He would be needed to communicate with the dragons once found and gain their confidence. Of course Lias, as a Draconas, could speak with the dragons, but he would not be trusted by them as easily as Torik. They did not know how much time they actually had and therefore they did everything based on the assumption that time was short at best.

Lias changed into his Draconas form, spread his wings, and took to the sky. He skimmed the treetops to reduce the risk of being seen and set off across the forest near the abandoned farm they had taken refuge in towards the capitol of Erewyth. Eventually he gained enough distance that his ability to communicate with Torik was no longer an option, leaving him with his own counsel should anything occur.

It didn't take long before he reached the end of the forest and the outskirts of the town that surrounded the city proper. Seeing no one in sight, he took the chance to fly closer to his goal to save more time, knowing that with the sun up he would blend into the sky without being seen unless someone knew to look for him and was doing so at that particular time. Once he came into sight of the city, he found an appropriate place to land that appeared void of any activity. Upon landing he glanced around once again to ensure that he had not been seen. Once he was satisfied, he changed into the nondescript older woman. Her age was hard to determine; her shoulders slightly stooped and long gray hair bound in a braid descended down her back. His old woman wore a basic cotton dress with a shawl about her shoulders and carried a large basket with which to carry home her day's purchases. She was almost too average and might possibly have caused a second look from those familiar with magical illusions to use a reveal spell. It was always best, when creating a secret identity, to remain as close to the truth of things as possible...and so if anyone asked, his alter ego was named Liasala. As an elf Lias was fast and agile. As Liasala he needed to slow his speed and lose his agility completely. It had been many, many years ago since he had used this ability and he usually just changed his appearance. This change demanded so much more and the importance of his mission was weighing heavily on him.

He made his way to the outskirts of the city and decided that in addition to his physical appearance, everything he did must appear to follow some purpose. Keeping this in mind, he made his way to the market which had been open for more than an hour. Being an elf, Lias was also practical enough to use this time to purchase items he actually needed for his journey, as well as items that were expected of an old lady. He made his way through the market up and down between the vendor's stalls, keeping his excellent Draconas hearing attuned to the conversations around him in the hopes of learning something of value. He had traversed approximately two thirds of the market when he heard two men arguing about the dragons.

"I don't give a damn about the extra pay anymore. The dragons may be workin' with the King, but it doesn't feel like it. Every time I feed them, I feel as though they would just as soon eat me. I want me old job back...less money and less chance of bein' et."

"I know what you mean, but you can't be sayin' stuff like that aroun' here. The boss is liable to feed you to 'em 'isself if'n he hears you complainin' like that."

"Yeah, yeah I know. They make me nervous is all. You're right though. It is what it is and there ain't nothin' to be done about it. Shit, we better be gettin' there for our shift. Those dragons will be up soon and they's gonna be hungry after they was worked most the night from what I hear."

"You heard right. They seem to be in a hurry to finish the addition. I don't know what he is needin' with more space. I hear there be more empty rooms in that castle than they can count, but I, for one, am not so fool as to ask what they're for. Some things are better left alone."

The two men continued to walk through the city in the direction of the castle which was perched high atop the tallest area in the city. Unless you were directly in front of a building, you could see the castle from anywhere in the city. Not unlike the castle in Amjukar, the castle in Erewyth was surrounded by a body of water, only it was a mote as opposed to a lake. The castle had only one entrance which was obtained by a heavily guarded drawbridge. Recently this drawbridge had been kept in a lowered position to allow easy access of the workers onto the castle grounds, such as the two men that Lias was following. King Baldor was not worried about an attack. Not one of the other kingdoms had tried to take the crown from him in the thousand years he had reigned and he had no fear of anyone trying to do so now.

The men walked together towards the castle and Lias did his best to appear busy as he followed close enough to keep them in Draconas hearing range. They walked fast enough and far enough that an old lady purchasing her wares in the market had no chance of keeping up. He found an abandoned building to stash his basket and change his appearance.

Lias was once again on his way. This time he appeared as a middle aged man of average height, weight and features. He wore a face that no one would recall. He was unaware that he had been seen until a hand fell to rest on his shoulder and hot breath brushed the side of his face. Once the hand touched him, the illusion was gone for that soldier. Before the startled soldier could react, Lias unsheathed the blade he kept in the small of his back and slit the soldier's throat. He killed the soldier silently to avoid alerting any others to what was happening. As the soldier began to fall, he caught his body and pulled him into the doorway of the abandoned building to conceal him. He felt remorse for killing an innocent man, but what he was doing was too important to risk being found out. Under any other circumstance he would have knocked the soldier unconscious, however, the man had seen him without his disguise and he just couldn't take the chance. He continued in the direction the two men he had been listening to had gone. The closer he got to the castle, the more pronounced was the smell of dragons. He didn't see anyone being checked prior to entering the castle grounds, so he acted as though he were one of the workers that helped remove the debris made by the dragons. He integrated himself among the others, this time calling himself Lasal if asked. He knew that if he came too close, the dragons would know him to be a Draconas and he was unsure of the reaction that would cause. Lias kept his distance and watched while working. They had temporarily lifted wards and other means of protection near the castle allowing the workers easy access to the area under construction. All other areas of the castle grounds not currently under construction were still heavily guarded with both soldiers as well as magical enchantments. There was no access to the inside of the castle from where they worked and so it was deemed an acceptable risk. After a while it became clear that they were building an addition to the castle that would house approximately a hundred or more dragons. Where King Baldor thought he would come by the dragons to fill the aerie, Lias had no idea. There were many dragons being used to build the aerie, though not nearly enough for the enormous structure currently under way. The dragons were used to cut and shape the stone with their fire. They were also being used to move the stone into place, saving a significant amount of time not having to do it with men and machines. Even the use of magic would take a good amount of time and effort. The more magic performed and the larger the object, the faster the wizard's, elves or Draconas' magic was depleted, creating down time while they regained their strength. The dragon born, however, had natural strength and their magic was stronger as well allowing them to work that much harder and longer.

Lias was in the process of loading yet more stone into a wheel barrel which would be removed by another, when a sudden quiet fell over the work area. Lias, like those around him, looked up to watch the dragons enter the work area by their handlers. Lias had to agree with the worker he had heard earlier. Not one of the dragons appeared to be happy with their circumstance. You could see it in their stance and most importantly in their eyes. The handlers looked nervous and the feeders appeared even more so. Probably, Lias speculated, they wondered the same thing as the worker earlier had expressed regarding whom or what the dragons would really like to eat. That being the case, he wondered why they were working for King Baldor at all. Baldor was strong but not strong enough to control so many dragons. What hold did he have? Based on the description he had been given, Lias recognized Torik's father, although he did not find his mother. She could be working elsewhere perhaps. It was all only speculation at this point. He worked at a distance until a halt was called to break for water and rations, giving him the opportunity to fade into the background. After gaining sufficient distance, he turned back into the old lady. He made his way back to the abandoned building to retrieve his basket and took the time to hide the soldier from a cursory look. Staying in character, Lias walked through the market to the outskirts of the town until he once again found a place of seclusion. With the day's purchases in hand, he changed into his Draconas form and took wing to head back to Torik and tell him what he had learned.

Torik was a dragon and as such he should have been patient to an extreme. However, Torik was a young dragon and had not developed such patience, so he barked at Lias when he returned,

293

demanding that he tell him what he knew, and that right quick.

Lias smirked at the young drake, finding much amusement in the dragon's reaction. Torik looked chagrined at his outburst and requested an update on the day's events in a more civil tone.

After Lias brought him up to date on all he had learned and seen, the young dragon curled up placing his snout atop his front legs and looked intently at Lias. He considered what Lias had seen and what it meant. Lias went about stoking the fire by hand, although it could have been more easily done as a Draconas, just to allow the young dragon some time with his own thoughts. Eventually Torik spoke and Lias gave him his full attention:

"Obviously the King of Erewyth is expecting more dragons into his fold. Otherwise, what use would an aerie be of that size? My father would never willingly work for Baldor, so there is something forcing them into what is nothing less than slavery. With that being said, we need to find the reason and determine a way to eliminate it. I cannot just fly there and ask, or whatever they are using to keep my father could be my downfall as well. You will need to speak with him. He will be leery at first, but you will have two things that will help pave the way. First, you are a Draconas and as such you will have that in your favor. Additionally, and more importantly, you will have something from me that will convince him that we are together. " The drake looked at Lias for his input.

294

"I agree with all that you have said. The only thing standing between me and your father is the ability to gain closer access. They use the same men to feed the dragons; this would be the easiest way to get close to him. I could incapacitate one of the feeders and take on his appearance and therefore his job. Although I would appear as one of the feeders he is used to seeing, he, along with every other dragon within close range would know me for a Draconas. Hopefully that will help when I explain the reason that I am there impersonating a feeder. Our plan is also dependent on the dragons not revealing my cover. What were you planning to provide me to prove to your father that I am there at your request?"

The young dragon reached with his talons under his breastplate and broke off a scale from that area. He handed the scale to Lias and said, "This scale is close to my heart and will tell my father two things---that I know you and that I trust you. Before you say anything to him, show him the scale. That should cause him to pause long enough to hear you out with any luck."

"Very encouraging," Lias grumbled.

The day opened with fog and rain as Lias bid Torik good bye. His plan required that he impersonate someone that was already a feeder. His hope was to intercept the men from the day before and pretend to be one of them, since he already knew the way they spoke as well as their mannerisms. The feeders worked in pairs, which was fortunate, since he did not know the entire process and he could simply emulate the person he worked with.

Because the fog and rain made visibility almost nonexistent, Lias once again took on the disguise of a very average man that would go unnoticed until such time that he was able to locate his target. It was a chilly miserable day. Despite this, he was hopeful that the weather would stay for the duration, making his job easier. The fog and rain may have been a visibility issue for those that he was searching for, however, as a Draconas, Lias' eyesight allowed him to see through the weather as though it did not exist. Before long, the man who had complained the day before came into sight and as fortune would have it, he was alone while making his way to meet up with his partner.

Lias looked in the direction the man was headed to determine the best area for the switch. He had no intention of harming the man. Lias had prepared a vial, with crushed dream weed, that he would blow into the man's face. This would cause the man to sleep for not less than twelve hours, providing Lias the time he needed. When the man woke up he would be confused and disoriented and most likely would just go home and sleep it off.

Lias noticed an abandoned building that allowed more rain to enter through the roof than it kept out. Apparently abandoned buildings were prevalent throughout the kingdom of Erewyth which didn't say much for the local economy. A thriving town would have most or all buildings put to some use or purpose. No one would have a reason to enter the building. Having found an acceptable shelter, he made his way towards his soon-to-be temporary doppelganger. Lias approached the man who felt his presence and turned to see who was following him so closely. As soon as he turned to Lias, the dream weed was blown directly into his face. Lias had used more than usual to accommodate for the rain. The man dropped like a rock; the dream weed's effect was instantaneous. He threw him over his shoulder and took him to the abandoned building. Once inside, he propped the man against the corner on the floor where the least amount of rain entered. With nothing more than a thought, he assumed his form, left the building, and continued to the dragon feeding area. The rain and fog were letting up slightly but still creating a visibility problem which was alright by Lias.

When dream boy's partner showed up, Lias ran to catch up. He fell into step with his doppelganger's partner and followed in silence to the feeding ground. Lias was sure that the partner never expected anything was amiss.

The feeding area was adjacent to the work area and was void of anything other than dirt and rocks; any vegetation having been trampled beneath the dragon's feet. Lias and his partner waited patiently while the handlers brought the dragons forth. His plan was dependent on being able to speak with Torik's father. He waited as the handlers brought a dragon before them that was not Torik's father, and Lias had no choice but to hope the dragon did not give him away. He quickly spoke to him with mindspeak catching the dragon off guard for just a second before he settled in as though everything was the same.

"I am Draconas Lias, one of The Seven of Amjukar," he began and was interrupted by his partner.

"What are you standing there for? Give me a hand with the meat."

Lias followed the man to the distribution area where carcasses were handed out with quick efficiency and helped carry it back to their dragon. On the way back, Lias spoke to the dragon urgently to make his intent known, "As you can tell, I am not the regular feeder. I am here to find out why the dragons are working for King Baldor. I am here with Torik, the son of Gorrel. He wishes me to speak with him and has sent me with a heart scale to show I am friend." Lias managed to say all of this while his partner was oblivious to the mindspeak taking place and before tossing the meat to the dragon. The dragon eyed Lias while he ate gauging the truth of what was said. After deciding that the Draconas spoke truly, he replied, "I will have Gorrel speak with you." He left and was replaced by another dragon waiting for his day's meal. Lias was concerned that he would need to repeat himself yet again, though found that each dragon they fed from thereon was already aware of who he was. Finally Gorrel made his way to the feeders. His feeders were two pairs down from Lias but well within mindspeak range. Lias flashed the heart scale to Torik's father and watched his eyes widen ever so slightly at confirmation that Lias had told the truth.

"Why are you here?" Gorrel asked.

"I have the same question. Why are the dragons working for Baldor?" Lias questioned back.

"We have no choice but to do so. Our eggs were stolen by the king and he has indicated that they will all be destroyed if we do not help him. All I know is that this addition is clearly meant to house more dragons. I feel as though we are helping him to enslave even more of our kind, yet I have no idea of what we can do. Prince Quintos was also enslaved and is being used as a common horse. There is nothing more demeaning than a prince drake being used as a means of travel, yet he is in the same predicament. Our eggs must be protected at all cost."

Just as Lias was about to reply his partner started to punch him in the arm. Luckily Lias saw this just in time to move away from the punch before his true self was revealed to his partner. Lias silently scolded himself. He needed to be more alert.

"What you be doin', day dreamin'? Get a move on!" his partner groused.

Lias helped with the next carcass, this one being unrecognizable and he pushed it out of his mind. He continued to speak with Gorrel as he moved away,

"I am here to help. My kingdom is greatly concerned about this and knew that the dragons would never ally themselves with Baldor of their own free will. We shall do whatever is within our power to get your eggs back so that you will be able to free yourselves without fear of reprisal. I shall start right away. With your permission, I would like to take Torik with me. I feel that he is in danger whether he stays in the mountains of your home awaiting discovery or whether he is with me. I believe that he would follow me anyway and perhaps we can help each other."

"I would be proud to have my son be a part of rescuing our race. He is a new hatchling---just one thousand years old from the previous mating season, despite his youth, he is resourceful, cunning and will serve you well."

"Thank you." Lias started to bow his head in respect to the older drake but had to stop himself due to their current situation. The gesture was not lost on Gorrel and he bowed slightly in acknowledgement.

Lias spoke little the rest of the day leaving his partner perplexed at his quiet demeanor. Apparently, the man he currently impersonated never shut up. When his doppelganger showed up the next day feeling "off," it would not seem so out of place after today.

He turned down his partner's request to join him for an ale, yet another obvious change in habit, though it couldn't be helped, and headed back to Torik when the coast was clear.

Torik was waiting anxiously. Unlike the day before, he did not verbally attack Lias as soon as he was back. Instead, he waited until Lias had shifted from his Draconas form and sat down.

"I spoke with your father. The dragons are being coerced into slavery because this season's dragon eggs were stolen by King Baldor. He is threatening to destroy them if they do not cooperate. Additionally, the king is having an aerie built to house the new hatchlings for what I am sure is to be an army under Baldor's control. The only way to save your race is to locate the eggs and retrieve them without their being damaged in the process. Only then will the kingdom of dragons be free to go against Baldor's wishes and perhaps even retaliate."

Torik knew the implications of what Lias had discovered. "What is your intent Draconas Lias of The Seven of Amjukar?"

The use of his formal title was not lost on Lias. It had been used to invoke a promise and commitment from not only Lias but his kingdom as well.

"I intend to locate the horde of eggs and steal them back, with your help if you so choose."

"I so choose." He paused and remembered something he had yet to ask, "What of my mother? Did you speak with her? "

"I'm afraid that in all that was going on I neglected to ask. However, all of the dragons being used in the construction of the aerie are male. That leads me to believe that perhaps some of the female dragons are being used to oversee the care of the eggs. As I understand it, they must be kept at a certain temperature at all times, depending on which ones are designated as female and which are to be male. Also, why would Baldor waste the use of his own people when he can force the dragons themselves? If given the opportunity, I am sure they would want to do so...in as much as the hatchlings are their own. Who better to ensure the eggs' safety? It would be perfect, a few of the female dragons caring for their own eggs, under the watchful eye of Baldor's men."

Torik admitted to himself that it made sense and hoped that his mother and sisters would be found with the eggs. The two spoke into the night regarding the possible places the eggs and dragons were being held. They also agreed that taking all things into consideration, the best place to keep the eggs would be somewhere large, inaccessible by foot and with access to a natural heat source that could be regulated as needed. They agreed that since he was building the aerie for the intention of keeping the dragons that hatched, they were sure that the eggs were well tended. Additionally, the chance of Baldor having the eggs destroyed was remote since the next chance he would have to fill his aerie with the hatchlings would not come for another thousand years. Still, losing the eggs was a much greater risk for the dragons than it was for Baldor, and they needed to work on that premise.

There was a volcanic mountain further west of the mountain range Prince Quintos called home. The volcano was active, constantly spewing forth lava that gradually made its way to the base, and once cooled, became black glass which was coveted by those that knew how to work the material into objects of use and beauty. Only those that had grown up in the region and knew of its deadliness dared to travel to the mountain and acquire the black glass. It was rumored that the volcanic mountain was home to a series of chambers that no man could survive due to the heat and gases that built up within and were released periodically through vents in the volcano's sides. A dragon, however, would have no problem residing within the mountain and perhaps would even find it to be ideal for those very reasons.

It was decided. They would fly to the volcanic mountain···known simply as Fire Mountain···with all haste.

Chapter 21

Commander Farris of House SeKar furrowed his brow in concentration. He would have been much happier knowing why he was about to traverse one of the most inhospitable environments in the realm. What were they to gain? All he had been told was to intercept the group from Amjukar and determine the reason for the impromptu trek through the desert. Once that information had been received, they were to eliminate anyone seen as a threat. Commander Farris had cultivated a relationship with Prince Tomlin for the sole purpose of providing the prince with a confidante. Pretending a friendship with the man had been nauseating though necessary. Ever since Prince Andres had been killed by a person or persons unknown (although it was widely believed Tomlin took part, although no one would have believed the man was capable of wielding the knife himself...), Farris had taken it upon himself to stay as close to the center of events as possible. He considered it his personal responsibility to protect the kingdom from a bad ruler. Thankfully, Queen Teserath had been in control since then. He noticed his wife looking at him questioningly and forced himself to relax and smile at her as though he had not a care in the world. Corinne was his life. He loved her with all that he was and hoped to one day be able to take the time to have a child or two to carry on his name.   Perhaps if their mission was successful in its conclusion, they would be able to take a break from their current demands to start on their family. Farris was hopeful that it would be sooner rather than later, since his wife was an elf only, not an elf and wizard like him, and her lifespan would not be as long as his.   He tried not to think about the years he would be without her and concentrated only on the years to come and the children they hoped would be a part of that.

He rubbed the neck of his horse, calming them both before he turned in his saddle and gave the signal to move forward.   He had been in the desert closest to the Kingdom of Valsara many years before without incident.   He realized, however, that they were working their way towards a possible confrontation with the Knights of Amjukar.   Neither he nor any of the Elven Elite were even remotely concerned about a knight. Farris was aware, though, that an elf Draconas was one of those they pursued, and he knew exactly who she was and their relationship to each other. Farris had known Andres as well as Anya and had cared about them both.   He knew that if Prince Tomlin or even Queen Teserath knew of his actual allegiance, not only would another have been sent in his place, he would most likely be spending the rest of his days in the dungeons beneath the castle. Farris believed Queen Teserath to be a good queen. She, however, was not as strong as she needed to be where her brother was concerned.   Farris knew her brother, Prince Tomlin, for the snake he was. A concern of both his and his wife's, as well as several others, was what would happen in the event that Queen Teserath died whether of natural causes or no. As it stood now, her brother would be crowned King of Valsara, since the queen had yet to marry and produce an heir. Tomlin on the throne was something that neither he nor his wife could bear to think about. Farris planned to discuss the situation with his cousin when the opportunity presented itself. As far as Farris was concerned, it was Elle's responsibility to ensure Valsara's future. And Farris, for one, would make sure that she realized it.

***

Elle was oblivious to the thoughts of her cousin not far away from their current location, but as circumstances would have it, she was thinking along the same lines. She occasionally thought about the responsibility of the crown of Valsara and wondered if the responsibility might become hers to carry. She knew that it had been her father's wish that she would take the throne when the time came. Although, at the time her father had still lived, her rule would not have taken place for hundreds of years.

Since she had received the calling of The Seven, she believed it to be a sign that the Kingdom of Valsara was in a position to take care of itself. She was not naïve, however, and knew that if Tomlin were to take the throne that she would need to reevaluate her position on the matter.

***

King Baldor kept his soldiers outside the town of Horarti-Sol while he sent Lt. Commander

Andal into the town for information and supplies. Although Andal's appearance frightened the shop keeps it was preferable to having to stoop to such a common chore himself. The change in Andal was just enough to scare anyone into telling the truth, and instead of paying top dollar for their supplies like all other travelers, they were made an incredible deal on all that was needed. When asked about the party from Amjukar, they were told that they had left the town more than a week before. As far as the residents were aware, the party was following the well-worn road through the dessert, although one shop keep did let it be known that the supplies purchased from his store were over and above what was needed to get to Gardwell.

King Baldor chewed on this information and decided that they would need to keep a close lookout for a deviation from the normal trail. They were obviously going to strike out in a different direction at some point. Donnal should be contacting him to make him aware of their movements, and if he didn't hear from him by day's end, he would contact him. If Donnal didn't have the information he required, then Baldor would have no choice other than to believe that his commander had turned on him and when they met again, Baldor would make Donnal regret that decision with every bone in his body.

***

Prince Strom followed closely behind Commander Lorn making sure to keep him in sight. The dwarves had eliminated the cloaking and dampening spells to allow for ease of movement since King Baldor and his "soldiers" had so easily overtaken and passed their position despite the pace they had kept. The general mood was foul; dwarves prided themselves on their ability to march and run for long periods of time with little rest. Their talent extended to battle. They may not have been the fastest race, but their stamina was unmatched by any in the realm. Dwarves could often win a contest just by their ability to outlast their opponent. Elves had stamina as well, and usually used magic to enhance their ability, in the end causing even them to tire before a dwarf.

All the dwarves could do was continue in the direction they knew they needed to go and hope that they were able to locate the trail of those that they sought. They would soon find out that any path left would be obliterated by the elements. They would continue sending out the Draconas in their party to search far and wide for any trace to indicate the direction in which to proceed.

***

Draconas Markim paced in his study as he always did and worried about the unavoidable confrontation that was sure to take place when the kingdom's representatives came together in the sands of the desert wasteland. Had he been foolish to send such a small group? Baldor was arriving with one hundred soldiers that were a slap in the face to the gods who had created the creatures of this world. It was not for a mere mortal, whether they were a wizard or not, to change the laws of nature. Nothing good could come from their

309

creation. He could only hope that the other kingdoms that had joined in the quest would understand the importance of working together when the time came. Men were unpredictable and the races were not known for their cooperation with each other. Still, if men, elves and dwarves could live together in Amjukar perhaps there was hope.

There was nothing to be done for it so he ceased his pacing and pushed the thoughts from his head.

***

Queen Teserath retrieved the delicate tea cup from the tray and drank the slightly bitter tea that she requested when she needed to relax. The taste was a little off from what she was used to, but she attributed that to an inferior batch of leaves. She would need to talk to the kitchen about it when she had the opportunity. She placed the cup on the tray and picked up the tart that was sweet enough to take away the bitter aftertaste of the tea. As she was about to take a bite, she began to choke. She looked at the tart dumbfoundedly; she had yet to take a bite so why was she choking as though something was lodged in her throat? Her eyes began to water and she began to choke in earnest. She was having trouble getting air. The Queen began to panic and tried to reach the rope to summon help; that's when she noticed that the rope had been placed just out of her reach. She fell to her knees as her face began to mottle and turn blue. Her eyes appeared to enlarge and become too big for their sockets. As Queen Teserath finally collapsed, she saw movement from the corner of her eye. Her brother walked into the room from a hidden door in the wall, and with a look of complete apathy he released the cord returning it to its normal position and watched his twin sister die.

Chapter 22

The party from Amjukar continued their passage through the desert wastelands, no one knowing how much longer their trek would be. No one knowing what would happen when and if Desne Mar was found. No one allowing themselves to think of what would happen if the land was never found or the gods forbid, if King Baldor found it first.

They had turned off the main route that was commonly traveled through the desert and began making their way in the direction that Elle's senses were telling her to go. Changing direction was of great concern because no one knew what lay ahead. It made sense to change direction because it was believed that if Desne Mar did exist and was in the path most commonly taken then it stood to reason that someone would have discovered it long ago. Every person in the party felt some trepidation in making their way through unchartered territory. At the same time, there was a sense of thrill of the unknown.

They began their southeasterly route with all water skins filled and all the provisions they could carry. They could only hope that they either had more than was needed or they would be able to replenish them along the way.

Magic could be used for the acquisition of many things, though that did not include food and water. Elle did have the ability to work the elements, however rain in the desert was not the norm, and trying to change the natural order of things would come at a cost. She genuinely hoped that things did not come to that.

When they first began their trek through the desert, they worried that their prints would stand out like a beacon and gain the attention of those that were following. They soon realized, however, that sometimes the sand simply fell in on itself; sometimes the wind wiped the prints, and more often than not the sand worms crossed their paths and obliterated any sign of their passing.

The sand worms were much more prevalent in this area of the desert and they could only assume it was due to the inactivity of the area. Elle had been told that nomads moved from watering hole to watering hole in the desert allowing the resources to replenish themselves before they were completely drained, so they never stayed in one area for too long, which would have caused the sand worms to abandon the area.

After travelling for a few days, they realized something that the nomads had known for all time. If sand worms were in an area, then that area had a food source as well as a water source nearby. The more there were, the better the area's resources. In effect, the nomads followed the path of the sand worms when travelling the desert. The group from Amjukar could only hope that they saw sand worms on a daily basis. When they allowed that thought to come about, they knew that their perception on things had changed indeed.

***

The sun was directly overhead, seemingly causing everyone to slump forward in their saddles. No one was talking or joking. Everyone was too hot to talk, or move, or breathe or.....

Elle looked sideways and saw Donnal riding there. Even Donnal, who never appeared flustered, looked as though he wished he were anywhere but here. And that is what got her to thinking: *Why was Donnal still here?* When they had first met him, he had indicated that he had something of his own with which to contend. Since that time, however, not a word more had been discussed regarding the subject. The party from Amjukar had taken a detour from the well-travelled path, in the desert, used by most people. So, it stood to reason that Donnal was no longer on his own mission, but that of the Amjukaran's. Why had she, or for that matter, anyone else, not noticed this before? Should she address this with him? Or, should she bring it to Sir Devin's attention first?

Donnal could feel Elle's eyes boring into him. He was afraid to look her way. He was getting a vibe from her direction and it wasn't a good one. Had he blown it? Somehow, had he slipped up, let loose an errant thought, or was it something else? Damn, first this god's blasted heat; then Elle's close scrutiny. He wasn't sure what was causing the most heat, the sun or Elle's attentive stare.

Donnal could not believe a woman could cause him this much trepidation···it was something with which he had no means of comparison. When he finally gathered his nerve, he turned his head in her direction.

Elle was caught off guard by the sudden move from Donnal when he turned to face her. She never understood why, of all people, Donnal was the only one that could catch her off guard like that. With everyone else, she knew what they were going to do, sometimes before they knew it themselves.

Donnal appeared almost lost to Elle and she couldn't help but soften her features, even if only a little. He noticed the slight change in her demeanor and was the first to speak:

"Ask your questions. I will hold nothing back," he said with quiet resignation.

Elle just studied him for a moment, and knew that what she was looking at was a man··· who had finally come to terms with something··· and was ready to be done with it, whatever it was.

"I was going to call a halt," she began, "due to this oppressive heat. We can speak then and resume our journey when the sun decides it is time to rest."

Donnal nodded his head in acceptance.

Elle spoke with Sir Devin and a halt was called to the sounds of whispered comments: "Thank the gods," "About time," and grunts of approval.

There was no shade to be had, so the knights broke out their tents. They used their tents for the purpose of shade and rest. All would enjoy at least a quick nap, if they were able to fall asleep in such heat. Some of the knights whispered in low tones to their neighbors to pass the time, while others wished for complete peace and quiet. Any movement seemed to ruin the small amount of relief they had. As a result, never had the camp been so quiet in all the time they had travelled.

Due to the quiet nature of the camp, Donnal suddenly became self-conscious about his upcoming talk with Elle. He felt as though no matter how quiet their conversation, it would be heard by the entire camp. He wondered, if he asked, would she use the dampening spell he had seen them use before, to keep their conversation private. Or, once he told her everything, would it no longer matter since he would be asked to leave, at the very least. He didn't have long to find out; she was approaching his makeshift camp.

Elle set up her tent directly across from Donnal in order to gauge his reaction to her questions, while staying out of the sun herself. She was glad that this long overdue conversation was about to take place. She was also leery of it as well. Elle knew, on some basic instinctive level, that what he would tell her was not going to be a good thing. It didn't matter; she had to know. When all was ready, she sat across from him and waited.

Before Elle could speak or ask a single question, Donnal put forth his request:

"Would you mind, before we start, placing a dampening spell around us so that our conversation may remain private?"

Elle looked at Donnal in surprise and said, "Anything that you and I speak of today will most likely be repeated to Sir Devin and Draconas Akhena. Especially, if I believe it will affect our group in any way."

"Of course," he replied, "though will everyone be privy to the information? Or, to put it another way, perhaps it may not be in everyone's best interest to know all that is spoken. If, however, it is overheard from the start, you no longer have a choice in the matter. At least, with a dampening field in place, you may tell only those you see fit."

Elle saw the logic in his argument and erected the dampening field around the two of them.

Akhena and Borg watched the interaction between Elle and Donnal, trying to decipher what was happening. Once Elle put the dampening shield in place, they continued to keep an eye on the two, leaving them to their privacy.

With their tents placed slightly away from the others, and the dampening field in place, Donnal began to relax and ready himself for what was to come. He wondered if Elle would ever forgive him.

Elle looked at the handsome man/draconas in front of her and asked, "Is your name really Donnal?"

Donnal let out an audible sigh at the easy question. "It is," he answered.

"Where are you from?" she asked.

"I was born and raised in the Kingdom of Erewyth," he stated.

This statement was not expected, and Elle could not help but to show the surprise on her face. She collected herself and changed her next question to ask, "What was your mission when we met you, and why is it apparently no longer a priority?"

This was the crux of the problem. This was what would cause this beautiful elf to look at him with disdain. He licked his chapped lips, and said, "I was sent here by the man that raised me, after my father accidentally killed my mother, in a drunken fit. That same man has been my Lord, my father if you will, and my king. His name is..."

"Baldor!" she breathed in fear.

"Baldor," he confirmed, with his eyes downcast, unable to look at her.

Donnal had expected Elle to immediately bolt from the tent; to find the other leaders of their party. Instead, she just sat there and looked at his downturned face. She said not a word. She just waited.

Finally, after what seemed like an eternity, Donnal lifted his eyes to Elle, expecting to see hatred and betrayal portrayed there. What he saw, instead, was betrayal, yes, but also confusion and··· was that pity? What had he become to elicit pity for the god's sake?

Elle could see, feel and hear the array of emotions coming from Donnal, although she normally had a hard time hearing him. She wanted to know more. The important thing, at this place and time, was finding out why Donnal was here and how had that changed, if at all?

Elle didn't need to ask more questions, Donnal knew what she wanted to know, so he began:

"I am, was, King Baldor's 1st in Command, his right hand man, so to speak. As I said, he found me as a boy on the day I lost my mother to a father's drunken fit. He was tall, strong, and had a commanding presence. I was in awe. He offered to take me under his wing and live in his castle. I was young and poor, and my father was killed by King Baldor in retribution, effectively leaving me homeless as well. It never occurred to me to say no." Donnal took a breath, it was still extremely hot, and just talking made one very tired. He continued: "I grew up in the castle. I wasn't loved; Baldor does not know love. I was well provided for, however. Even when his daughter was born, there was no change to my position in his household. I believe that had I grown into a weak or scrawny child, he would have rid himself of me. However, I grew not only into a strong man; I became a draconas as well. Unfortunately, my worth to him increased dramatically. I am his property, as far as he is concerned, and it is time for me to repay him for taking me in." Again, Donnal paused.

Elle could tell that this was probably one of the hardest things Donnal had ever done. She told him to wait, then rummaged through the supplies, and brought water to him. He thanked her and took a drink before handing it back. She took a drink and tucked it away, turning her attention back to Donnal. "Go on..." She encouraged.

Donnal nodded and continued, "King Baldor heard that something was going on in the Kingdom of Amjukar; something to do with a party of knights and a scroll. He was extremely frustrated at the lack of information, so he sent me to get the information for him. I ran into your brother, whom I overheard speaking, and knew he could be a way in to your group. I must say, I really was concerned for your safety from him. I know he's your brother, however, the man is unbalanced, not to mention lazy."

Elle smiled a little at this last, and he allowed a small smile in return.

"I'm sorry, I venture off course," Donnal said, then, "I have never cared for King Baldor, but always felt that I owed him my allegiance. Nevertheless, when I found out about the land we are searching for, I knew in my heart that a land such as that could never fall into that man's hands. He is evil, make no mistake. He will roast you alive with no remorse or regret. He invents new ways to torture people; it is a game and favorite pastime of his. And his power---his power is unique in that the more suffering that surrounds him, the stronger he becomes." Donnal was quiet for a moment before continuing, "When he realizes that I have betrayed him...."

"In what way have you betrayed him exactly?" she asked.

"He reaches me with a speaking stone. The last few times he has contacted me, I withheld information from him. I knew there was no way I could allow him to claim Desne Mar, and...."

She waited for him to continue. After several long moments he finally said:

"And then there's you, Elle. I care about you, and if I'm not totally mistaken, you care for me as well." He looked at her with an intensity that made the warmth of that day's sun pale in comparison.

Yes, she cared for him very much. But what was she to do? This man was sent by King Baldor, the enemy of the entire realm. One did not just simply let that go. Donnal had, quite literally, infiltrated their camp, and done so on her recommendation. She felt the fool. After all, she was the one with the ability to read emotions, not to mention thoughts. Granted, Donnal had been difficult for her to read, to say the least. That, however, was no excuse. She had always suspected that he was holding something back. She should have pursued this a long time ago. Elle felt as though she had let everyone down, herself included. Now, what was she to do? Donnal seemed to be sincere in all he had told her, but she had her doubts···doubts in her own abilities for having missed something so important, and doubts about Donnal.

Donnal watched the play of emotions cross Elle's face. He knew Elle regretted that she was unable to hide what she was thinking and feeling. Donnal, though, thought it was endearing. It made her more approachable, which she probably took to mean vulnerable, and perhaps she was right. He knew she was upset, and he was the reason for her being so. He regretted having been the one to make her feel that way. He waited patiently for Elle to process her thoughts and draw her own conclusions.

Elle knew Donnal was waiting for her to make a decision. However, the decision was not hers to make. All she could do was follow her instincts, speak with the others, and allow everyone to voice their concerns and opinions before the matter was decided. And so she told him:

"It is not my decision to make. I must confer with all of the leaders on this."

"I am not concerned with the opinions of the others, not much anyway, as my concern lies with you. Will you give me the chance to prove myself?"

"Honestly, I do not know. I want to, Donnal. I really do. But we're not just talking about you and me here; we are talking about the realm. The Realm, Donnal. What would happen if you were to go back to Baldor due to your feeling of allegiance owed? Would you be able to go against the man that raised you if we find ourselves in a fight for this land? And how could you be sure? How could we be sure?" Elle ran her hand through her hair in an uncharacteristic show of frustration and

322

continued, "I know...and I believe that you really do care for me. I know how I feel about you. But, like I said, this is not about us. It can't be about us." She paused when a thought occurred to her and asked, "The speaking stone, where is it?"

Donnal pulled the stone from under his shirt, where it was attached to a leather thong.

"How often does Baldor contact you?"

"Every few days. I believe he will contact me more often now. I have not given him our direction in the desert and he is getting upset with my excuses."

"Donnal, you need to prove yourself, to both myself and everyone else. I want you to stay by me at all times, on the ground and in the air. When it's not possible, I want you to open yourself to me so that I can read your thoughts. When next King Baldor contacts you, I want you to feed him misinformation. Do you agree to this?"

"I will do whatever it is you ask of me," Donnal said with all sincerity.

"I hope that you do. Now, I have the unfortunate business of speaking with the others regarding this matter." She stopped and turned back to him, and held her hand out for the stone. Donnal removed the thong from around his neck, and draped it over Elle's hand.

Donnal watched her as she left her tent to find Sir Devin and decide his fate.

Elle walked up to Sir Devin who was speaking to the knights that were charged with the next watch. They would be breaking camp as soon as the sun set, which was thankfully not long in coming. When Devin caught sight of Elle making her way to him, he finished what he was saying, and turned to her.

Without preamble, Elle said, "We need to speak privately."

"Come to my tent."

Sir Devin and Elle proceeded to his tent. They passed Sir Borg and Draconas Akhena on the way and Elle indicated that they should follow. Draconas' Corvus and Sakira were asked to attend as well.

When they reached Sir Devin's tent everyone turned to look at Elle with a questioning look.

Before Elle could begin, Draconas Akhena asked, "We are missing Draconas Donnal. Do you wish me to get him before we begin?"

Elle was not fooled. She knew Akhena had asked the question on purpose. "It is because of Donnal that I have called this meeting," she said.

The look between Akhena and Borg was not lost on Elle, and she didn't know how to feel about it. It mattered not; she knew what she had to do.

Elle continued, "I brought you here to discuss what I have just learned. I have been speaking with Donnal and he has shed light on some things that I know we have all had questions about." This was harder than she had thought. She gathered

324

her courage and continued. "As you know, we have all felt that Donnal was holding something back. Admittedly, he has been a productive member of our group and is well liked by the men. Unfortunately, the reason he came to be here, is why we are now meeting. And, before anyone starts off on a tangent, please allow me the courtesy of saying all I wish to say."

With that, Elle placed the dampening spell around the tent and told them all she had learned. Sir Borg, being the dwarf that he was, did not want to hear anything after the words "sent by Baldor," other than the sound of his axe removing Donnal's head. It took both Akhena and Devin several minutes to calm him down before Elle could continue. She explained everything. How he came to be there. How he came to be with Baldor in the first place. And why his loyalties had changed. She showed them the speaking stone which he had used to communicate with and Baldor and explained what Donnal had agreed to in order to redeem himself. She asked that they think on what they had learned. She also encouraged them to speak with Donnal, and ask questions themselves, to help with their decision. She did warn them that what was said was not to become public knowledge. So, if anyone did ask questions of Donnal, they were to insure complete privacy. Elle looked pointedly at Borg as she said this. The group broke up, everyone lost in their own thoughts once again.

Elle walked back to Donnal's tent. She was able to really 'see' him before he became aware of her presence. He looked dejected, a strange look for a man who was usually more than able and competent. She felt sorry for him. If what he said was true, he had just lost the only real family he had ever known. She saw his back straighten, as if he hadn't a care in the world, and she knew he was aware of her presence.

She sat down across from him and said, "I spoke with the others. Don't be surprised if they ask you questions. Also, don't be surprised if Borg tries to kill you."

"I would expect no less from him. In fact, I would be disappointed in him otherwise."

"Be patient," she said. "Let everyone come to their own conclusion, in their own time. Meanwhile, just be the same person we have come to know and depend on. When we resume this evening, I, for one, would like to do some night flying...."

"Sounds great," he replied, with less enthusiasm than was usual.

In what seemed like too short a time for everyone, with the exception of Donnal, they were once again on their way to Desne Mar, the Land of Magic, with the coming of nightfall and the realm's kingdoms giving chase.

Desne Mar

Land of Magic

Book Two

Coming in September 2016

www.ingramcontent.com/pod-product-compliance
Lightning Source LLC
Chambersburg PA
CBHW020229180626
46810CB00006B/2101